"ATTACK of the 50 FOOT WALLFLOWER"

Screenplay by

CHRISTIAN McKAY HEIDICKER

Based on a Story by

CHRISTIAN McKAY HEIDICKER

Guest starring
Daniel Framsky

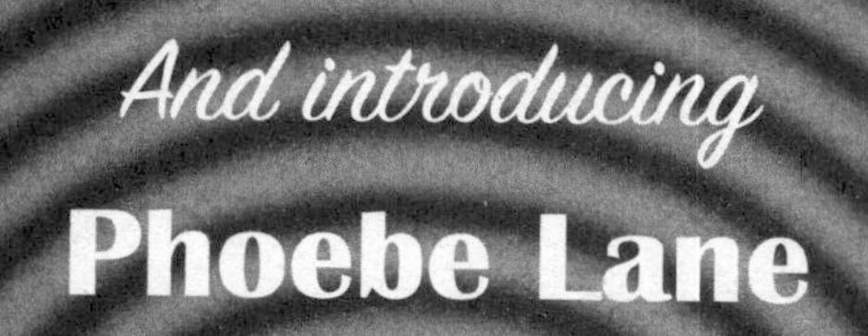
And introducing
Phoebe Lane

"Throw your arm across your eyes and scream, Ann! Scream for your life!"

—Carl Denham, *King Kong*

"Hey! You! In the dress. Wanna hear a joke?"

I was smoking in the shadow of the big top tent when the carny started to flirt with me. The wind changed directions, so my cigarette changed hands. Ma'd just about kill me if she knew I was smoking in my new sheath dress.

"Ah, come on," the carny said. "One little joke won't hurt ya."

He was coiling rope with arms like stretched taffy. He sported a Boy Scout haircut and smiled uneven teeth beneath an uneven mustache. And here I'd hoped my new dress would attract a different sort of fella—my age maybe.

"Tell you what," the carny said. "I'll tell the joke. If you laugh, you gotta tell me where I can find you when I get off work tonight. If you don't, then"—he placed a hand on his chest, like his heart might break—"I'll leave you alone forever."

I took another drag and blew the smoke upward. Daddy filled the western sky, faint as faded denim and tall as a mountain in a land ironed flat. He was eating popcorn in his bathrobe while the sun set near his knees. His eyes, the size of moons, were fixed on the eastern horizon. Ma always called this a "fair-weather day" because it meant there were no Shivers anywhere near these parts.

Still, if Daddy's eyes moseyed south and landed on Pennybrooke before this carnival could begin—and me and Ma had to flee instead of sit through another audience hooting and leering while she showed off half her bra—I wouldn't have been too broken up about it.

"So a blind guy staggers into a woodworking shop," the carny said, coiling a new rope. "Y'know, dark glasses, swinging his cane, bumping into things, the *works*. And he asks the owner for a job. The owner looks this guy up and down, and thinks, 'No *way* am I giving a blind guy a job in a woodworking shop. We got *power tools* here.'"

I smoked and listened. Well, half-listened anyway. Why couldn't Ma take us to Paris? Or New York City? Carnies don't flirt with you in New York City. Worst flirt you'd get in Paris is a mime, and they'd be charming about it—throw an invisible lasso around your waist and present you with an invisible ring or something. Besides, a big city like that has got a lot more people in it, so there's less chance of getting killed in a Shiver.

The carny ignored my bored expression and continued his joke. "So the owner asks the blind guy how he'd be able to tell the difference between types of wood. And the blind guy just taps his nose, like he's got this great sense of smell, right? So the owner decides to give him a test. See how good this guy's sniffer really is."

I took a final drag from my cigarette, let it drop in the dust, and ground it out with my pump.

"You ever think about how you're gonna die?" I asked the carny.

"What's that now?" He seemed taken aback, like he didn't know I was able to ask my own questions. I was just there to listen and laugh at his joke like a doll with a pull string.

"How you're gonna die," I said again. "And when you think it'll happen."

The carny snorted and let the coiled rope flop off his shoulder. "Old and drunk and in bed," he said, "hopefully with the right lady by my side." His gaze dipped below the hem of my dress. "I don't mind a little dough on 'em."

I tried to think up a retort about how he should go to the bakery and choke on a loaf of bread, but I never was as quick with comebacks as Ma. Instead, I found Daddy's eyes in the sky again.

"I'd say you got three weeks. A month tops."

The carny saluted the clouds and blinked. Even though Daddy was as tall as a tornado, he was still invisible to the carny's eyes. "That's, uh, some pretty dark subject matter for a girl young as yourself."

"You didn't seem too worried about my age when you asked what I was doing later."

The carny scoffed. I smiled too, at my own little joke.

Ma was a lightning rod for monsters. She said so herself. If this carny was going to travel in the same carnival the famous Loretta Lane was starring in, then a Shiver would catch up to him eventually. Only Ma and I would have plenty of time to escape when Daddy's eyes wandered this way to warn us, like thunder before the lightning.

"Where'd you get your confidence, girlie?" the carny asked.

I wished I'd inherited enough of Ma's good looks that it would be obvious, but I sighed and nodded to the billboard on the edge of the field. "Runs in the family."

The billboard was painted with tall, screaming letters: COME ONE! COME ALL! FEAST YOUR EYES ON THE EMPEROR OF APES! GASP AT THE TOWERING BONES OF OOK, THE APE THAT NEARLY TOPPLED A SKYSCRAPER! JUST 50¢! And toward the bottom:

(STICK AROUND TILL EVENING TO SEE THE STUNNING LORETTA LANE IN HER ICONIC TORN DRESS!).

"Say," the carny said. "You're that *Lane* girl."

I struck a match, lit another cigarette, and then shook out the flame. "Guess you better watch what you say around me then."

The carny scratched the back of his neck and hauled up the coiled rope, tossing it into a wheelbarrow. "Nah. My uncle runs this carnival. They couldn't fire me if they wanted to."

I smirked. I could tell he was rattled.

He scooped up the last rope and started winding. "The boys say you stay cooped up in that motel room all day. Why don't you get out? Live a little?"

I took in the dusty air, the tattered tents, the rusted carnival rides, the near-flat skyline. "You call this living?"

Without another word, I spun on my heel and headed back into town.

"Hey!" the carny called after me. "Don't you wanna hear the end of the joke?"

"I'll survive."

• • •

Whenever we reached a new town, Ma always made us stop by the tourist center to watch the promotional film. She said it gave us *culture.*

"And here we have Pennybrooke. Ah. Peaceful Pennybrooke. Don't let the harsh desert horizons fool you. For our city is a veritable oasis, rejuvenated by . . . shops . . . fine dining . . . roller skating . . . baseball . . . and even a lovely park where you can take that special someone for a stroll. Ha-ha. Hold on to that one, fella!"

They couldn't fool me. Pennybrooke was just another in a

long list of cookie-cutter towns on this tour—Cherrywood, Merrycreek, Sunnydale, Happy Oak—each the spitting image of the last. I could walk these streets with my eyes closed and still tell you everything the town had to offer.

Exiting the carnival field, I passed the dull white walls of the church and then crossed the street, turning my head away from the gray brick of the high school. On Main Street, I passed the lackluster record shop with the sign that read NO RACE MUSIC and the drugstore with its display of Slinkies and Hula-Hoops, jawbreakers and lilac water, and a spinning rack of comics with Captain America socking the Gill-man right in his fish lips. I continued past the frying grease smell of the diner where the Coke was warm and never mixed right, and finally the sock hop hall with its chrome and neon lights and a jukebox that played "In the Still of the Night," causing slick-haired boys to rub noses with girls in voluminous skirts.

A bunch of people were gathered in front of the appliance store, staring at a display of television sets that showed the evening news.

"This is Jimmy Jamboney reporting on Downingtown, Pennsylvania, where a goo*—a goo out of* space*, ladies and gentlemen—is devouring citizens at an alarming rate and growing more expansive with every victim."*

The crowd of Pennybrookers covered their mouths. I rolled my eyes. They may have acted shocked now, but after the broadcast was finished, they'd return to their daily lives, buying the latest blenders and dishwashers and chocolate malteds, assured that a Shiver would never come to their town.

"This globular entity has encased a diner like a famished jellyfish," the reporter continued, *"slowly suffocating the citizens*

within. Authorities cannot say where one of these molten meteors bearing the blob may crash next, but they are warning parents not to let their teens form groups, nor create gangs of any sort, for that is how they are most susceptible."

The people on the corner mumbled to one another accordingly. "That's what you get when your son's in a gang," one woman said.

I was just grateful Ma and I hadn't been anywhere near that Shiver; otherwise, I might not have been able to chew bubble gum for a month.

I continued beyond Main Street, past the Penmark Roller Rink, which had a sign that read NO COLOREDS. I walked the sidewalks of the ranch-style houses with their big shiny windows and sharp, angled shadows pointing toward the motel.

If anyone looked at me as I passed down Main Street, I didn't notice. In a couple weeks, Ma and I would be on to the next town, following the carnival on its six-month tour of the Southwest. Unless Daddy's eyes flashed us a warning, that was.

Either way, Pennybrooke and all its inhabitants would soon be out of our lives. Easy as the click of a channel changer.

• • •

As I walked up the driveway of the motel, a woman nearly made a pan-cake of me with her Chrysler convertible. She slammed on the brakes, the bumper stopping inches from my knees. We glared at each other through the windshield

She was pretty and pregnant and wore cat's-eye sunglasses, a taffeta dress, and a paisley scarf tied around her head. She scowled as I stepped around the car and then screeched down the road, leaving a foot of burnt rubber behind. I guess I'd be upset too if I looked like a watermelon stuffed in a sock.

I stormed up the motel steps. To think I almost died in a town like *Pennybrooke*. Ma had a lot of making up to do. I'd demand she replace each and every record I was forced to leave behind in the last town we fled, including "Rumble," which was banned from the radio. While we were at it, she needed to take me back to the department store and replace this sheath dress with a sack. After that carny's dough comment, my flesh felt like it was going to bust through the dress's seams like a popped Pillsbury container.

And if Ma refused to meet my demands . . . well, then I'd ditch her. No more Ma. I'd get by somehow. And I'd never have to run from another Shiver so long as I lived.

I practically kicked down the motel room door.

"Ma, this town's the bunk. And don't tell me how much that carnival's paying us, because it isn't worth a nickel more than—" My breath left me when I saw the blood.

Wait. My heart started to calm itself. Not blood.

It was Ma's nail polish, darkly spattered across the bed cover. The room held a tangy, woozy scent. I put a hand to my chest and pushed the door shut.

"Ma?"

There was no answer. Other than the nail polish, everything about the room felt normal. Ma's suitcase was on the floor. The dresses swayed in the closet under the flow of the AC. *American Bandstand* was on the television, with a hundred teens dancing to "At the Hop."

I peeked under the bed, half expecting to see Ma's dead eyes staring back. But there was nothing under there but an old crumpled Kleenex.

No Ma.

When I'd left that afternoon to stretch my legs, she had been smoking and ironing in her Maidenform bra, breathtaking even in curlers.

"Knock 'em dead, darling," she'd said, spritzing her polka-dot dress.

I'd given her a look from the doorway.

"I'm just saying you could command armies in that dress is all," she'd said.

I'd crossed my arms.

"Sorry," she'd said. "I know it doesn't mean much coming from your old ma."

"No," I said. "It doesn't."

And then I'd left.

I clicked off *American Bandstand*, and the music cut—the dancers swallowed in darkness. I searched for a note, and when I didn't find one, collapsed on the bed, making the springs squeak. The faucet dripped and echoed.

Maybe it was a steak-at-the-Automat kind of night. Maybe Ma had heard me whine about these suburban towns one too many times and had to get away awhile. She just did it so quick, she spilled her nail polish and forgot to clean it up.

Yeah, I assured myself. That was what happened.

I wrapped myself up in Ma's electric blanket and flicked the TV back on to distract myself. I tried to keep up her sunny kind of thinking through the Sunday-night feature—even after the network signed off for the night and the motel room filled with a cold *beeeeeeeeeeeep*.

Outside the window, Daddy stared at a cloud that looked just like an open pack of cigarettes.

The next afternoon, I stood in the parking lot of the Pennybrooke police station, debating.

Before I was born, Ma told the police all about Daddy. She marched right into the station and described the invisible man in the sky, from his La-Z-Boy to his bathrobe, right down to the number of wispy hairs covering his bald head. The only part she left out was that he had appeared almost three months earlier, right around the time she'd become mysteriously pregnant.

Ma told the police she thought she might be hallucinating until she started paying attention to the giant man's gaze. "His eyes drift across the country, slow as clouds, and wherever they land, something bad happens. About a month ago, he was looking to the east, and then they had all those victims in Massachusetts. You know, the ones with the gray marks on their throats? Then about a week ago, he was looking right at Manhattan, and they had all those reports about that woman who supposedly turned into a jaguar every time she was kissed by a fella."

"And what would you like us to do about it, Miss Lane?" one of the officers asked.

"Well, what if I were to tell you where he was looking, and then you could send the military and, y'know, get a jump on the next disaster?"

The officers gave each other looks. "With all due respect, ma'am, just because the air force saved you from the top of the

Chrysler Building doesn't mean they're at your beck and call."

"I'm not crazy," Ma said. "I'm just trying to save lives."

"You have to understand how this sounds, ma'am. Sure, we've got viruses. We've got mutations. We've got critters that blow up to the size of a battleship when exposed to radiation. Heck, we all saw the pictures of that Rhedosaurus thawed out by the atomic bomb. But all of that's science, plain and clear. None of them have to do with some *magic* man in the sky."

"And what if you're wrong?" Ma said. "What if you listen to me and you end up saving lives? Isn't that what you're here for?"

"We're here to protect and serve, ma'am," the policeman said. "That includes protecting some people from themselves."

And that's how Ma wound up in the psychopathic ward at Mercy Hospital for her second trimester with yours truly. She managed to keep her pregnancy a secret by blaming her swelling belly on the lack of exercise, fearing the nurses would take me away when I was born. She played nice with the doctors and was released on good behavior three months later. Ma never did much trust authority figures after that.

I paced through Pennybrooke's police station's parking lot. Television told a different story about policemen, of course. If a Shiver showed up in your town, officers would be there to save the day with their sirens and their guns and their badges. If filling the monster with bullets didn't help, then by golly, they'd gladly fall in the line of duty if it meant fewer innocents had to die.

After ten minutes of pacing, I quietly opened the door to the police station. It didn't look like the stations on TV. The walls were stained, the spackled linoleum floor was chipped, and there were bits of insects in the windowsill. Piles of papers drooped on the edges of desks, along with a newspaper whose upside-down front-page headline read BLOB GETS A BAD CASE OF THE CHILLS. The air smelled of sour coffee and cigarettes, which was good because it would cover up the fact that I'd been chain-smoking all night.

The two officers on duty didn't look like the cops on TV either. One looked thick as cement and had his boots up on his desk, while the other, a weasel of a man, was straddling his chair backward, finishing a joke.

"By this point, the shop owner's getting nervous, y'know? Because the blind guy'll probably saw off his own *finger* or something. Ha-ha. So here's what he does. For the final test, he sneaks off and tells his secretary to come in and take off all her clothes and lie down on the table. So she does. Ha-ha. She strips and lies down, naked as a jaybird. Of course, the blind guy's none the wiser. He just sniffs her and says, 'This one's tough. Could I smell the other side?' So the secretary turns over face down, and the blind guy, y'know, ha-ha, he smells the *other side*. And then he stands up straight and says, 'I think I got it.' And the shop owner says, 'Oh, yeah? What kind of wood is it?' And the blind guy says, *ha-ha*, he says—" The weaselly officer could barely contain his chuckling now. "'That's a craphouse door off a tuna boat!'"

He fell into fits of laughter, stomping his feet and clapping his hands at his own joke.

The thick cop smirked. "So did the blind guy get the job?"

The weaselly officer waved him away. "Ah, get lost. If you had a lick of sense you'd bust a gut." He took a sip of coffee and noticed me over the rim. "Don't look now, Shelley."

The thick officer quirked his eyebrow in my direction. "Hey, girlie. You paying our gas bill?"

"Huh?" I said.

The officer gave a nod. I looked at my foot, still safe on the sidewalk outside, and brought it in, the door clicking shut behind me. The two men stared as I crossed my arms over my stomach, thoughts escaping like steam.

"Well, out with it," Officer Shelley said, swinging his boots off his desk. "Puss stuck up a tree? Need us to chase it down for ya?"

The weaselly cop sipped his coffee, amused.

I considered hightailing it back to the motel right then and there. But then I remembered the dead glow of the television and the drip of the faucet. I couldn't sit in that room another second without shattering the windows screaming.

"I'd like to file a missing person's report," I said.

Officer Shelley smiled, expanding his pale mustache. "So, not a cat?"

"It's my mother," I said. "She disappeared last night. She'd never leave me alone this long. Not unless something . . ." My words failed.

Neither officer reached for paperwork.

"Standard procedure is to wait forty-eight hours before filing," the weaselly one said. "Otherwise, our drawers would be flooded with married men who slept one off at a buddy's house, if you catch my drift." He winked and sipped his coffee.

My shoulders unclenched a little. Here I was fretting like a chicken with its head cut off, and it hadn't even been a whole day. For all I knew, Ma was collapsing on the motel bed right that moment, recovering from her first post-Phoebe bender.

I nodded at the officers. "Thank you for your time."

I turned to go, but Officer Shelley said, "Hold a minute. Aren't you that gorilla woman's daughter?"

I paused in the doorway. Officer Shelley eyed me while the weaselly one stood and stepped close so he could get a better look.

"You know, Shell, I think you're right. I can almost kinda see the resemblance."

I managed not to scowl.

The weaselly officer stroked the fuzz on his chin. "Hey, here's something none of us at the station can figure out. What kind of respectable woman keeps her daughter cooped up in a motel room? Why hasn't she settled down yet?"

"Daddy was killed by the Gila monster," I lied. Ma and I whipped up a new tale for every town we went to. "Saved a busload of kids in the process."

"Shame," the weaselly officer said, shaking his head. He recovered real quick. "Well, is she seeing anyone now? I seen pictures in the magazines, and *wowza*. Not to mention she's *famous*!" His brow wrinkled up with a thought. "Say, you don't suppose one of her fans kidnapped her, do ya?"

Officer Shelley smiled. "Woman like that? I wouldn't rule it out."

"Like you said," I said, squirming a bit, "Ma hasn't been missing long. I'll just go back and wait—"

The weaselly officer caught my arm, pinching tight. "Hold on a second. We can't just let a young thing like you go back to that motel room all alone now, can we? Not with no one around to keep an eye on ya."

I glanced through the station window. Daddy was frozen

halfway through the sneeze he'd started that morning, the clouds roiled toward the horizon as if blown by his nostrils. His watchful eyes never did count as a father figure to anyone but Ma and me.

"Pennybrooke's a quiet town," the weaselly officer said, "but what with all the spooky stuff happening in the world today, you never can tell when evil will show its face." He pinched my arm harder. "But don't you worry. We'll keep you safe. Why, we stopped some greasers from stealing the juke-box just the other night with nothing but a hard look."

A Shiver would crumple you like an old gum wrapper, I wanted to say—would've said if Ma weren't missing.

Still gripping my arm, he nodded to Officer Shelley. "We could make one of the cells comfy, at least till her ma turns up, right, Shell?"

My back pressed against the station door. Ma was right. These officers were just trying to lock me up where they could keep an eye on me. The blob headline screamed out from the newspaper on the desk. With one Shiver dead, another could be on its way. And if Daddy's eyes wandered to Pennybrooke, I'd be locked up. I'd come to some horrible end involving aliens or giant insects, and I'd die a virgin who never got to see Paris.

Officer Shelley sniffed. "She doesn't want to sleep in no musty cell." He looked at me with eyes as dull as gunmetal. "I got a couch at my place that's fit for a king."

The weaselly one chuckled. "You'd know, too. Your wife makes you sleep on it often enough."

"Shut your mouth before I shut it for you," Officer Shelley said, and the weaselly one fell quiet.

A chill went through me.

Never trust an older man who tries to get you alone, Ma once said.

A police officer wasn't just some carny I could shoo away like a mosquito. I reached behind my back and found the door handle.

Officer Shelley stood and ambled toward me, adjusting his holster, which held a silver-and-oak revolver. "And if my couch is fit for a king"—he placed his hand on my shoulder—"it's good enough for a princess, too." His thumb grazed my collarbone, sending a thrill of fear through my body.

I turned the handle and pushed back against the door, breaking free from both officers' grips and stumbling outside. I started walking across the parking lot as fast as my pumps would carry me.

"Hen outta the coop!" the weaselly one called, laughing.

Heavy boots came stomping out the door. Halfway across the parking lot, a hand caught my wrist, stopping me with a jerk. I whirled and jammed my finger right in Officer Shelley's eye.

"Gah!" he cried out, and covered his face while I backed away.

He blinked at his palm a few times. His face burned up with rage. "Now, that's funny," he said, not laughing. "If you weren't a young lady, I'd drop you faster than a hot coal." He fixed his tearing eye on mine and unclipped his handcuffs. "Not saying I'll be soft with ya."

He came at me but was stopped by a burst of laughter from the station door.

"Ha ha ha!" The weaselly officer was laughing so hard he nearly fell over. "A teenage girl—ha ha ha ha—teaching *you* a lesson! Boy, she pulled a real *Curly* on ya, eh, Shell? Ha ha ha! Wait till the others hear! Ha ha ha!"

While Officer Shelley stood stunned, the handcuffs dangling from his fingers, I ran.

"Ah, let her go!" the weaselly one called. "Girl who looks like that? Don't much need to worry about *her* getting kidnapped."

I ran all the way to the motel, my heart beating like a butterfly, narrowly escaping through a hole in a net. I scaled the motel steps and flopped onto the bed, blood fluttering through me, tip to toe.

A knock came at the door, and I jerked upright.

"Miss Lane?" an urgent voice said. "Miss *Lane!* I've been trying to call, Miss Lane. You missed our first rehearsal for the big event!"

It was the carnival owner. He knocked again, louder this time. *"Miss Lane!"*

I sat in silence until he huffed and his shoes clacked down the motel steps. Once my heart had found its regular rhythm, I got up and examined myself in the mirror.

Ma once told me how she'd managed to get released from the asylum.

I had to erase myself, Phoebe. Become a blank slate. A wallflower. As harmless as a woman in a painting. If I acted too chipper, the doctors thought I was manic and might pick up a chainsaw and discover what people looked like on the inside. If I was weepy, they thought I was depressed and might drink a Drano cocktail. But if I was nobody special, not too happy and not too sad, then they could stamp my file with a big old smiley face and safely release me into the world.

I tried on a smile in the motel mirror, just like the girls on TV. I needed a story to tell while I tracked down Ma—one so convincing the police wouldn't be tempted to lock me up.

"Ma's back," I told my reflection. "She forgot to mention

she had an errand out of town, and she turned up this morning with a smooch and a new braid belt just for . . ." Tears began to tremor in the corners of my eyes. I sucked in deep, then continued. "Ma's back. She forgot to mention she was visiting a friend for a few days. Everything's perfectly—" I sniffed, started over. "Ma's back. . . ."

The next morning, I gave up on sleep. I put on my cotton knit T-shirt dress, white stockings, and buckled shoes, and then reached under the bed and pulled out the suitcase where Ma kept all the cash from her Ook appearances. I counted out six dollars and then checked my expression in the mirror. I looked about as pleasant as a mortician recovering from a root canal. So I pinched my cheeks, forced on a smile, and then threw open the door.

If the police weren't going to be any help, then I'd find Ma myself. I'd ask everyone in town whether they'd seen the famous Loretta Lane, acting as sunny as if I'd only just misplaced her. If that didn't work, I'd walk into the desert until I was out of earshot and ask Daddy if he'd seen what happened.

This would be an act of desperation, of course. I hadn't tried to talk to Daddy since I was eight years old, showing my paint-by-numbers to an empty sky until Ma called me inside to keep other people in the motel from whispering.

When I was older, Ma told me that when I was just a lump in her belly, she borrowed a friend's Model T, drove it out to the middle of the salt flats, pointed to her stomach, and screamed, "Hey! What's the big idea?" It wasn't until she unbuttoned her frilly top, flashed her chest to the sky, and still got no response that she realized Daddy was about as reachable as the end of a rainbow.

Still, I wasn't about to overlook any possibility of getting Ma back. The sooner I found her, the sooner we could ditch this town and get one step closer to New York. I'd be a regular Nancy Drew in Pennybrooke that day—only one who interviewed the clouds as well.

When I walked into the motel manager's office, a puffy white Pomeranian started yipping and jumping at my legs.

"Good morning," I said to the manager in a chipper voice, sidestepping the dog and laying the money on the counter. "I'd like to pay for another night, please."

Ma never paid for more than that in case Daddy's eyes looked our way and we had to skedaddle.

The manager smiled like a wrinkled apricot and then furrowed his eyebrows at the register. He didn't seem to notice that his dog was putting runs in my fifty-cent stockings.

"You didn't happen to see Ma yesterday or this morning, did you?" I said, nudging the Pomeranian away with my shoe.

"Don't believe so," the manager said. The register made a *ding* and spat out the drawer. "She gone missing?"

"Oh, no, nothing like that," I said, hiding my disappointment. "It's just she's terribly sick—pale as a moon and leaky at both ends."

The manager flinched, which was just what I'd intended. I didn't want him snooping around the room, seeing the spilled nail polish and the missing Ma, and getting any ideas to phone the police.

"Would you mind canceling the maid service?" I said while the Pomeranian leapt and licked the spaces between my fingers. "I'd like her to get some rest."

The old man scratched the corner of his lips and nodded.

"Ethel won't complain. You're our only guests on the second floor, and her knees have been acting up of late. You want I should give you some extra supplies?"

"I would like that, thank you."

While I tried to keep the Pomeranian from shredding my stockings for good, the manager opened a cupboard and loaded up my arms with fresh towels and two rolls of bathroom tissue.

"Tell your ma I said get better, and let me know if you meet anyone missing a dog."

I frowned at the Pomeranian. "It's not yours?"

The old man shrugged. "Just showed up in the parking lot a couple days back. I wanted to drown the thing, but Ethel's got a conscience."

I took another look at the dog, its tongue dangling out the side of its mouth. It was as white as marshmallow fluff with a personality twice as sugary. Now that it had my attention, the dog spun in an excited circle, and I noticed a dark smudge on its back, right at the base of its tail. Kneeling, I touched the smudge and then stifled a gasp. It was Ma's nail polish. Had this dog been in our room when she disappeared? If I found its owner, would I find Ma?

"You mind if I take her?" I asked the manager. "Ma could probably use the company while she's sick."

"You'd be doing me a favor," the manager said. "I don't want any messes in the room though."

"Oh, I don't think you'll have to worry on that account." I looked at the dog and forced a cutesy voice. "This little sweetie is made of nothing but cloud fluff."

The dog lolled her tongue in agreement and then trotted

alongside my heels as I exited the office. I nearly dropped the towels and bathroom tissue when I saw the man standing in the parking lot. Officer Shelley leaned against the hood of his police car. He wore his civilian clothes—jeans, a cowboy shirt, and boots—and was chewing a toothpick to splinters.

I remembered to smile. "Why, good morning, Officer Shelley," I said as if this were an episode of *Leave It to Beaver* and I had never jabbed him in the eye.

Shelley hooked a thick thumb through his belt, making his pants droop. "Your ma show yet?"

"She sure did," I managed without a waver, thanks to hours of sitcoms and mirror practice. "You know, it was the *darnedest* thing. She was plum certain she'd told me that she had a TV interview in Sherwood. When she got back late last night, I was so mad I could've spit. I told her if she didn't remember to tell me where she was going in the future, *I* would have to start giving *her* the hiding."

Officer Shelley's expression didn't thaw an inch. I remembered how his eye squished under my finger—like a hard-boiled egg—and I grew nauseous.

"I'm glad you're here," I said. "I wanted to apologize for yesterday. I was in a right state, and you gave me a bit of a shock. I hope I didn't hurt you any."

His bruised eye twitched, but he said, "No harm done." He glanced up the motel steps. "Your Ma decent? I'd like to have a word with her."

"She's terribly sick at the moment," I said. "Probably contagious."

Shelley thumbed his nose like he smelled a rat. "In that case, why don't I poke my head in and wish her well?"

"Isn't that kind of you. Um . . ."

Before I could come up with an excuse, the Pomeranian let out a tiny growl. I wondered if dogs could sense evil in real life just like they could on TV. Then I had a revelation.

"Oh, I haven't forgotten about *you*, naughty thing," I told the dog in my cutesy voice. "Officer Shelley, you simply wouldn't *believe* the mess she made all over the bed up there. Why, it looks like someone tossed an A-bomb in an outhouse. Doesn't it . . . Pan-Cake?"

Whether I named the dog after Ma's makeup base or a breakfast item because I hadn't eaten for two days, I wasn't sure. But Pan-Cake panted up at me, as if she was proud of the imaginary mess.

I gave Officer Shelley the most innocent of looks and held up the towels and tissue. "You wouldn't want to help me clean it up, would you? Or is that not in your job description?"

He shook his head. "It is not."

"Well, thanks for stopping by," I said, starting up the steps. "I feel just as safe as a bug in a rug with you around."

His eyes narrowed. "But why don't I see to it you make it safe to school this morning?"

I smiled so big I thought my teeth might break. Ma and I moved around so much that school was nothing more than an inconvenience. I learned everything I needed from books and television.

"And ruin my reputation?" I said. "If I show up to school in a police car, everyone will think I broke the law or something, and my good name will be soiled forever."

"Well, then I'll follow behind," he said. "It's no trouble at all. I wouldn't want to have to pick you up for truancy later."

Ma was right. This is what I got for involving the police in the first place.

I wrinkled my nose at him in what I hoped was an adorable way. "Just let me get this little devil's mess cleaned up."

While trying to figure out an escape, I poured a bowl of water, opened a box of Cracker Jacks, and then shut them in the bathroom with the dog. Then I walked down Main Street toward the high school with Officer Shelley's police car following behind like a shark. In the sky, Daddy was digging in his nostril. He was no help at all in situations like this—only as a weather vane for Shivers.

Before I could make a run for it, I was passed like a Frisbee from Officer Shelley's watchful gaze right into the sunken stare of Freeman High's principal. He stood seven feet if he was an inch and had long, thin limbs and a bald skull. "Miss Lane," he said, giving me a grin as wide and eerie as the dummy from *Howdy Doody*. "This *is* a surprise. And here I thought the actress's daughter was above schooling."

So much for playing Nancy Drew that day.

• • •

Freeman High looked like an old insane asylum, because that's just what it used to be. The halls were filled with boys and girls who seemed to be near-perfect photocopies of each other—greasers or jocks, knee-high skirts or plain dresses. All of them glanced at me with that familiar disappointment. *That's* Loretta Lane's daughter. It was only a matter of time before one of them whispered, *Daughter of Ook*. I sat through home ec, American history, and nukology, all of which might as well have been in a different language.

All morning, I kept a smile plastered to my lips like a

tightrope walker, grinning ear to ear but terrified I'd tumble into tears at any moment. Ma was out there somewhere. She needed me.

The moment the bell rang, I hustled into the hallway, slid into the shadowy space between the lockers and the water fountain, and buried my face in my hands.

"You must be Phoebe Lane!" a voice said above me.

I pushed myself upright against the wall, brightening like a rising sun. "Why, yes, I am."

"I'm Beth," the girl said. "It's *so* good to meet you."

The girl had a lisp, so I couldn't tell if her name was *Beth* or *Bess* at first. She wore Buddy Holly glasses, a ponytail, and a black skirt and polka-dot blouse that buttoned up to her throat. She smelled like flowery lotion and had the kind of bust that was so big Ma said it gave girls back problems.

"Um, how do you do?" I said.

Beth hooked her arm through mine and led me down the hallway. "When I first heard Loretta Lane had a daughter, I thought you might be spoiled. But after I heard about what you did to that police officer? I thought, *I just* have t*o meet her now!*" She pulled me in close. "You're a real *rabble-rouser*, aren't you?"

"That was an accident," I said, hoping I wasn't getting a reputation for assaulting police officers. I needed to stay invisible until I found Ma.

Beth winked at me like she didn't believe a word. "Sure. Some accident."

She continued to guide me down the hall, past lockers and classrooms and greasers combing their hair. No one had held my arm like this since my best friend, Katie, when I was in the second grade. It made me squeamish. I wanted to pull away, but I didn't think that's what normal girls did in this situation.

"Officer Graham is my brother," Beth said. "The guy who looks like a weasel? We don't look anything alike 'cause I was sorta adopted a couple years back. He's got a heart of gold, but you'd never know it because he's always trying to impress the other officers. It's just one big boys' club."

Heart of gold, huh? I wondered if Beth had ever heard him tell the joke about the blind carpenter.

"Anyway," Beth said, "he said your finger was as well aimed as a *rocket ship*." She gave a little shudder. "Boy, that Officer Shelley gives me the *chills*. And not the good kind. He's *always* staring at my chest. I'd give him a good poke in the eye myself if it wouldn't get my brother in trouble. Some men, right? If they can't get it anywhere else, they go for the young and helpless." She squeezed my arm. "Or maybe not so helpless."

That made me smile a little.

"Did your ma make it back?" Beth asked.

"She sure did."

"Glad to hear it."

Beth led me straight out the school's back doors and into a fenced enclosure with a trash bin that smelled like turned orange juice. She glanced back toward the school to make sure no one was around and then closed the gate.

"If you need to cry, do it back here," she said, giving me a sympathetic look. "That way the girls don't make fun of you and the boys don't try and offer you their smelly jackets."

So this was why she grabbed me from the lockers. My eyes watered up.

"You want to talk about it?" Beth said.

I shook my head and fumbled in my purse for a cigarette.

Beth watched me smoke. "Those things will kill ya, you know."

"What do you mean?" I'd heard of girls accidentally setting their hair on fire with a flicked ember, but nothing beyond that.

Beth leaned against the bin. "Forget I said anything. You mind if I ask a couple questions? Get your mind off things?"

I sniffed and smoked. "Shoot."

"How'd your ma get the monkey smell off?"

"He was an *ape*," I said, exhaling smoke. "And she said he didn't smell too bad, actually. Like a breeze off damp grass."

I'd seen Ma onstage enough times that I knew just how to answer these questions. After her dance number, she would smile in the spotlight in her light cream dress with the big black buttons, the sleeve torn away like a candy wrapper or a banana peel, and she would answer the same questions over and over again.

"Were you frightened for your life, Miss Lane?"

"I was scared witless! But I knew the United States Air Force would pull through!"

"How do you feel about gorillas now?"

"I try to avoid them, along with heights."

"Is there a special fella in your life?"

"Why? Was someone in the audience asking?"

The crowd would whistle, laugh, and clap the same every time. And every time, an audience member would call out, "Will you do it for us, Loretta? Please?" And Ma would say, "Oh, very well," and throw her arm across her eyes and scream like the life was about to be torn from her breast. And the audience would burst into applause. Every time.

Meanwhile, I'd be watching from the back of the tent, and wondering what it was like to hang there between Ook's giant forefinger and thumb, heels dangling thousands of feet above the pavement, the ape's massive leathery face sniffing at me, the air from his nostrils tugging at my dress.

I would have had a heart attack. Ma turned it into a stage show. How would I get by without her?

"Did she wet herself?" Beth asked. "I would've."

That ape was nothing but a big softy, Ma would tell me after she'd stepped out of the spotlight. *You could see it in his eyes. Gentle as an infant, with palms soft as coconut oil. Shame what happened to him.*

"I don't think so," I told Beth. Then I swallowed. "I'll have to ask her."

Beth blushed. "Did she see his . . . *thing*?"

Beth might as well have tossed a bucket of ice water over me I was so surprised. No one had ever asked Ma that question before. No one except her curious daughter, that was.

"She said it was bigger than a *school bus,*" I said.

Beth laughed and snorted. I laughed a little too.

"Boy, having a famous actress for a ma," Beth said. "All that traveling around. You must be so . . . *lonely.*"

Again, I was at a loss for words. The girls in these suburban towns always asked me if life on the road was glamorous or exciting. Never this. I took a final drag of my cigarette just as the lunch bell rang.

"Well, we'll make sure you aren't lonely while you're in Pennybrooke," Beth said, and took my arm again, squeezing it in the soft space between her arm and her side. We left the trash area. "Are you free this afternoon? The Girl Scouts are meeting at the church at three thirty, and I think you'd fit right in."

"Ma needs me this afternoon," I said, which wasn't a lie, really. The second school let out, I'd be back on the hunt. I'd spend the night searching the storm drains if I had to.

Not that I would have joined the Girl Scouts anyway. Beth was sweet, but I'd learned not to make friends when I'd just have to leave them behind in a couple weeks. Or worse, watch as a Shiver swept through and killed anyone I'd grown close to. I'd learned that the hard way with Katie.

"Ah well," Beth said. "Another time, then."

As we walked to class, I left my arm in hers. But only because that's what girls on television do.

• • •

"Yoo-hoo!"

The moment Beth and I entered the lunchroom, a blond girl waved us over. Her hair was styled in famous bangs with braided pigtails.

"That's Rhoda Penmark," Beth whispered as we walked toward the girl. "When she was eight, her mom slipped her enough sleeping pills to knock out a herd of cows and then shot herself. The hospital pumped Rhoda's stomach in the nick of time. Isn't that *wild*?"

"Yeah," I said. "Wild."

And to think I'd been upset with Ma just for dragging me to Pennybrooke. It was easy to forget that some monsters didn't have fur or tentacles.

"Then again," Beth whispered, "Rhoda also claims she was struck by lightning. So who knows?"

"What were you saying about me?" Rhoda said with a smile when we reached the table.

Beth's face lit up like a traffic light. "It wasn't anything about you. I was just saying—"

"You were telling her about my mother, weren't you?" Rhoda said, laying one hand on top of the other. "That's all right. I don't mind. Mother was very confused, the poor dear. She thought she'd try to protect her one sweet daughter from the cruelties of the world by replacing my vitamins with pills that make you so sleepy you won't ever wake up again." Rhoda sharpened her smile at Beth. "She wanted to keep me safe from the monsters and the murderers and the little girls who whisper secrets about me."

Beth bit her lip and stared at her shoes.

Rhoda was pretty but unsettling. She wore a gingham dress and a heart-shaped silver locket and had a look so cool it wouldn't melt butter. Her hair wasn't blond so much as white. I might've believed she was an alien if schools didn't test students for that sort of thing.

"So," Rhoda said to me, "you're the girl who nearly had Officer Shelley's eye as a souvenir. I'm not sure about your flirting tactics, Phoebe Lane. I prefer it when the boys can actually *look* at me."

I remembered the gunmetal gray of Shelley's gaze. "He's at least fifteen years my senior."

Rhoda shrugged. "To each her own, I guess."

For having a mother who tried to murder her before shooting herself, Rhoda seemed unruffled by the world. Every line she spoke was light and airy like she was planning a picnic.

A boy with curly hair and a ratty jean jacket approached the table and set a cup of tapioca and a spoon in front of Rhoda. "One tapioca. And one spoon, so clean you can see yourself."

"Thank you, Calvin," Rhoda said.

Calvin noticed me and smirked. "Who's the new broad? She looks like someone told her her cat exploded."

I quickly wiped at my eyes while Beth gave him a sizzling look.

"What?" Calvin said. "I didn't mean nothing by it. Exploding cats are a national tragedy."

"This is Phoebe," Beth said. "Loretta Lane's daughter. Isn't she pretty?"

I blushed. The only people who ever complimented me were Ma and gross old carnies who couldn't get it anywhere else.

"So your ma's the actress with a thing for apes," Calvin said. He stroked his chin and sized me up. "I don't see the resemblance. To the gorilla, I mean."

I snorted. Rhoda scowled and peeled open her tapioca.

Most boys were over the moon when they heard that *the* Loretta Lane, a true-blue celebrity, had moved to town, and that her daughter might be found at the local malt shop. But their excitement died every time they saw how much like Ma I was not. And one of them would always come up with the same tired nickname that never stopped stinging: "Daughter of Ook."

"I'm glad you're around, Phoebe Lane," Calvin said. "We could use some new flavors at Freeman. Besides, you can keep Beth here from toppling over. It's a miracle of science that she keeps upright with those things."

Beth crossed her arms over her chest. "It's almost like I'm not standing right here."

"I was talking about your glasses!" Calvin said.

"You're excused, Calvin," Rhoda said neatly.

"But you said if I bought you a snack I could sit with you."

She took a bite of her tapioca. "Yes, but I didn't specify what day."

Calvin sighed. "Next time I'm getting it in writing. On a *napkin*. In *blood*." He flipped up his collar and was about to leave, but then a thought turned him back to Rhoda. "I'm gonna be on TV someday. A comedian. *Famous*. And all the women will be knocking down my trailer door just to get a lock of my hair. So you'd better get a taste while you can."

Rhoda gave him a look as cold as a January icicle until he left. Then she licked her spoon and stared at me. "My dad used to be a colonel, but now he owns the roller rink. If you're nice to me, Phoebe, maybe I'll let you in for free."

I tried on my TV smile. "Sounds like a blast."

She pointed with her spoon. "You might want to touch up that nail polish though."

I looked at my nails, flaking after days of neglect. "Oh. Yeah, sure."

A deafening sound wailed through the lunchroom. The school siren. My fingers flew to my ears as kids ducked under the tables. I followed them, cradling my trembling knees in the shadows. The Shiver couldn't be happening now. Last I checked, Daddy's eyes were still fixed on the horizon.

The siren died away, and Beth patted my leg.

"You never been in a duck-and-cover drill before?" she said.

I took my fingers out of my ears and shook my head, rattled. The lunchroom doors flew open, and figures swept through the cafeteria in fluttering capes and scowling masks.

"The drama team," Beth said, grinning. "Last month they made a giant tarantula, each one playing a leg. I'm guessing this is banshees."

We watched the figures as they fluttered by, making *whooooo* sounds.

"And everyone just hides under the table?" I said.

"Fun, right?" Beth said.

"Sure, a real *crack*-up," I said, then thought, *until a real Shiver shows its face.*

Rhoda hadn't said a word since the drill began. She watched the figures like they were the most romantic thing in the world, eyes flickering as if lit by candlelight.

I'd almost forgotten I had a leaping creature made of marshmallow fluff waiting for me back at the motel. I thought the Pomeranian might nip my nose clean off it was so excited to see me. The Cracker Jacks were untouched, and the dog hadn't made a spot of mess in the bathroom.

"Good dog," I said, but didn't pet it. "Let's get you some real dog food and find your owner."

I grabbed my purse, opened the door, and then stopped abruptly. There was Officer Shelley, fist raised, about to knock.

"Hello again," he said. "Thought I'd check in."

My mouth stopped working. Pan-Cake started to growl.

"Your ma make it back?" Shelley asked, peering over my shoulder.

I hoped my shadow was blocking the nail polish stain.

"She's just out picking up a couple TV dinners and Coca-Colas," I said, my lips too tense to smile. "Should be back in a jiffy."

Shelley leaned against the doorframe. "In that case I'll wait."

My mind sent fishhooks out the door, trying to snag something that would rescue me. A storm welled on the horizon, bruising the sky with storm light. In the parking lot, the motel manager sprayed out the gutters with a hose, but he only smiled and waved, figuring I was safe with the man with a badge.

"Strange for a mother to leave her child alone so long and

so often," Officer Shelley said. "I have half a mind to drag you back to my house and make a proper lady out of you." He laid his hand on my shoulder just like he had at the station, thumb resting on my clavicle. "My wife's with her sister for the weekend."

Just then one of my fishhooks snagged something. "I appreciate the invitation, but I'm actually on my way out." I ducked the officer's hand and pushed past him. "I've been invited to join the, um, *Girl Scouts*."

"That so?" Shelley said.

He didn't look too happy about letting me go, but the dog was snarling between us.

"Yep, imagine that," I said, backing down the stairs. "Little old me in Girl Scouts. Toodle-oo."

I took off down Main Street, Pan-Cake trotting by my side.

• • •

Clouds swept overhead, blanketing the sky in layered grays and obscuring Daddy's face. I was headed toward the church because I didn't dare get caught by Officer Shelley anywhere else, when a voice called out to me.

"Phoebe! Oh, Phoebe!"

My shoes stuttered to a stop. There was Rhoda standing in the open doorway of one of the Levitt ranches, flapping her hand at me.

"Come to me, will you?" she called. "All I have is socks."

I walked up the perfectly straight sidewalk that cut through the perfectly mowed lawn.

"My shoes are at the cobbler's getting new cleats put on," she said. "Apparently, I walk harder than anyone else and wear my soles right down to the leather. Isn't that funny?"

"Funny," I said, imagining Rhoda stomping the heads of baby birds. I was in no mood for smiling. I'd spent my entire TV personality at school that morning.

"Why, who is *this* darling girl?" Rhoda said, crouching down and opening her arms.

Pan-Cake ran up and placed its front paws on Rhoda's knees while Rhoda combed her fingers through its fur. I guess the dog couldn't sense evil after all.

Beyond Rhoda I could see into a living room with flowered wallpaper and plastic-covered furniture and a coffee table with a little glass dish filled with candy. I didn't get many chances to see inside normal houses.

"I just *love* little dogs like this," Rhoda said in a syrupy voice. "But Dad won't let me have one." She squished Pan-Cake's face, rubbing her nose against its wet black one. "I'll bet if he came home and saw something as beautiful as *you*, he'd just *have* to let me keep you, wouldn't he?"

Was Rhoda trying to take this dog right out from under me? I needed it to find Ma.

"I'm afraid I've grown attached," I said, kneeling myself and touching its soft hair.

Rhoda rubbed the dog's velvety ears. "If she was mine, I'd shampoo her hair *every* day, and then I'd tie it up into little bows. Why, I might even paint her nails. What's her name?"

"Um, Pan-Cake."

Rhoda scowled. "You mean like something you eat?"

I shrugged. "Or a makeup base."

"*Well.*" Rhoda became prim and proper. "*I'd* name her Queenie."

I stood and patted my leg. "Come on, Pan-Cake."

I could feel Rhoda's glare as we headed down the sidewalk. The clouds woke with flashes of light, and scattered raindrops tapped my hair. I was starting to like the name Pan-Cake.

• • •

By the time I reached St. Maria's, the clouds were releasing a torrent. As I ran to the front entrance, trying to keep my head covered, the church's clock tower bonged three times.

I was half an hour early.

The church's double doors were locked, so I knocked while Pan-Cake shook herself dry beneath the eaves. One of the doors creaked open and the smell of dust and Pine-Sol mixed with the rain. A pair of horn-rimmed glasses glowed in the darkness. The reverend was small with thin black hair and clammy-looking skin, like he'd been dipped in wax.

"Yes?" he said in a pinched voice.

"Can I come in?" I said, wringing out my hem. The knit-cotton dress was soaked through and clinging to my body.

The reverend's eyes scanned the street. "It would not be becoming to invite a young girl into the church alone." He began to close the door. "Now, if you'll excuse me, I must iron my bookmarks."

"Wait!" I said.

The door stopped at a crack.

"I'm part of the Girl Scouts," I said. "They're meeting here in thirty minutes. I just need to stay dry till then."

"You are the . . . *actress's* daughter," the reverend said through the narrow opening.

"Yeah?" I said, hugging myself and shivering.

"I fear your mother's wantonness will bring death upon us all," he said. "Good day."

The door clicked shut.

I scoffed and looked at Pan-Cake, like, *Can you believe he just did that to us?*

Ma may have been a lightning rod for monsters, but it didn't have anything to do with her looks, I didn't think. Besides, she was "as chaste as a nun's knickers" up until the day she married Brad, the pilot who saved her from the Chrysler Building. That's what she claimed anyway.

The church's door creaked back open and then shut again. An umbrella fell by my feet. I opened it over my head and watched the rain clean the dust off the Lincoln sitting in the parking lot. When Beth arrived, her smile just about banished the storm.

• • •

The rain pelted the windshield while the squeaking wipers did a miserable job of keeping up. There were four of us in the station wagon, plus Pan-Cake, who sat on Beth's lap and watched the desert plants whiz past the window.

"We're simply *tickled* that you could join us this afternoon, Phoebe!" Beth's adoptive aunt Gladys said in the driver's seat.

"Tickled!" Susannah said from the passenger's.

They seemed like the kind of women who would be tickled by a trash compactor. Their skin was pale as milk and their beehive hairdos brushed the car ceiling. I thought I might drown in their lavender perfume.

I didn't want to participate in community service. I wanted to look for Ma. But my search was rained out anyway, and joining the Girl Scouts sure beat being ogled by Officer Shelley in the motel room of gloom.

"So!" Susannah awkwardly rotated in the passenger seat so

she could address me. "Loretta *Lane's* daughter. How *exciting*. Where's your father in the picture?"

"He was part of the expedition to Alaska in fifty-one," I said, thinking fast. "He was one of the first to dig up the saucer."

Gladys sucked through her teeth. "He wasn't one of the ones who . . . burned alive, was he?"

"She probably doesn't want to talk about it, Auntie," Beth said.

"Where are my manners?" Gladys said. "Phoebe, today we're going to the *Nava-Joe* reservation."

I had flashes of the boy I'd met when I was twelve. The one with his arm in the sling. If my heart got one more pinch that day, I swore it would pop.

"Not many girls are interested in going to Gray Rock, unfortunately," Beth said. "That's why we're only four today."

Susannah flipped on the radio. "*—individuals in Switzerland have been mysteriously decapitated, losing their heads to what people are describing as a* strange mist *which has crawled its way—*"

"Blech," Susannah said. "Always bad news."

She tuned it to "Twilight Time" by the Platters.

Out here in the desert, the horizon so distant, I could see all the way down past the black box in Daddy's hand to his towering shins, covered in flannel pajama pants. It was an unfortunate angle because it was obvious where I inherited my legs, which didn't pinch off at the knee, but continued in wide columns right down to the ankles.

"Now, Phoebe," Gladys said, adjusting the rearview so she could meet my eyes. "I want you to listen to me *very* carefully. These people we're about to visit aren't in what we'd call an *ideal* position." She spoke in a low voice as if the Navajo people might hear her across the long desert miles. "That's why it's our job as good Christians to save this, um, *tribe* from their *untamed selves*. Is that what we're calling it now? Tribe?"

"Yes, tribe," Susannah said.

Beth mumbled something that sounded like "*Nation*."

"Don't get me wrong," Gladys said. "Those Nava-Joe code talkers were *very helpful* in the second war, but after the fighting was over those people didn't *behave* themselves, now did they? Doing peyote and performing those *ceremonies* and . . . well, *goodness* knows what else. If they aren't careful, they'll invite God's wrath and drop a disaster the size of *Ook* on all of us. Oops, excuse me."

"It's okay," I said.

"The only part that's okay," Beth mumbled.

"Besides," Gladys said more quietly, "we need to keep up relations to make sure their tribe keeps digging up that uranium."

I looked out my window through the rain at Daddy, whose eyes never seemed to fall on an Indian reservation. I wondered how Gladys would explain that.

We rode in silence for a while. Pan-Cake tried to crawl from Beth's lap into mine, but I pushed her off.

"Oh!" Susannah burst out and started ruffling around in a paper bag between her legs. "I almost forgot! I figured since it was our first time visiting the Nava-Joes, we could try to blend in." She sat up, wearing a feathered headdress. "How, Chief!" she said, raising her hand with a mock Indian accent.

"Oh, you're *too much*," Gladys said.

They laughed in pitches so high, I worried my eardrums might break.

"May I see that?" Beth asked with a strained smile.

Susannah handed her the headdress. I turned away for a split second when Beth said, "Whoops!"

When I looked again, the headdress was gone, and Beth's window was open. I followed her eyes through the rain-streaked rear window to see the headdress rolling along the highway like a struck bird.

"Oh, *shoot,*" Susannah said, craning her neck around. "That cost me three dollars."

Beth shrugged. "The wind stole it right off my head."

I had this funny feeling like Beth had tossed it out the window on purpose. But why, I had no earthly idea.

"Ah, well," Gladys said. "We still have the Bibles."

• • •

After a half hour of driving, the rain calmed to a drizzle. The highway spat us out onto a muddy road, which wound its way to a wide valley lined with mesas and plateaus that looked like sandy birthday cakes. We passed a military base with a banner that showed a picture of a winking cadet and read SO LONG, MOM! I'M OFF TO DROP THE BOMB!

Beth yawned awake beside me and petted Pan-Cake. "Are we there?"

"We sure are!" Gladys said. She pointed a sparkly fingernail at several eight-sided wooden houses with mud roofs scattered around the base of a small hill. "Phoebe, your and Beth's job will be to read stories to the little ones."

I grimaced. I never saw the point in children. How could anyone in good conscience bring kids into this world when they might just get gobbled up by a Shiver?

As we pulled up, a man exited one of the houses to greet

us. He wore jeans and a flannel shirt and his hair was tied in a bun with white yarn. A woman in a black dress and a suede jacket watched from the doorway. I was suddenly glad Beth had ditched the headdress.

"Wait here while I work my magic, girls," Gladys said.

She got out of the car and smiled brightly. "Why, good afternoon! Looks like we dried up all the rain!"

The man looked at the sky and scratched above his eyebrow like he didn't necessarily consider this good news. Still, he extended his hand. "My name is Eugene," he said. "I'm the chairman here at Gray Rock." He gestured to the woman. "This is Darcy."

"Oh!" Gladys said. "Why, what nice names."

"Could be worse," Eugene said, chuckling. "What can we do for you?"

"Well," Gladys said, laying a hand on her chest. "My name is Gladys, and I am the head of the Girl Scouts of Pennybrooke. In the car is Susannah, Beth, and Phoebe. Oh, and Pan-Cake. Wait till you *hear* what we've brought you today! It's Bibles. And they are an absolute *steal*."

"We already have Bibles," Darcy said from the doorway.

"Not like these, you don't," Gladys said, shaking her finger.

While she tried to sell the Navajo people on Bibles they didn't need, something about the woman caught my eye. My heart lit up. She was wearing Ma's jacket. It had the hole in the elbow and everything.

I popped open the car door.

"Phoebe?" Susannah said. "Maybe you should wait until—" I slammed the door on her.

"Tell you what," Eugene was saying. "We'll be happy to

purchase some Bibles if you consider buying some of our blankets. Darcy's weaving provides warmth to the body and the soul."

"Oh!" Gladys said, wringing her hands and laughing nervously. "Well. Um—"

"Where did you get that jacket?" I said to Darcy, running up to her.

She clasped it around her chest and pointed toward the highway. "I found it. In the road."

In the car, Pan-Cake was yapping her little lungs out, leaping and scratching at the window.

"Phoebe?" Gladys said. "I think your dog needs to go tinkle. Perhaps you should—"

The moment Beth opened the car door, Pan-Cake leapt out and took off running across the highway right in front of a speeding truck.

Beth covered her eyes. "I can't look!"

The truck swerved, nearly making a pan-cake of Pan-Cake, but she made it safely across the road and continued into the open desert, barking.

It was like she was onto a scent. Like she remembered something.

I took off running after her, across the highway and into the desert, my pumps kicking up mud.

"Phoebe?" Gladys called after me. "Phoebe! You'll ruin your dress!"

My legs were on fire. I'd never run so far in all my life. The ground was still soft with rain and the sucking sands had stolen one of my pumps, but still I chased Pan-Cake into the desert.

My anger gave me strength. I was ready to yell Ma's ear off the moment I found her. Finally, I'd have enough leverage to abandon these suburban towns forever and make her take me to New York or Paris or better yet both. Of course, I wouldn't start shouting demands until after I hugged her for an hour at least.

I followed Pan-Cake past sandy mounds and scrub oaks and every now and then a fenced-in water pump. When the desert was aglow with twilight and the Colgate constellation was fading in above Daddy's head, we arrived at a rocky outcropping. Pan-Cake sniffed around the rocks' outer edge and then started to bark.

"What is it, Pan-Cake?" I said. "What did you find?"

My heart took a tumble. There, set into the rock, was a steel door. It was as dark as the space between the stars and seemed to swallow moonlight. The desert insects played strange music. A fierce wind whipped through the Joshua trees. I was suddenly afraid.

How many coincidences had to happen for me to find this door? The Pomeranian, Officer Shelley, the Girl Scouts, Ma's jacket . . . It was as if this door *wanted* me to find it.

Still, if Ma was here, there was only one way to get her back.

I reached for the rusted handle. It was cold and it was locked.

Pan-Cake spun in circles and barked.

"*Hush,*" I said.

If there were people in there, I didn't want them to hear me coming. But Pan-Cake wouldn't stop yapping.

"Quiet!" I said.

Her bark grew even louder. I was about to grab her muzzle and clamp it shut when there came a *thunk* from behind the door, deep and echoed. I heard someone climbing stairs. I hid behind the shadow of the rock just as the handle turned and the metal door scraped open. A rectangle of light was thrown across the sand, and a man's silhouette fell over Pan-Cake.

"You little devil," he said.

Pan-Cake took off into the desert, and the man ran after her. The steel door started to fall shut, and without thinking I slipped inside. Two handrails led down a steep metal staircase, every third stair lit by a bright, caged light. The man could return at any moment, so I stepped lightly down the stairs, my shoeless sock squishing with every other step. At the bottom of the staircase was a round concrete passageway lit by more caged lights.

Beneath each light was a grenade-gray door, alternating on the left and right sides of the hallway, each with an inset wired window. Crouching, I slid along the curved wall to the first door. It was warm to the touch, and I could hear the whirring of belts and screaking of gears. I peeked into the window.

The room was filled with machines I had no words for: antennae crawling with worms of electricity, bright grids of blinking lights, and circular screens with wiggling lines. I ducked when a man with a clipboard stepped into sight. He tapped one of the screens and then scribbled something down.

"Let's put another rabbit in the disintegration chamber," he said to someone I couldn't see.

I shuddered and continued down the hallway. The smell changed from something warm and electric to something like mildew and bleach cleaner. I peeked through the window of the next door on the opposite side.

This room was filled with aquariums and cages holding creatures of all sorts—frogs and lizards and birds and fish. A monkey nervously paced in a wire cage. A brain that I hoped wasn't human floated in a fish tank half full of murky liquid. As I stared at it, thoughts echoed through my head: *help . . . toothpaste . . . help . . . cornflakes . . . help . . .* I got away from that door quick.

The room after that had a bit of what looked like living gum trembling inside a terrarium. *The goo from space,* I thought. But this little blob was not frozen like the headline at the police station claimed it was. And that wasn't even the most upsetting thing about the room.

The far wall was made of glass, guarding a massive web of plastic tunnels. An ant farm. It brought back the worst Shiver Ma and I had ever escaped. Those things had torn through the town like it was made of paper, leaving no survivors.

Katie.

The window of the next door was foggy. Inside I could barely make out a garden nursery of sorts with rows of what looked like giant eggplants with leathery gray leaves sprouting out their tops. *Pods* . . . The kinds of pods that could grow a perfect copy of a human like they were a vegetable. Hadn't these all been destroyed when the military carpet-bombed Santa Mira?

The next door was filled with a glittering spray that almost looked alive the way it licked at the windowpane.

The door across from that stood beneath a flickering light and was as cold as a refrigerator. Inside the window was a sleek metal disc like a giant Frisbee. Beside it was a twisted figure frozen in ice. The sight raised goose bumps on the back of my neck.

The final door was big enough for a bus to fit through. Its window showed nothing but a wide dirt tunnel leading into darkness. The smell of wet soil wafted around the doorframe, and piled in the middle of the tunnel were giant sacks of sugar. What were they feeding down there?

Behind me, at the top of the staircase, the steel door scraped open again. I whirled, searching for a place to hide. None of these rooms were safe. I didn't want to be blobbed or nibbled or have my body replaced by a vegetable copy.

The footsteps grew closer. On the back wall of the tunnel was a simple wooden door—a janitor's closet maybe. I ran to it and pressed my ear against the wood. There were no sounds. I threw it open.

The light inside nearly blinded me. There were three people in the room. A man with glasses and a goatee saw me. His coffee fell out of his hand and splattered across the floor.

"Kill the lights!"

There was a deep *chok!* and the space fell into darkness, save the slanted rectangle of light from the tunnel that framed my elongated shadow.

I turned to run, but a rough voice said, "Stay right where you are!"

I had no idea if they had guns or what, so I froze in the

doorway. In the darkness came a shuffling, the screeching of metal, the moving of something heavy, and someone whispering, "Where's the darned—*oof.* I told you to tape that wire down!"

Finally, the rustling and scraping settled. There was another *chok!* and a ceiling lamp cast a circle of light around a chair in the middle of the room. A speaker above my head crackled and thumped as someone fumbled with a microphone. *"Close the door and sit."*

I gazed back down the passageway. At the bottom of the staircase stood a man in a leather jacket, staring at me with his head tilted, Pan-Cake lying still in his arms. There was nowhere to run.

I reminded myself that I'd come here to get Ma. And I wasn't leaving without her.

I swallowed, smoothed my dress, and walked toward the circle of light. Silence stretched in the darkness as I approached the chair, trying not to show fear. I sat and folded my trembling hands between my legs.

A speaker on the ceiling crackled and thumped. *"What do you know about us?"*

The voice was hoarse with whiskey and cigarettes.

"I don't know anything," I said. "I swear." My heart was beating a hundred miles a minute.

The darkness said nothing.

"Hello?" I said.

"How did you find this place?"

"Um, a dog. A . . . Pomeranian. I followed it here."

The speaker made a ruffled sound like the microphone was being covered with a hand, and there came more whispering. *"I'll shoot that dog myself, I swear."*

Another pause and then more static. *"What is your name?"*

"Um, Phoebe. Phoebe Lane."

This was met with a flurry of whispers.

"Did she just say Lane?" a British voice said.

"Someone get the chloroform," the rough voice said.

"Stop it. She's just a child."

"There was no mention of a daughter on the report."

"Somebody's getting canned."

There was more scuffling, and then a new voice came over the microphone.

"Phoebe?"

This voice was neither rough nor British. It was a woman's voice—firm and confident, the kind where you can tell she's pretty just by listening.

"Can you see the man in the sky?"

The question stole the breath right out of me.

"Do not say another word, Miss Link," the rough voice said without a microphone. "You are compromising our entire op—"

"Let her speak," the woman said.

The rough voice sighed, and then a cigarette lit in the darkness. The microphone clicked off.

"Phoebe," the woman said again, "can you see the man in the sky?"

"Um . . . ," I said.

The last time I'd told someone about Daddy I'd been six years old. I sat on the curb of the motel, squinting up at the blank sky, trying to follow Ma's instructions. *"If you focus on the bright bellies of the clouds until the sky sorta fades away, then you'll see him. That's your father. Pale like frost on glass."*

I was trying to figure out if the faint sliver of the moon was his fingernail clipping.

The motel manager came out of the office and adjusted her cat's-eye sunglasses at me. "Honey, you keep looking up with your mouth hanging open like that, a seagull's gonna lay an egg in it."

"I'm trying to see my daddy," I told her, and then crossed my eyes like I was at a 3-D movie, hoping he would pop out of the sky.

"Aw, baby, has your daddy gone up to heaven?"

"Nah. Momma got knocked up by the man in the sky. She says I'm a . . . 'maculate conception."

The manager pulled her jacket tight around her throat, swept into the office, and slammed the door. Ten minutes later she phoned our room, asking us to leave the motel and never come back.

"What were you thinking, telling her that?" Ma asked, stuffing her nylon leggings into her suitcase. "That woman thinks I'm so hopped up on drugs I believe I'm the Virgin Mary!"

"I didn't know!" I said, crying on my hard-shell suitcase.

Ma made a flutter with her lips. "No, I guess you didn't. Serves me right for telling you jokes that are beyond your years. Look, from now on, your father's a secret, you hear? People just can't understand. Now count out ten cents for the bus. Lord knows where we're staying tonight."

"You *can* see him," the woman's voice in the darkness said, "can't you?"

Was this a test? I imagined the figures in the dark room holding clipboards with two big boxes, one with CRAZY written beside it, the other with NOT CRAZY. In my mind, three pencils hovered over the CRAZY box, awaiting my response.

"Answer, kid," the rough voice said. "Otherwise you'll never leave here again."

My jaw trembled, trying to make words. The woman saved me from speaking.

"This is silly," she said. "You aren't scaring her into *anything*. You're just making a fool of yourself. Turn on the lights, Mason. I want her to see us."

"Do not turn on those lights," the rough voice said. "We must take every precaution not to compromise the lab. We must extract any pertinent infor—"

"With all due respect, Mr. Peak," the woman said, "the only thing you're going to extract is pity from me. Now turn on the lights before I rattle off everyone's full names and you're faced with the moral dilemma of having to *murder* this poor girl."

There was a husky sigh in the darkness. "Go ahead, Mason."

The lights popped on, and the space filled with light, making me squint again. I was in what looked like a small warehouse. A checkerboard floor stretched to the four distant walls, like a chess game that didn't know how to end. In the middle of the room was a table with three people sitting in chairs.

The British man with the goatee and the lab coat sat to the left. In the middle was the rough-voiced man with the microphone. At first, he held up a piece of paper to cover his face, but then he let it drop, hopeless. He had clownish hair and sagging cheeks like Droopy Dog, which he tried to make up for with a trim haircut and a nice suit.

The woman sat to the right. She was as beautiful as her

voice had promised. She wore a cheongsam dress, and her hair was as black and elegant as calligraphy, pulled back under an airwave hat. She had dark circles under her eyes, but otherwise looked as light and thin as Lladro from Macy's.

But then my eyes continued down and caught her stomach, which bulged into her lap beneath the table. This woman had a bun in the oven, and it was nearly cooked.

"Hello, Phoebe," she said. "I'm Elizabeth Link. But you may call me Liz."

"You were at the motel," I said. "The day Ma vanished."

The woman's eye gave a little twitch, like she remembered me but didn't know who I was at the time.

"Where's Ma?" I said, rage building in my trembling voice.

Droopy Dog, *Mr. Peak*, I guessed, glared at the woman.

She responded to me without looking at him. "Your mother is on a special mission."

I crossed my arms. I loved Ma to pieces, but the only mission she was any good at was wearing torn dresses and letting fellas hoot at her.

"You kidnapped her," I said. "There was nail polish spilled all over the bedspread."

"Actually, she was cleaning that up when we arrived," the woman said.

"Why didn't she leave a note?" I said.

"Probably because she didn't want us to know you existed. To protect you."

It was true Ma had been overprotective since being released from the hospital. That was part of the reason she'd never registered me for school. She couldn't make herself trust I'd come back to her.

I wanted to challenge this woman further, but she seemed to have an answer to everything.

Liz interlaced her fingers on the table in a businesslike fashion. "Phoebe, I think you might be able to help us."

The British man with the goatee smiled at me. Mr. Peak scowled.

"Help how?" I said.

"Well," the woman said, leaning in, "you have a gift that few people in the world have. You can see the man in the sky."

My leg started working like a jackhammer. I leaned on my knee to make it still. "I don't know what you're talking about."

The woman smiled. "That's fine. You can take your ti—" She winced and doubled over. She laid one hand on her pregnant stomach and the other flat on the table and breathed in and out a few times.

"Are you all right, Miss Link?" the man with the goatee said.

"I apologize," she said in a strained voice.

Mr. Peak rolled his eyes and then called up toward a microphone in the ceiling. "I said it, didn't I? It's one thing to have a woman on the payroll. Another to have one that's knocked up six ways from Sunday."

The woman flashed her eyes at him. "Would you prefer I take *maternity leave* during our little emergency?"

"Don't get smart," he said. "I'm not the one who knocked you up."

The woman straightened herself, and even though her face was pale and strained, she remained upright. "Perhaps it would be best for me speak to Phoebe alone."

Mr. Peak licked his teeth beneath his lips. He didn't seem to want to budge, but he must've known something I didn't about this woman because he tapped his papers into a neat pile, and then walked toward the exit. The man with the goatee followed.

"That's just great," Mr. Peak said in the doorway so the woman could hear. "The world'll get clicked off all because you can't handle a couple of kicks from a baby's feet. Hey, kid." He looked at me and pointed to the microphone in the ceiling. "Let us know if her water breaks."

When the door shut, the woman managed half a smile. "Why don't you come closer, Phoebe?"

I sat in the chair next to her while she slowly turned her belly toward me, like it was the rotation of a planet or something.

"May I?" she said.

Before I could answer, she tilted my chin upward, turning my face side to side.

"The spitting image," she said.

I knew she meant Daddy and took my chin back.

"I haven't got much sleep lately," I said.

Liz gave me a pitying smile. "I suppose I ought to start by telling you that you and I are sisters. Well, *half* sisters."

I studied her face, looking for any resemblance to Ma or Daddy to figure just which half she was talking about. I couldn't find a trace of either. Every inch of her was delicate and smooth. Here was proof that some people did win the lottery when it came to genes.

Liz gathered my hands between hers and set them in her lap, which was uncomfortable because while her hands were icy cold, her thighs were burning up. *Must be a pregnant thing,* I thought.

"I can see him too, you know," Liz said. "Our father. In fact, as far as I know, you and I are the only two. Well, and our mothers. But my mother is dead, and yours . . . well, as I said, she's on a special mission."

I looked at her skeptically but kept my mouth shut.

"You're smart keeping quiet," she said, squeezing my hands with her icy ones. "Your mother must have taught you well. Come with me."

She pushed herself up off the chair and then led me to a dark little room in the corner. The walls were a tangle of pipes, and hanging in the center was a periscope that looked plucked straight out of a submarine.

"Go ahead," Liz said.

I pressed my eyes to the rubbery eyepiece. There was Daddy, in two blurry circles, closer than I'd ever seen him.

"How does he look?" Liz asked.

I pulled my eyes back. "You tell me."

"Bored," she said, without looking.

"How many hairs does he have on the mole on his right cheek?" I said.

Liz gave a smirk. She blinked her pretty lashes and then gazed through the scope. "It isn't on his cheek. It's on his chin."

I had a lot of feelings then. Heartache. Affection. Like I wasn't so alone. Things I'd kept myself from feeling since I was eleven.

"So," I said, "Daddy keeps you safe too?"

The woman wrinkled her eyebrows in confusion.

"That's why he looks at us," I said. "To warn us when a Shiver is coming."

"Shiver?" the woman said.

"That's what Ma and I call monster attacks. They always leave you with a chill."

The woman's expression turned from confusion to pity. "Oh, you sweet, innocent thing."

I scowled at being talked to like I was in kindergarten, but a dreadful feeling started to well in my chest.

"Is that what you believe?" Liz said. "Is that what your mother told you?"

My teeth clenched. This felt like the time Katie told me there was no such thing as Santa, and I had to pretend like I knew all along while my heart was breaking.

"How do I explain this?" Liz tapped her teeth with her fingernail, thinking. "Best to be blunt, I suppose." She gave me a sincere look. "Phoebe, our father doesn't protect anybody. He only has three interests: violence, monsters, and women of a certain type."

"What do you mean?" I said, not sure I wanted to know.

"Our father's eyes drift toward these . . . *Shivers*, as you call them, because he likes to watch them kill. We are his entertainment. He doesn't care any more about you and me than you would about squishing an ant at a picnic."

I opened my lips to argue, but I couldn't. Realization dripped over me, cold and numb. I thought of Daddy's expression: bored or tired or pleased as punch. He had never been watching out for me and Ma. He'd been watching for his own pleasure.

Katie. The boy with his arm in a sling. He was *enjoying* it.

"Violence is Father's favorite thing in the world," Liz said, "right after scantily clad women. In fact, that's where you came from. Father liked the look of your mother in that torn dress so much that he—"

My face crumpled.

"I apologize," Liz said. "I've known that Father is a debauchee for so long that I've grown used to it."

I rubbed my face, remembering all the times Ma had told me to avert my eyes because Daddy had his hand down his boxer shorts. Then I dropped my hands and stared at Liz's pregnant belly in horror. "Is that . . . *his*?"

"What? Of course not. Our father may be a pervert, but that doesn't mean he's incestuous."

I studied the pipes in the small room. "Did Ma know about this place?"

"She was as surprised as you are," Liz said.

Why had Ma lied to me all these years? Did she think I wasn't grown up enough, even now at fifteen, to handle it? I felt so stupid for not putting it together before now. My mind tried to fill in all the parts of the story Ma had never told me. Maybe when she went to the police station, she was actually trying to get them to protect her from the creepy man in the sky.

As if reading my mind, Liz said, "Your mother didn't necessarily lie to you, Phoebe. It's more likely she's been lying to herself. She first caught Father's eye when she was kidnapped by Emperor Ook. Father's been searching for her ever since. Well, her and a few choice other women. Every time his eyes tracked your mother down, she knew just when to escape. So in a sense, he *was* protecting you. Just not purposefully."

I'd been blaming Ma for robbing me of a good life. But it wasn't her fault at all. It was Daddy's. If she was the lightning rod, his gaze was the lightning.

Liz shook her head. "Here I am discussing family matters when we have mountains of work and mere days to do it. You know about Father's remote control, right?"

My mind was spinning so fast I couldn't quite figure out what she was asking at first. But then I remembered the black box sitting in Daddy's lap. Ma and I could never quite figure out what it was, but we took turns guessing. A box for a diamond necklace? A wand? Neither of us had ever guessed a remote control. It didn't even have a cord.

I adjusted the periscope. The remote was as clear as a mountaintop in sunlight. Usually it was rested on his knee, but right then, on that thawing spring afternoon, he was lifting it. And it was pointed straight toward Earth.

"And you understand what that remote implies?" Liz asked.

When I was seven years old, the motel manager insisted on showing me and Ma up to the room so he could demonstrate the "wave of the future."

"Is it magic fingers?" Ma asked. "'Cause I'm all out of nickels and those beds rattle the fillings right out of my teeth."

"Better!" the manager said, and with a chuckle, he carried my suitcase and led us past the icemaker down the hallway. He opened the door for us and set my suitcase inside, then flipped on the lights and rubbed his hands together. He went to the nightstand and picked up a small rectangular box with four white buttons and a wire leading to the TV. It said ZENITH in electric letters across the top.

He held it out to us with both hands like he was wielding Excalibur.

"Ladies, may I present to you . . . the *Lazy Bones*."

Ma gave the box a funny look. "What is it?"

In answer, the manager walked over to the television and flipped it on. A news anchor was speaking rapidly about a giant Gila monster attack in Little Winnipeg.

He walked back to me and crouched down low. "You like the news, little girl?"

I wrinkled my nose. The news was what happened to towns me and Ma abandoned. It was never good.

"What *do* you like?" the manager asked. "*Howdy Doody*?"

I bit my bottom lip and nodded.

"Well then, let's see if it's on, shall we?"

I reached up to turn the TV dial to channel three, but the manager said, "Ah ah ah." He held out the Lazy Bones. He tapped one of the four white buttons, second from the right. "Push *that* one."

I did. The button didn't go very easy, but I pressed and pressed until my thumb hurt, and then the button sank with a satisfying *Click!*

To my great astonishment, the TV changed. It leapt from boring old news to Ed Sullivan smiling in front of a curtain.

"Well, it isn't *Howdy Doody*," the manager said, winking, "but close enough."

My fright quickly melted away as I realized the magic that I had cast with my very own thumb. I smiled up at Ma, who didn't look so impressed.

"Is this thing why the room costs an extra dollar a night?" she'd asked.

The remote control had been the most enthralling thing I'd ever seen in my young life. But peering through the periscope, I took on Ma's skepticism.

There in the sky, Daddy's thumb was moving toward the only button on the remote that I could see. A big button right at the top. The power button.

"But," I said, slowly removing my eyes from the eyepiece, "if that's a remote control, then . . ."

Liz nodded.

All I could think of was what happened whenever I clicked off a TV for the night. All those smiling faces and newsreels and puppets and laughter collapsing into a single line and then shrinking to a bright blip that flashed like a dying star or an atomic blast before . . . nothing. Just a blank screen with a warped reflection of yours truly.

I'd waited my whole life to have the perfect kiss on the Eiffel Tower or the Empire State Building. But if Daddy turned off the world, I'd never get there. I'd never see Ma again. My legs went numb, ready to collapse.

"I find it's best not to consider our insignificance in the universe," Liz said, steadying me. She squeezed my arm. "Perhaps it's best if I explain what we do here."

She exited the room, and I followed in a daze. We walked down a different hallway to the room I'd seen through the wire window with all the machines and weird static. The man in the lab coat was gone.

"Our job in this lab," Liz said, punching buttons on a panel, "is to ensure that Father never grows bored."

Several wavering images appeared on a row of screens, each showing a close-up of a different part of Daddy. There was one for each of his drooping eyes, one on the corner of his lips, and one on his thick fingers holding the remote control—almost like a Picasso painting.

Liz adjusted dials until the pictures became clearer.

"Because I'm the only one who can see him—well, until you and your mother came along—it's my job to keep an eye on Father's expression and report what I see."

She punched another button and the images changed to

what looked like a sundial. Only in place of a shadow was an illustrated silhouette of Daddy, his arm lifting the remote.

"This is our Doomsday Dial," she said. "If Father's remote is pointed downward at six o'clock, then we're safe as houses. But if it rises to three . . ."

The whole world becomes nothing more than a blip on a TV screen.

Right then the remote on the Doomsday Dial was pointed at three thirty.

"As you can imagine," Liz said, "the men in this lab are losing their minds over our current situation. But don't fret. I can't tell you how many close calls we've had. I'll bet we've prevented this remote control from rising a dozen times at least." She seemed distracted by something on the screen. "Father is very predictable. Perverted men usually are."

My mind was sifting through the information as fast as it could. "How do you stop him from getting bored?"

Liz flipped a switch, and the screens fell into darkness. "Simple. We turn up the excitement."

Something crackled overhead, nearly making me jump out of my skin.

"Ease off, Link."

So there was a speaker in this room too.

Liz gave an exasperated sigh, while I collected my thoughts. *Turn up the excitement* . . . I peeked through the wire window into the hallway with its rooms full of monsters and oddities.

"You caused the Shivers."

Liz's head turned quickly in my direction. "Oh, my dear, *no.* The monster disasters are perfectly natural. There's nothing in this lab that wasn't already crawling on God's gray Earth. This lab was built to understand how these creatures came to be. Then we re-create them ourselves using radiation or atomization or—"

"Link," the speaker said. *"No specifics."*

The woman gave the ceiling a cold look, then warmed to me. "Imagine if Godzilla waded his way over from Japan and appeared off the coast of San Francisco. We could fight it off with an army of Gill-men that we personally generated. You understand?"

I took a step away from the window, imagining webbed claws and slimy lips. "You have Gill-men here?"

"Don't be silly," Liz said. "They're an aberration of evolution. That was just an example." She hit more buttons, and images of blueprints of all sorts of monsters started to flash across the screen. Antennae. Tentacles. Claws. Suction cups. "Over time, these creatures came to serve an even more important purpose. Keeping Father entertained. If things become too dull for his tastes, then—"

"Link," the voice through the speaker said. *"What did I just say?"*

Looking up, Liz muttered, "A rock and a hard place." She took my hand and smiled. "We need you to do something very simple for us, Phoebe—simple as playing I Spy. Do you know that game?"

I took my hand back. "I'm not six."

"No, no, of course you're not. I apologize." She nodded at her round belly. "This is my first, and I've never been good with children. I suppose I should be as straightforward with you as possible." Her eyes bounced around the room. "Father is growing bored more often lately. There's going to be a war.

A big war . . . and lots of people are going to—"

"Link," the speaker said, *"you are endangering that girl's life."*

She scowled at the speaker and then regained her composure. "All I'm asking you to do is watch through that periscope and keep an eye on Daddy's expression."

I gazed around the room with its screens and switches and concrete walls. "You want me to stay *here*?"

"In the lab, yes. We'll make up a room for you. A few times a day, you'll peer through the periscope. If it appears as if Father's thumb is about to move away from the button or if it looks like the remote is lowering at all, then you'll inform Mr. Peak, and they'll start to wind down the attack."

"What attack?" I said.

The speaker crackled again, and Liz gave it a sharp look. "I *know*." Again she smiled at me. "Just know that the sooner you tell someone that the remote is descending, the more lives you'll save."

"Is that . . . Ma's special mission? She's watching Daddy too?"

Liz nodded. "Precisely. We have her squirreled away in a different base. She's doing very important work, keeping an eye on the eastern side of our father's face. We just need someone to keep an eye on the western side. That's your job. We'll be trying out different experiments around the country. If Daddy isn't interested in one type of monster, he might be interested in another."

"Why can't you do it?" I asked.

She patted her pregnant stomach. "I'm due any day. And I'm certainly not as alert as I was a couple months ago."

I leaned against a switchboard, feeling light-headed. "Do I have any say in this?"

Liz looked at the microphone on the ceiling. "I'm afraid not, my dear."

So this was my life now. I would live in this concrete hole, among the creatures and caged lights and smells and beeps and electrical currents. I imagined myself peering through the periscope while Peak stared at me from the corner with his saggy expression.

One of these days, I might be staring at the end of a remote control pointed straight at my heart. Daddy's giant thumb would press down on that big button, and the ground would rise like a pulled shutter while the sky fell like a dropped sheet. Both would meet in the middle in a single line on the horizon before shrinking to a bright point of everythingness before it faded to nothing.

And there I was, spending my final moments with a man who looked like Droopy Dog.

"Guess the answer's 'yes' then," I said, wondering how I was going to escape.

If the world was really coming to an end, I wanted to live the life I'd always imagined was waiting for me in the big cities. Or at the very least have a milk shake with Beth. Maybe go on a date with Calvin and get one last laugh.

A knock came at the door right before it opened. Pan-Cake ran into the room with a wet branch in her mouth and started leaping at my legs.

A handsome man entered behind her and kissed Liz on the cheek. "Hello there, star eyes," he said in a Texas drawl.

"Stop," Liz said, fighting a smile. "You saw me twenty minutes ago."

It was the man who had opened the steel door. He'd seemed hostile with Pan-Cake at the time, but it turned out he was just going to play fetch with her. He wore a bomber jacket, Levi jeans, and leather boots. A matchstick hung from the corner of his lips.

"Peak got me caught up on Phoebe here," he said, flashing me a smile and sticking out his hand. "Heck Halberstam. But you can call me Hal. Pa signed the certificate before Ma got the chance, and she wasn't the type of woman to raise no Heck."

I shook his hand and smiled, which felt odd in a situation like this.

Hal thumbed his nose toward Pan-Cake. "Lucky-13 sure seems to have taken a fancy to ya."

I couldn't bring myself to pretend like I was excited about the dog right then. Or anything, for that matter.

Liz put her arm through Hal's. "Do you have any questions for us, Phoebe?"

How could you take my life away like this?

"Phoebe," Liz said carefully. "No one else can do what you do. In fact, if I go into labor, then you might be the only one in the West who can call off the attack."

And save thousands of lives from the Shivers you made, I thought.

Liz suddenly brightened. "Let's just pretend this is going to work, shall we? You're going to have a short vacation. Right here in the lab. You're going to perform a simple job, and then when it's all finished, you'll get to go to a normal school with kids your own age."

Not if Daddy gets bored, I thought. Then all the motels and all the schoolkids and the Navajo people, the parks and the television sets, Calvin and Rhoda, Officers Shelley and Graham, Beth and Ma, wherever she was, even the motel manager and his wife. They'd all get swallowed up in darkness.

"In fact," Liz said, "I'll bet we can arrange it so that if you help us out, you'll be given protection for the rest of your life. You and your mother. You'll never have to flee another town again."

My heart fluttered as the speaker crackled. *"Miss Link, I don't think offering—"*

"I'm *sure* we could arrange it," she said, staring daggers at the ceiling. She smiled at me again. "That way you wouldn't have to worry about these *Shivers* anymore, and you could just focus on you things." She squeezed my arm. "Whatever they might be."

I got a flutter of hope, but it died just as quickly. It was easy for Liz to say. She already had a handsome fella. She got to leave the Buried Lab. I was just a glorified canary in a coal mine.

"Let me show you to your room," Liz said, and then looked at my one wet sock. "And my goodness, let's find you some shoes. Hal, we might need to borrow yours. I'm not sure any of mine will fit her."

She and Hal led me and my big feet deeper into the lab. Right then I'd take Rhoda or the two beehive hairdos over being buried in the desert with Droopy Dog, a bunch of monsters, and a pregnant lady who talked to me like I was six.

I was still awake when the sobbing echoed down the hallway.

"*Ma*?"

I threw my feet off the bunk and waited to hear the crying again. The concrete floor of my windowless cell was littered with excelsior, as if they expected me to use the bathroom like a guinea pig. It smelled like the last occupant had.

The sobbing came again, muffled and distant. I leapt up, grabbed my dress, and then remembered Liz had locked the door.

"For your own safety," she'd said. "If there's an emergency, we'll be able to hear you scream down the hall. Rest well."

Obviously, she didn't have much experience as an older sister.

The sobbing continued. *Was* that Ma? I'd only seen her cry a handful of times in my life. It was mostly about Brad, who had divorced her after she got miraculously pregnant when they'd been trying for kids for almost ten years.

I decided to take a chance and slipped on my dress. When Liz had closed the door, I hadn't heard it click. I stood up and tried the handle. It was locked. But when I pulled on it, it came open.

This hallway had no lights save a faint glow rounding the corner at its end. I crept as quietly as I could. As the hall started to bend, the sobbing grew louder. Then it crackled. I looked up. It was coming through a speaker on the ceiling. . . .

I nearly jumped out of my skin when someone stepped around the corner.

"Oh!" Liz said, putting a hand to her chest. "Hello."

I froze. "Um, hi."

"What are you doing awake?"

I glanced at the speaker. "I thought I heard crying."

Liz wiped her cheeks. "That was me, I'm afraid. Pregnant women should be in bed, not assisting a buried laboratory in saving the world."

I nodded like I understood.

Liz sniffed and smiled. "I see I could have done a better job locking your door. Ah well, you're here now." She cradled her belly. "We can't sleep either. Shall I make us all some tea?"

I followed her to a closet kitchen where she boiled some water and prepared a tray with a flower-painted teapot, two fragile cups, and a tin of butter cookies. "We have a few creature comforts in this wretched place," Liz said. I followed her down the hallway, the lid on the teapot clinking delicately. "I find a little chamomile stops the fussing in its tracks. I'm expecting a snob, I guess."

What she really meant was a *cultured* baby, I thought. Ma once said she alternated Olympia beer and Coca-Cola every other night while she was pregnant with me. I didn't know what those drinks made me, but it sure wasn't a snob. Or cultured.

We came to a door with rounded corners and a big wheel on it, again like something stolen off a submarine.

Liz lifted the tray toward the wheel. "You mind?"

I turned the wheel, first to the right, then remembering "lefty loosey," quickly turned it the other way, hoping Liz hadn't noticed. I never made these kinds of mistakes in front of Ma. The door made a hissing noise as it creaked outward.

I held it open while Liz carefully stepped over the lip of the frame.

She set the tea tray on a small table that already had two chairs on either side of it and said, "Would you seal the door again, please? I don't want anyone breaking up our party."

I turned the wheel—the right way this time.

Liz sat in the far chair and I sat in the other. A band of light crossed her eyes, leaving the rest of her face in shadow, making her even more beautiful somehow. She filled the cups with tea and said, "This is pleasant. Two sisters getting to know each other."

I looked around the room, whose walls were made up of tiles like charcoal pyramids, all pointing inward, right at us.

"Why are we in here?" I asked.

Liz picked up her teacup, holding it just with her fingertips. "Because this is the only room with no microphones."

I picked up the other cup and tried to hold it just as delicately, but it made the porcelain feel slippery. "How do you know?"

"I was here when they built this place."

We took sips of the chamomile, and I set mine on the tray, trying not to make a face.

"So," Liz said, "now that we're alone, tell me about yourself."

I held my arm. "What do you wanna know?"

She shrugged her pretty shoulders. "Anything."

I felt about as vulnerable as a frog with its guts splayed open. I didn't have any good stories. Not like Ma. That was the problem.

"Perhaps you'd like to ask me a question first," Liz said.

"Okay, um . . . do Daddy's eyes follow the monsters? Or do the monsters pop up wherever his eyes go?"

Liz sipped her tea. "There's no real way for us to tell, is there?"

"I guess not," I said, feeling stupid for some reason.

"Anything else?" Liz said.

My cheeks darkened. I'd had a question burning inside me for years. "So how does Daddy . . . how did our moms, um . . ."

Liz smiled. "Let's just say there was no actual physical contact. They were just beautiful and standing in the wrong place at the wrong time."

I scratched at my clavicle, trying to piece that one together.

"Why didn't you get locked up?" I said.

"What do you mean?"

"Ma was tossed in the loony bin the minute she breathed a word about Daddy. Why weren't you?"

Liz set down her teacup with a small clink. "I suppose that had to do with my mother. She never told me about the man in the sky. She was a geisha, and they're trained never to speak of untoward things. The man in the sky was a taboo topic, like sex or that time of the month. She simply pretended he wasn't there. Although I'm quite certain she could see him. I could tell by how she didn't look at the sky. Mother avoided clouds the same way she avoided the eyes of her clientele."

All of a sudden I wasn't much jealous of Liz anymore. How would it be having a mother who never shared the secrets of life with you, who kept them tucked up and hidden within the folds of her kimono?

"I managed to keep it a secret for most of my life," Liz said. "But then I married a military man. You met Hal earlier this evening. I told him where Father was looking, and he started reporting it to the military as hunches. Over time, the secret service grew to trust us. Eventually, I learned to make myself indispensible."

Did that mean I was indispensible too? A part of me hoped not. I wanted this lab to dispense of me immediately.

"They thought I was the only one," Liz said. "The military, that is. But then combing through old police files, we found a woman who claimed she saw a man in the sky who caused disasters with his eyes. And to think it was the famous *Loretta Lane* herself. So we summoned her to the nearest town, Pennybrooke, by setting up the Emperor Ook tour."

"*You* planned the carnival tour?"

"Of course," Liz said, like it was the most obvious thing in the world. "Ook is tired news these days. But you'd be surprised at what a couple phone calls and a little money will do."

Ma had been surprised when she'd received the call saying she was back in demand. She'd been out of the limelight since 1943 when she got pregnant. But a job on the road was too enticing for a woman and her daughter always on the run.

"You were a *complete* surprise, of course," Liz said. "I'm impressed your mother managed to keep you a secret."

There were so few things I understood about Ma right then. I wondered if she had hidden me to keep me safe or if she was just ashamed.

"So your mother never registered you anywhere?" Liz asked, sipping her tea. "Not so much as a birth certificate?"

"I don't know," I said. "I suppose not."

"Interesting. You must have been so . . . *lonely.*"

It felt strange having this pointed out twice in one day. This time felt less comforting because Liz wouldn't be doing anything to solve it, like Beth did. I felt a chill from the concrete walls. The way things were looking I might be lonely for the rest of my life.

"How are they going to stop him?" I said. "Stop Daddy from ending the world?"

Liz's fingernails made rhythmic notes on her porcelain cup. "There were things I couldn't tell you earlier. Things I was *kept* from telling you because they were listening in. Hence the reason for my bringing you in here." She gestured at the black pyramids. "The men upstairs are trying to solve Father's boredom the only way that men do."

"How?"

Liz leaned in like she was letting me in on a secret. "Imagine every catastrophe that's happened in this country. The plants. The aliens. The giant insects."

I'd known people who'd been killed by every one of those things. I took another sip of the disgusting tea to hide my sadness.

"As I said," Liz continued, "their hearts were in the right place initially. Any time a disaster struck—or a *Shiver* as you call them—the military swept in and took careful notes on how it happened. Maybe it was a mutation. Or a freak occurrence in nature. Or gamma rays. They recorded every detail to try to prevent these tragedies. But once Hal and I made them aware of Father, that's when things took a turn. Any time the remote started to rise in the slightest, they released one of their own copy creations, just to pique his interest."

I thought of all the times that monsters had returned inexplicably, even though they were said to have been wiped out. Like when the son of the doctor who accidentally spliced himself with a fly was tricked into getting spliced as well.

"But," I said, "people *die* in those attacks."

Liz nodded. "That's men's thinking for you. They refer to it as *collateral damage*. And they forgive themselves by saying it saves more lives in the long run."

Ma never did think much of men's thinking. *At any given moment you can't trust they have enough blood knocking around upstairs,* she'd said. I didn't know what she'd meant at the time, but I noticed she always did exactly what men asked of her for fear they'd lock her up again—forcing her to hug herself in a straitjacket through the long lonely nights.

Liz sighed. "And perhaps the men are right. So far their copy creations have convinced Father to lower his remote every time. Heaven forbid he changes the channel or turns us off completely."

I nearly choked on my tea. "Changes the channel?"

Liz's cup paused before her lips. "Throwing our entire world into another dimension."

The thought made my vision blur. The first time I held a Lazy Bones I'd spent the rest of the night flipping between channel after channel—news, Ed Sullivan, news, *American Bandstand*, the Sunday night feature, news—until Ma pinched the bridge of her nose and said, "*Enough*, Phoebe. You're going to start talking in incomplete sentences."

"Best we remain in this dimension, hmm?" Liz said, reading my expression. "Anyway, Father has become increasingly more difficult to entertain lately. With familiarity comes contempt. He's almost completely lost interest in single monster attacks. So now . . ." She glanced nervously toward the door. "Well, now the men here want to try combinations. Two different monsters at the same time. Or three. They want to release the past terrors of the world and start a war so bloody and terrifying it will convince Father to set down the remote control and continue watching for the foreseeable future."

I tried to imagine a Shiver that involved more than one type of monster—a blob and a flying saucer, a Gila monster and flesh-eating plants, Ook and a storm of scarabs—but my mind couldn't seem to hold it all.

"Where's it gonna happen?" I asked, thinking of Pennybrooke.

Liz finished her tea and set down her cup. "That's classified information, I'm afraid."

I glanced at the ceiling. "I thought you said there were no microphones in here."

"Trust me, Phoebe. You're better off not knowing some things. These men are kind enough, but you don't want to give them any excuse to keep you locked up here for good."

"But more and more people are going to have to keep dying all the time, just to keep Daddy entertained."

It was odd making this argument. I'd never let myself care about the people Ma and I left behind. After losing people I loved, I'd grown a thick skin. But that was when I thought all the Shivers were natural. Now that I knew humans were causing some of them . . .

"I know," Liz said. "It's hideous. The men argue that death and violence are what created this world in the first place and that without them we don't have Father's interest. And without Father's interest . . . well, our lives simply won't continue."

"If that's men's thinking," I said, "then what do *you* think?"

Liz smiled and poured herself more tea. "I think

Father—*Daddy*—can't know what he wants if he's never seen it before. But what that is . . ." She gave a small shrug.

"You mean like . . . romance?" I said.

Liz hiccupped, nearly spitting out her tea. "I think it's safe to say he'd shut us all off at the first bashful bat of an eyelash."

My cheeks grew hot. "I guess you're right."

Liz's cup clinked on the tray. Her chair scooted back. "Brainstorm a minute. I'm going to go get you some sugar."

A circle of light wavered on my full cup of tea. So much for looking cultured.

Liz loosened the wheel, stepped out, and the door fell shut behind her.

Outside, Daddy's remote was rising higher by the hour. I wanted to come up with a solution. Not a stupid one, like romance. A real one Liz and the men of the lab could use, instead of releasing every horror in God's—or whoever's—creation on all the quiet towns of the world.

There were still so many Katies in the world I hadn't met yet. So many boys with arms in slings. The thought of all of them being torn apart and smashed flat and bled dry as part of Daddy's entertainment made my head heavy and my teacup blur. The light in the room dimmed. It had been a long day.

A minute later, the wheel turned, and Liz reentered with a bowl full of sugar cubes. She plopped two into my tea. "See if that helps." I swished the cup around a little until the cubes disappeared in white whirls, then took a sip.

"Mm," I said. But I wasn't thinking about tea.

Liz's hand reached out and took mine. "It's not your responsibility, Phoebe," she said. "Not alone, anyway." When I didn't respond, she pulled my hand across the table and set it on the swell of her stomach. "If this all goes well, you'll be an auntie soon. Or half of one."

Something tugged at my heart. I'd never had any family besides Ma.

Liz touched my cheek. "Take the night and see if anything comes to you, and we'll meet back here for coffee in the morning. Okay?"

I nodded, and Liz's eyes smiled in the band of light. Her mother must've been a real knockout. Enough to knock out Daddy's genes.

She leaned in conspiratorially. "Perhaps we women can come up with something the men never would have thought of, huh?"

I nodded as a tear dripped into my tea.

Katie Bryer came into my life in the summer of 1954, after Ma and I narrowly escaped the meteor crash at Sand Rock. Katie was the first girl who took the time to teach me how to play hopscotch *and* fire a slingshot.

Her mother stuffed her in poofy dresses and shoes that glowed like bowling balls, tying her hair in tight ponytails to try and wring the tomboy tendencies right out of her. Katie looked as bright and cheerful as a fruit salad when she left her house and like lint from the dryer when she returned. I'll never know why she took a shine to me.

For the first time in my life, I had a whole two months to make a real friend. It seemed disasters were happening everywhere but in our town for once. Katie and I explored every nook and cranny of Alamogordo, New Mexico, singing "Diamonds Are a Girl's Best Friend" near the old White Sands test site, daring each other to dance the Cha-Cha on street corners, and even flipping through the first issue of *Playboy* in her brother's room so we could sneak a peek at Marilyn Monroe, who had nothing on except the radio.

One day Katie suggested that if a boy wanted to kiss me, to make him eat a sucker first. "If he's a looker, he can get away with apple. If he's funny but not so easy on the eyes, make him eat grape." As far as I was concerned, Katie was the best thing since Wonder Bread.

When I came home one day to find Ma boxing up her feather hats, my heart turned over.

"Pack up, Phoebe," Ma said. "Daddy's looking our way."

I froze in the doorway.

Ma zipped up her suitcase. "Hop to!"

I turned and ran.

"Phoebe, come back!" she called after me, but I was already halfway down the street.

I ran all fifteen blocks to Katie's house and pounded on the door. Vera, the Bryers' help, answered, baby Jason swaddled in one arm.

"Why, it's *Phoebe!* If I'd known you were comin', I'd've baked a cake! Ha-ha. Come in, come in. Katie'll be back from Girl Scouts in ten."

Of course. It was Wednesday. I hadn't joined the group because Ma was worried we'd have to leave before I could sew my first badge.

I stepped into the foyer, trying to catch my breath.

"Child, you're blushing bright as the sun," Vera said. "What's going on?"

Words drained out of me. I'd hoped Katie would answer the door, so I could wrap my arms around her neck and hold on tight until she agreed to come with us or Ma said we could stay put for once.

"Come on," Vera said, rubbing my back. "I'll make you a sandwich."

I followed her into the kitchen. At the motel, Ma and I only ever ate precooked canned food, but at the Bryers' I was spoiled with oven-cooked Swanson dinners, Jell-O salad, Cheez Whiz, raspberry Kool-Aid, and Betty Crocker with Reddi-Wip for dessert.

Vera bounced Jason in her arm while spreading marshmallow fluff on the bread. I wanted nothing more than to sit and relax and gobble up everything she pushed my way, but there was no time.

"Vera?"

"Yes, dollface?"

"What if I told you that you and the Bryers had to get out of town now? This afternoon?"

"Why, Phoebe"—Vera set down her knife—"you're pale as a sheet. Whatever's the matter?"

I looked at the clouds through the window above the sink and tried to organize my thoughts. I couldn't actually *see* Daddy at that point, but I knew he was there. The newspapers had proven it every time Ma made us flee another town. But any talk about him could land me and Ma in the rubber room.

"Just pack everything up," I said, "and when Katie gets home, come to the motel. If you stick with me and Ma, we'll keep you safe."

Vera studied my face like it had algebra on it. Then she gave me an admonishing look, like I was a toddler playing games.

"This is a God-fearing town, Phoebe," she said, cutting the crusts off the sandwiches. "Nothing bad will happen here. And if there is an emergency, we'll be kept safe. That's what the police officers are for." She set the sandwich in front of me. "*There.* This'll make you feel better."

I took a bite. I didn't know what else to do. The marshmallow fluff and Wonder Bread grew soggy on my tongue. I wanted to believe Vera. Sometimes the disaster was small, easily solved by the military. Or it only affected a person or two. Ma and I would skip town only to hear about the man who accidentally spliced himself with a fly. No one actually got hurt . . . except him and the fly, of course.

Other times, the disaster was too big to imagine. Ook or Godzilla or the Rhedosaurus would go on a city-smashing spree. Ma said it was never worth the gamble.

I hadn't swallowed the first bite of my sandwich when the knock came at the front door. Vera went to answer it.

"Why, good afternoon, Miss Lane! Your daughter's trying to convince me that we need to get out of town without so much as a fare-thee-well."

Ma laughed, her voice a strained sort of casual. "The girls must be playing a little game or something. You know the drills they run kids through at school these days."

Vera chuckled. "Any break from boys and doo-wop is a blessed relief." She called down the hallway. "*Phoebe*? Your momma's here."

When I stepped into the foyer, Ma playfully shook her finger at me. "No more late-night TV for you, young lady." She scraped a bit of peanut butter from the corner of my lips, her smile twitching just slightly.

As we stepped off the porch, Ma called back, "Sorry for the interruption, Vera."

"It's nothing at all!" Vera said, and waved.

When we reached the end of the driveway, I spotted Katie coming down the sidewalk. I broke free from Ma, sprinting fast as my buckle shoes would allow. By the time I'd thrown my arms around Katie's neck, Ma was already trying to pry them off.

"Come on, Phoebe. None of this now."

I wept into Katie's hair, and Katie was such a good friend, she started crying too.

"What's happening?" she asked. *"What's happening?"*

"Nothing's happening," Ma said, tugging my arms. "Phoebe and I are just heading on a little vacation, and she doesn't want to go."

My grip was loosening against my will. If Ma had let me, I swore I could have picked Katie up and carried her out of town with us.

But that's not what happened.

Just before Ma pulled me away, I whispered *I love you* into Katie's hair so soft I don't know if she heard. As Ma dragged me down the sidewalk, I couldn't stand looking back at my best friend's face.

We reached the gas station pay phone and Ma fished a nickel from her purse. "You're lucky I love you, otherwise I'd chain you to the radiator in every town we went to. Hello? Yes, we need a taxi from the Smithfield gas station to the metro just as soon as you can send it."

We escaped in the nick of time. People in the station were in a panic. Loud pops echoed down the city streets.

On the bus, I buried my face in my hands.

Ma's fingernails ran through my hair. "Shh, Phoebe. There there. Daddy's eyes saved us. We need to be grateful. He *saved* us."

I suddenly regretted not looking at Katie one last time and tearfully pressed my nose against the bus window.

Ma tugged at the back of my dress. "Look away, Phoebe. No use seeing that. And close your legs. Otherwise, people will know you got apples on your underpants."

Maybe it was my imagination. Maybe it was the spotted window and the distance. Or maybe the next day's headline played tricks on my memory. But I could have sworn I saw a cone-shaped hill rising above Alamogordo. Instead of sand grains it was made of bricks and car tires.

As the bus pulled out of the city, I remember seeing a silhouette—an ant the size of a tank—scramble to the top of the giant hill and wave its antennae as something—no, *someone*—wriggled in its jaws in the dying cloud light.

I woke up back at the motel.

At first I thought I'd dreamed it all. The trip into the desert with the Girl Scouts. The monsters in the Buried Lab. My half sister and the Doomsday Dial. But then I heard a light snoring. Pan-Cake was lying on the pillow next to me, her white fur covered in sand.

On the nightstand beside her was a ham radio with a glowing light. The knob to tune the frequency had been broken off, the metal underneath fused in place. The speaker made a crackling sound, almost like a voice coming through. I woozily pushed up to my elbows, picked up the radio's mouthpiece, and clicked the button on its side.

"Hello?" I said, then waited.

At the base of the nightstand was a pair of men's army boots. I guess Liz found some in my size. The boots blurred in and out of focus as I cradled my head. I didn't remember coming home from the lab. Was my chamomile drugged? Or the sugar?

"Hello?" I said again into the mouthpiece.

There was no response.

Pan-Cake let out a little snort, her paws twitching. We'd both done a whole lot of running the day before. Maybe I'd just passed out cold, and they brought me home when Mr. Peak came to his senses and realized a lab was no place for a teen girl. Or a little dog, I guessed.

There was a knocking at the door. I slumped to the blinds and peeked out, expecting to find Officer Shelley, but instead saw a stout bald man in a plaid jacket. The carnival owner.

"Miss Lane? Miss Lane! It's Mr. French, Miss Lane. You've missed three rehearsals now! And the show is *tomorrow night*." He pounded on the door. "Miss Lane!"

He was practically beating the door down when I opened it.

Mr. French huffed, dark as an eggplant. "Is your *mother* here?"

"Um, no, she's not," I said, supporting myself on the doorframe. My legs were drooping.

"Well, we have a *situation* on our hands. Everything is set up at the fairground, except we are missing our *main attraction*. I could try to fit Emperor Ook's bones into that dress, but I do not think our audience would be amused."

While he rambled on about the carnival, my eyes drifted past him. The sky was overcast, but in the glow of dawn, I could see Daddy's remote peeking over the mountains—the giant sundial about to announce the end of the sun. Was that what the ham radio was for? So I could report back to the lab if Daddy looked bored? What about the periscope? Why hadn't the lab left me a pair of binoculars, at least?

"I'm talking to you, young lady," the carnival owner said, snapping his fingers in my face. "When do you expect her?"

"Um . . ." My eyes drifted back to the remote.

I wasn't about to sit in this motel while the world made its mind up about whether it was going to end or not.

I met the carnival owner's eyes. "Ma quit," I said.

He paled. "But—but the billboards and the advertisements. We paid her three months' advance!"

"She sends her regrets."

I closed the door in his face. It was seven thirty. Time to go to school. It might not be the Eiffel Tower or Korvette's, but it sure beat waiting for the world to be shut off in the motel room of gloom. Besides, Daddy's movements were slow. If there were any changes in his expression, I'd be able to get back to the ham radio quick as a bunny and let the lab know.

I emptied Ma's makeup bag into the sink and followed her morning routine to the letter. I quickly learned that watching da Vinci does not a painter make. In twenty minutes, my face was stinging with alcohol from swabbing away all my mistakes, and I had to keep applying base to cover up my chapped skin. I wished Ma was there and not on some *special mission*. For a lot of reasons.

I grabbed the sheath from the closet because it was the best dress I owned, even if it was a little tight. But I was in for a shock. When I slipped it on, it swished around my midsection. I looked in the mirror and found that it no longer made me look like a teakettle in a cozy. My dough was nowhere in sight.

"Huh," I said to my reflection, turning to the side and giving my side a pinch.

My stomach started to gurgle, and I remembered I hadn't eaten a thing since Ma vanished—other than a heaping dose of butterflies. I'd gone on a three-day diet without even thinking about it, and now my dress fit like an absolute *dream*. But now that I knew she was safe on her special mission, I felt as empty as an inflatable doll. I grabbed a few dollars out of the suitcase.

"Be good, Pan-Cake," I said, but she was out cold even as I shut the door.

The day was beautiful—mostly overcast with a perfect

blend of flashes of sunlight and cool breezes. Ethel, the manager's wife with the knee braces, was rolling a cart filled with fresh towels.

"Why, good morning, dear," she said in a warm voice.

"Good morning," I said, and was surprised by how chipper I sounded without trying.

When I was little, motel managers were like grandparents to me. I adored the managers of one Comfort Motel so much, I asked Ma if I could call them Grandma and Grandpa. She had heartbreak in her eyes when she said, "I don't think that's a good idea, sweetie." She was right. That night, Daddy's eyes warned us to flee after someone started bringing people back from the dead with a monkey's paw.

No. Wait. Daddy didn't warn us. He *wanted* to watch those people die.

I wished it wasn't overcast that morning so I could flip him the bird.

On the way down Main Street, I stopped by the drugstore and bought a jar of Cheez Whiz, a can of SPAM, and two boxes of Cracker Jacks for breakfast. I picked kernels out of my teeth the rest of the way to school, my legs as trembly as a newborn deer's.

When I walked into Freeman High, I heard the squeak of shoes as two boys spun on their heels. One of them gave a low whistle like a bomb dropping. I looked around and realized I was gathering gazes like laundry static. I was about to explain that these army boots were the only shoes I had and that they should stop staring if they valued their eyeballs when someone threw their arms around my neck.

"I was worried *sick!*" Beth said, squeezing and pressing her chest to me a little too hard. "What happened? You just took off into the desert! Are you okay?"

"I'm *fine,*" I said, laughing and pulling away.

Liar, a voice said in my head. It spoke so clearly that I winced.

"Is Pan-Cake okay?" Beth asked.

"Um, yeah. She's fine. She's as beat as batter though."

"Where did you *go*?" Beth asked, adjusting her glasses. "The police combed the desert. They said they turned over every rock."

Not every rock, I thought. *Not the one with a door in it.*

"Well," I said, "see . . ."

Beth's eyes were all wrinkled up behind her glasses like we'd been best friends for just about forever. That's when I realized that nothing is lonelier than being the only one who knows the world is going to end. But if I told Beth, the men in the lab might come nab me. Maybe Beth, too.

The lunch bell rang.

"Can I tell you later?" I said. "I'm so hungry I could eat a horse."

"You're in luck," Beth said, hooking her arm through mine. "If I know Freeman's cafeteria, that's probably exactly what they're serving."

• • •

"Sheesh, leave some for the Africans," Rhoda said, sitting down across from me and staring at my lunch tray.

I had just about everything the lunch lady was serving up, from macaroni and cheese to drumsticks to buttered rolls to peas and carrots with gravy. But Rhoda couldn't faze me. Now that I was eating a solid meal, my skin felt gilded. This was good because Beth said she had to look something up in the library, so I was left to face the white pigtails and famous bangs alone.

"How's Queenie?" Rhoda asked.

I swallowed a chunk of chicken. "Who?"

"The Pomeranian, of course." Rhoda examined the end of her pigtail. "I only ask because she must feel so *cooped up* in that motel room. Father and I have a whole house and a nice big backyard she could run around in."

"Her name is Pan-Cake," I said, biting into a roll.

Rhoda flipped her pigtail over her shoulder and ignored me.

Calvin strolled up to our table and rubbed his hands together. "What about today?"

Rhoda bobbed her head back and forth. "I'll have to think about it."

"She'll have to think about it," Calvin said to me. "She's like one of those computers that fills a warehouse and takes a month to tell you one and one makes two. I'll be in a retirement home and old Rhoda will stroll in to join me for a game of bingo right before I die of cardiac arr—" His eyes did a double take. "Hey, did you cut your hair?"

"Um, no," I said. I hadn't washed it in a week.

He stroked his chin. "Something's different. Stand up."

I couldn't think of any reason not to. So I stuffed the roll in my mouth and stood.

"Boy, take her out of the sun and turn off the sprinkler," Calvin said. "This girl is *grown!* You're taller than me!"

I *was* taller than him. How had I not noticed that before?

"Say," Calvin said, "while blondie here is computing

whether or not to give the time of day to yours truly, do you want to hit the malt shop with me later?"

I was too shocked to respond. I'd never been asked on a date before. Also, my mouth was full of roll.

"Calvin," Rhoda said, "be a dear and get me a fruit cup, would you? Clean spoon?"

"Oh, um, yeah, sure. One fruit cup, coming right up." He snapped and pointed. "Think about it, Phoebe."

He jogged off to the lunch line while Rhoda got this look on her face, like the one the evil queen gets when the mirror first muttered the words *Snow White*.

"Maybe you could bring Queenie for a little visit later," she said.

"Huh?" I said, sitting back down.

"Your adorable doggie, of course," Rhoda said.

"She has other plans. Excuse me."

I took a massive bite of mashed potatoes and went to the lunch line, trying to still my pounding heart.

"Hey, Calvin," I said real low so the other kids in the cafeteria couldn't hear. "You know where the motel is, right? The one at the bottom of Main?"

"The one with the burned out *O* on the sign?" he said.

"That's the one." I swallowed deep and tried to tap into Ma's wellspring of confidence. "Why don't you show up there tonight around six? Room eight. Meantime . . ." I pulled him close and whispered into his ear. "Think of every dirty thing you ever wanted to do with a girl and write them down on a napkin. When you show up . . . we'll try 'em all."

Calvin tried to talk, but his jaw wouldn't work. I'd never left anyone speechless before. Let alone a wisecracker.

"Did Rhoda put you up to this?" he finally managed.

"You just show up," I said. "That's all."

He swayed, then took a step backward and sat on a stack of lunch trays. I blushed. Ma had told me about how boys have trouble standing whenever the blood relocates.

"What's your last name, by the way?" I said, trying to contain my giggling.

"M-Marple," Calvin said.

Phoebe Marple sounded like an eighty-year-old cartoon character. Ah, well. It's not like we were getting married or anything.

"Mr. Marple!" the lunch lady shouted. "*What* is your bottom doing on those trays? Stand up *immediately*."

I beelined it out of the lunchroom so I wouldn't have to watch that particular scene unfold. At least now I'd have some sort of life experience if Daddy ended up pressing the big button. In my imagination, I had always lost my innocence to some handsome tuxedoed man in New York. But with the world threatening to end, it would have to be hammy Calvin Marple instead.

I grabbed the rest of my food on the way out.

• • •

"Bye, Phoebe!" Beth called on the front steps of Freeman. "You coming to Girl Scouts today?"

"Um . . . yeah!" I called back, waving. "I think I will!"

I'd just need to pick up some food first. I was starting to get spots in my vision.

"Great! Don't forget Pan-Cake!"

I was almost to the bottom of the steps when a long-fingered hand landed on my shoulder.

"Miss Lane," Principal Toll said. "Would you like to explain to me what you're wearing?"

I followed his gaze to my legs and realized for the first time that the hem of the sheath dress was a couple of inches above my bare knees. Had it shrunk?

"I think it's time you paid a visit to Dr. Siley," Principal Toll said. "It's about time you're given your tests."

• • •

Girls and jocks and greasers alike stared as Principal Toll led me down the hallway. I realized they weren't staring at my army boots. They were staring at my *legs*. I didn't know what was happening to me, and right then I was too worried to care.

"Now, now, don't look so dour," the principal said as he led me down the hallway. "Seeing a psychiatrist is perfectly normal. Perfectly."

Principal Toll escorted me to a wooden door with a fogged window that read DR. SILEY, MD. The principal gestured to a chair and waited for me to sit before he left.

Voices murmured behind the door. Someone was crying. I thought I heard the words "nighttime," "blood," and "thigh," but the voice belonged to a boy, so that couldn't have been right. I crossed my legs, folded my arms, and prepared to act as natural as I knew how. The thought made me uncross and recross my legs the other way.

When the psychiatrist's door creaked open a minute later, my heart made a leap. There was nothing special about the boy—not in such a way that you'd put him in a Sears catalog or anything. He was bulky with low cheekbones and thick eyebrows, a squashed nose and a wide mouth, a cleft chin and a buzz cut, and a whole bunch of other unfortunate features that somehow came together into something that wasn't terrible to look at. When he saw me he wiped at his eyes with the back of a hand. In his other, he held a book called *Seduction of the Innocent*. He sniffed and the corner of his mouth made a sideways leap. It was so sweet, a girl could almost forget it was the end of the world.

The boy broke eye contact and clomped down the hallway. He hadn't so much as glanced at my army boots.

A throat cleared, making me jump. A man with a mustache, round glasses, and a white jacket stood in the doorway. He gestured inside, and I entered. The office was dark, barely lit by a window covered with wood slat blinds. The wall held a clock with a pendulum and portraits of Dr. Freud and Klaatu, the alien that made the electricity cut out across the entire planet for half an hour in 1951. The shelves were filled with books. One gave me a crawly feeling in my skin: *Sexual Behavior in the Human Female*.

"Sit," the psychiatrist said in a voice as low and soothing as a washing machine.

I sat. An hourglass lamp threw a circle of light onto a black leather desktop, illuminating a file. I saw a name, upside down at the top of the sheet: *Lear Finley*. The boy with tears in his eyes. I squinted at another line: *Father victim of vampirism*.

Oh. The boy was a Shiver survivor. I'd never met a survivor before. My and Ma's rule was that we never returned to a town that had been attacked. Too messy.

Before Dr. Siley could take his seat, I said, "Could I have some water?"

He gave me an irritated look, half squatted in his chair, but then pushed up off the armrests and went right back out of the office. The moment I sensed his shadow round the corner, I snagged the paper from Lear's file, folded it a few times, and slid it into my sock. I leaned back just as Dr. Siley reentered and set the glass of water on a coaster in front of me.

He sat and, lighting a cigarette, flipped Lear's folder shut and opened a blank one. "We're going to discuss your inappropriate dress, Miss Lane," he said, unscrewing the cap of a fountain pen, "but first I'm going to ask you a few simple questions. Have you or anyone you know exhibited a desire for blood, fear of sunlight, or an abhorrence to garlic?"

"No," I said.

He checked a box on the paper.

"Have you ever been in any type of illegal machine that instantaneously transported you through physical space, even if only a few feet?"

"No."

He checked another box.

"If you have been in one of these machines, is it possible that there was an insect or other creature of some type in there with you, and is it possible you were crossed with that creature, perverting your natural sense of humanity in any way?"

"Um, still no."

"Was that hesitation I sensed?"

"No."

Check.

"Do your sexual desires cloud your mind?"

Not more than any other girl, I didn't think. "No."

"Do you experience visions of a life that is not your own?"

"Doesn't everybody?"

"Hmm." The doctor did not check the box. "And finally, are you now or have you ever been a communist?"

"No."

Check.

My foot wouldn't stop tapping. I'd never had a test like this. I wanted a cigarette so bad I could've leapt across the table and snatched the psychiatrist's right out of his mouth.

Dr. Siley opened a drawer. "Now I'm just going to ask you to hold a few objects for me." He pulled out a clove of garlic, a silver bullet, a crucifix, and a cake of rotenone. For each one I picked up that didn't make my skin sizzle, he checked another box.

The doctor adjusted his glasses uncomfortably. "This next one is strange, but necessary. I promise you there's nothing untoward. I'm going to stand up from this chair and I'm going to come around this desk and I'm going to kiss you."

My whole body went cold. "Oh, I—"

He stood up, buttoned his jacket, and came around the table. I pressed back in my chair, thoughts swarming. What if I was really a cat person? What if I just never knew it till now because I'd never been kissed before? What if this whole time Daddy wasn't searching for Ma but *me* because he was waiting for me to transform? Also, this was my first kiss. I didn't want it to be my first kiss. Not with a guy with a mustache. Not with—

Dr. Siley bent over, and he pecked me on the cheek. It was quick and unromantic, and the saliva from his lips felt sticky on my skin. I felt relieved until he tipped my chin back and peeled open one of my eyelids and then the other.

"No sharpening of the pupils. Good." He returned to his

seat and checked another box. Then he screwed the cap back on his pen, placed the cigarette in his lips, and lifted a heavy box from the floor and plugged it in. "Where is your father?"

"He passed," I said, staring at the machine. It had a gauge with a needle and numbers ranging from zero to five hundred to two k. "He fought the great dinosaur in Japan. It clawed his plane right out of the air."

Dr. Siley nodded and flipped a switch. The machine hummed to life.

"What is that thing?" I said, uneasy.

"It's a standard Geiger counter. No need to be nervous."

He drew a metal rod from a clasp on the side and passed it over my head. The machine made a sound like stretching plastic. The needle leapt to two k.

Dr. Siley's cigarette dropped to the floor and smoldered on the carpet. He touched his Adam's apple. "Perhaps I should have waited to kiss you. . . ."

"What is it?" I said. "What does two k mean?"

The wall clock ticked away the seconds.

When I was nine I asked Ma what life was like in the loony bin. She grabbed an old sweater from the closet, pulled it over my head, slipped my arms into the stretched-out sleeves, and then tied the sleeves behind my back. She told me to lie on the bed and stare at the wall. She said I could have meals at eight, noon, and six. If I needed to go to the bathroom, I'd have to use the coffee can in the corner. Otherwise, I just needed to lie there and think about what made me go crazy.

"The problem is," Ma said, "how can you know? Is crazy a bug in your stomach? A scribble on your heart? A bruise on your brain? Whatever it is, you've got to try to make that crazy die inside you. You have to do it without ever feeling the sunshine or laughing with friends or even playing a round of solitaire. And if nothing is actually making you crazy, if all the doctors and psychiatrists think you're nuts for no good reason, well then you have to kill whatever part of yourself makes them think you're that way. Even if it's the best part about you."

I started to sob. I thought that just by asking the question, Ma had decided to commit me right there in our motel room, and that I would have to stay like that until I figured out what was wrong with me. At my first sniffle Ma immediately untied the sleeves, yanked off the sweater, and gathered me up in her arms.

"Oh, sweetheart. Sweetie. My Phoebe." She rocked me

back and forth. I couldn't stop sobbing. "I am so sorry. I didn't mean it. I was just playing." When my crying finally calmed, she cradled my face and wiped the tears away with her thumbs. "That'll never happen to you, do you hear me? *Never.*"

Turns out Ma was wrong.

I sat in the back of Officer Shelley's police car, my aching arms bound around my chest.

Officer Graham, Beth's brother, sat in the passenger seat. "Gosh, Shelley," he said through his hazardous materials suit. "To think we had an honest-to-goodness threat in our station and we let her go. Think of the damage she could have caused."

They'd been waiting for me in the parking lot when Dr. Siley and Principal Toll led me outside with special gloves. I kept asking them what was happening, but they wouldn't answer. They just stuffed me in the straitjacket and then stuck me in the back of the squad car. A part of me wanted to know what that machine, that Geiger counter, had told them, but another part wanted to ignore it altogether, like a zit or a scale that tells you you've put on a couple pounds. Whatever it was, they were going to lock me up for it.

I wanted to kick out the car's back window and sprint down the road, run into the desert until I reached the Buried Lab. But that was exactly the sort of thing that got you committed. According to Ma, I was supposed to sit here and act like everything was hunky-dory, even though my arms were tied underneath my armpits and they hadn't even told me what I'd done wrong. I was supposed to smile and play by the rules until the officers and the doctors decided I was a functional member of society and then released me from the loony bin.

But I had a sinking feeling they were taking me somewhere

much worse. My heart was pounding so hard, I could feel it thumping through the straitjacket. I tried to think sunny thoughts as I rested my cheek against the police car's window.

I thought I couldn't get more terrified. That was before I looked at the sky.

The clouds had cleared. Daddy was staring straight at Pennybrooke. His mouth hung open, a dumb expression on his face. Again, I had to remind myself that he wasn't warning me to get away. He was waiting for something. A Shiver was on its way. Right then.

I jerked away from the window.

Officer Shelley adjusted the rearview mirror so I could see his eyes through the clear faceplate of his plastic suit. "Uncomfortable?"

I wanted to scream at him to take off the straitjacket. I wanted to tell him that it was a matter of life or death and that I had to catch the next taxi out of town or else there would be dire consequences.

But I realized that's what every crazy person said. They all had an emergency that was right outside of the hospital, which they had to attend to immediately. The only thing the officers wanted to hear from me, the only thing that could possibly get me released, was sweetness and light. But I didn't have an ounce of either inside me.

I tried to relax. "It's nothing."

"Didn't sound like nothing," Officer Shelley said.

My brain was all fuzz and static—an ill-tuned television set. Ma had specific instructions for escaping a Shiver: Leave immediately. Don't say goodbye to anyone. Don't grab your record collection or anything special to you. Just take whatever's needed to get out of there and then *go*. You never knew what horrifying thing was going to come busting up out of the concrete or swooping down from the sky.

I wiggled a little, trying not to be conspicuous, hoping to loosen the bound sleeves. But they clung tight.

"Is that jacket strangling you, Phoebe?" Officer Graham asked.

"Yes," I said, hoping for a chance to escape. "Yes, it is."

"She's fine," Officer Shelley said.

So much for that plan. Somehow I had to get back to the motel and grab Ma's money. I had to use the ham radio to warn Liz that Daddy was staring straight at . . .

But that's when it hit me. They knew. The Buried Lab knew a Shiver was on the way. Heck, they might have even released one of their creations from that haunted hallway. I didn't have time to be all sweetness and light. I had to escape.

"I gotta see Ma," I said.

"No chance," Shelley said.

"She'll be worried sick," I said.

Shelley shook his head.

"Gee, Shell," Officer Graham said. "Don't you suppose we ought to go to the motel and tell Miss Lane we got her daughter in custody?"

My muscles eased. There was that heart of gold Beth was talking about.

"Miss Lane ain't at the motel," Shelley said.

"Well, where is she?"

"Beats me. But she ain't there."

Officer Graham rounded to get a look at me, his suit crinkling. I gave him the sincerest eyes I could.

"Well, maybe she wasn't there for *you*," he said. "But maybe she'd be there for me? What do ya think?"

Officer Shelley gave him a cold look. "Just to prove you wrong," he said, and flipped a U-turn.

• • •

A sports car was parked in the motel parking lot. It had flames on the hood and fins on the tail and fuzzy dice dangling from the rearview. Leaning against the side was Hal, heel propped on the tire, matchstick in his mouth, just soaking in the sunshine. Relief might have rushed through me if I understood what was happening.

Officer Shelley pulled into a space and got out of the car. He passed Hal in the parking lot and was about to head upstairs when Hal drawled in his Texan accent, "I'm gonna have to ask you to turn around and let that girl go."

Shelley gave him a look. "Oh, yeah? And why's that?"

Hal flipped the matchstick from one side of his mouth to the other. "You're not going to give her what she needs."

Shelley put his hands on his hips. "What does she need?"

Hal removed the matchstick and flicked it. "If I told you, you might be tempted to lock her up and keep her, and I just can't let you do that."

Inside the car, Officer Graham and I stared at the scene. In the background, Ethel beat the dust off an Oriental rug. *Whack whack whack whack whack.*

Shelley gestured to Officer Graham, and after fumbling with his seat belt a moment, Graham awkwardly climbed out of the car.

"This girl is in our custody," Shelley told Hal. "We're taking her in to—"

"Stop talking." Hal said it so forcefully it knocked the words right out of Shelley's mouth.

Shelley snorted and gave Officer Graham a look of disbelief. Hal was half Shelley's size.

Hal adjusted his sunglasses and spoke in an even voice. "Have you ever been spanked, Officer?"

"Wh—" Shelley began, but it turned out Hal wasn't done.

"I'm guessing it's been a while. I'm guessing you've cracked plenty of skulls during your time on the force, put a lot of people in cuffs, but that you're overdue for a whooping yourself." He lowered his sunglasses and gave a little grin. "I can tell. So I'm going to make a little deal with you." He started to unbuckle his leather belt. "If you say another word, I'll bend you over the trunk of my car, yank that plastic getup down around your ankles, and give you a hiding you'll never forget."

Shelley stood frozen. It was clear no one had ever spoken to him like that.

"Smart," Hal said. He ambled over to the police car and opened the back door. "Hello, Phoebe," he said, then started giggling like a schoolboy who'd just lit a firecracker in the girls' bathroom. "Boy, I hate cops. *Hate* 'em! They act like everything is a danger so they can swoop in and be the heroes. Lean forward for me."

I did, and he started to loosen the straitjacket.

"How's Lucky-13?"

"Um, she's fine?"

"Getting her plenty of water and sunlight?"

Water and sunlight? That's when I realized I hadn't seen the Pomeranian eat once. Or tinkle.

"It's okay," Hal said, undoing the first strap. "She's not your average dog."

I wanted to ask him what he meant, but there were more pressing issues.

"Daddy's looking at Pennybrooke," I said.

Hal glanced vaguely up at the sky and then started to loosen the next strap. "Don't I know it. Why do you think I'm—"

"Put your hands in the air and step away from the vehicle!"

Officer Shelley had stripped his plastic suit to his waist and had his gun pointed at Hal.

Hal rolled his eyes. He grabbed his belt and slid it out of his pants. "What did I just tell y—"

There was a pop. Glass shattered and warm liquid spattered across my face. Hal's hand leapt to his neck as he stumbled backward. I was so shocked I couldn't even scream, but Ethel was screaming enough for the both of us.

Hal bent over double, still holding the gash in his neck, then threw his head back and laughed. "Hoo, boy!" he said, and then winced. "Now, you see, this probably hurts your brain more than it hurts me."

I looked down at the liquid that had sprayed across my straitjacket. It wasn't blood but a clear goo. Almost like Hal was . . .

"W-w-what are you?" Officer Graham asked, his quaking voice muffled by his suit.

"Just a breeze through the desert, friend," Hal said and cracked his neck.

"Doesn't mean I want you to shoot me again though," Hal said, and then ran at Shelley.

Shelley was able to shoot Hal twice more in the chest before he was tackled.

Officer Graham tremblingly pulled down his suit and got his gun untangled from his holster. He pointed it at Hal. "F-freeze!"

"Don't shoot, you idiot!" Shelley said, wrestling on the ground, covered in goo from Hal's neck. "You'll hit me!"

He socked Hal in the chin and again in the chest, making a wet vegetable sound.

"Run, Phoebe!" Hal called to me. "Get out of here!" Pinning Shelley's arm with one hand, he reached in his pocket and then thrust his keys toward the trunk of his sports car. "*Git!*"

I jumped out of the police car and started backing across the parking lot. Even with Shelley wrestling him and Graham tugging on his boot, Hal managed to get his key into the trunk and pop it open. I glimpsed the tops of three leathery pods, just like the ones back at the Buried Lab, before I hightailed it down the road, still bound in my straitjacket.

• • •

I ran without direction. I wished I knew where Beth lived. I'd get her to take off this straitjacket and then ask if her aunt Gladys could give me a ride out of town in her station wagon before the Shiver arrived. Beth could even come with me if she wanted. Ma wasn't around to say no.

I heard the ringing of the church bell, and hoped Beth had shown up early to Girl Scouts. I ran along the sprinkler-damp sidewalk, keeping an eye out for monstrous shadows, until I reached the bright white walls of St. Maria's. Neither the station wagon nor Beth were there.

I had to remind myself that this was how it always worked

with a Shiver. Beth would be part of Daddy's entertainment while I, by some stupid luck, would not. For the first time in a long time, this unsettled me. And not only because I had no way out of this straitjacket.

I slipped behind the hedges growing along the side of the church. Hal had undone the top strap and loosened the second. If I could just . . . I wiggled and twisted and flexed my arms outward until I heard a metallic *plink* followed by another. The broken buckles fell around my boots. Whoever made these must have used cheap metal.

Unless . . . I dismissed the thought.

I slipped off the straitjacket, stepped out of the bushes, and then hesitated. I couldn't call a cab. I'd left all the money back at the motel. All I needed was a ride from some charitable soul. Once me and Ma were reunited, we could build a new life with nothing but the clothes on our backs. We'd done it before.

I pounded on the church door, and a few moments later, it cracked open, revealing the small waxen man with the polished glasses.

"Yes?" Reverend Marsh said.

"You really think Ma's gonna destroy this town?" I said.

"I do."

"Then here's your chance to get rid of me and her wantonness for good."

"Does this seat go back any farther?" I asked Marsh, trying to stretch out my legs in the passenger seat of his Lincoln.

"It does not," Marsh said, keeping his eyes on the road and clinging to the steering wheel with his waxen fingers as if for dear life. "It is a bench."

My skin felt tight on my bones. My limbs wouldn't stop fidgeting. Was I stupid for having the reverend drive me back into the desert, even though it was the only place I could think to go? Were Marsh and I going to be met by some creatures crawling down the highway on their way to Pennybrooke?

And then I realized that was what the dirt tunnel in the haunted hallway was for. Releasing lab-grown Shivers.

Either way I had to go back. I'd make Liz tell me why they'd brought me to Pennybrooke when they were planning an attack. I'd demand to know what other creatures besides the pod people they were planning to release on innocent people. I'd make them tell me where Ma was on her special mission.

I pressed my feet into the ground to stretch out my hips, making my body arch back over the seat. Marsh squirmed, clicked on the radio, and tuned it to a Bible station. A man shouted about forgiveness and how God would save non-sinners when things were at their darkest. I waited for him to be interrupted by an emergency broadcast about the catastrophe that had just hit a town called Pennybrooke. But the preacher kept on preaching.

I rolled down the window and stuck my legs out.

"Please do not do that," Marsh said.

The air rushed around my ankles, feeling just like heaven.

"Would you rather I put them in your lap instead?" I asked.

He was silent the rest of the drive.

• • •

When we passed the army base and the Gray Rock reservation, I pulled in my legs and pointed to the opposite side of the road.

"Pull off here," I said.

Marsh's eyes widened like I was asking him to drive off a cliff, but he didn't complain. The Lincoln bumped along a desert path that might have been a road at some point but was now overgrown with jagged desert brush.

"There," I said, pointing to the rocky outcropping.

Marsh parked the Lincoln, and I walked a circle around the rocks. There was no door. I made another circle, slower this time, running my fingers along the rock, looking for any openings or fake surfaces. Nothing. The door was gone. It was as if the entrance had never existed.

"It was here," I said to myself. "I swear it was."

Marsh stepped out of his car and wrung his hands. "I must return to the church. The stained glass must be cleaned for Sunday's service, and I am all out of Windex."

I turned in a circle, searching the desert. Did I have the wrong rocks? Had the lab moved somehow? *Had* I dreamed it all? I glanced into the sky, and my heart had a shock, as if it had been struck by lightning.

"Is there somewhere else I can take you?" Marsh called over the desert wind. "A gas station? A home for women perhaps?"

My jaw hung open as I stared into the sky, trying to understand what I was seeing.

Daddy hadn't been looking at Pennybrooke.

Daddy was staring straight down . . . at *me*.

For the first time in my life, my father was looking at me. The corner of his mouth was ticking up into a smirk. He was lowering his remote control.

"I am becoming very dirty out here," Marsh said.

I stood in shock as the reverend beat at his suit, sending up plumes of dust.

• • •

Daddy's eyes followed the reverend's Lincoln along the highway like a lighthouse beaming on a lone ship in the night.

I was the Shiver.

That's what the Geiger counter had told the psychiatrist.

That's how I had busted out of the straitjacket.

My tongue ran along the tips of my teeth. Were they getting sharper? My fingertips ran along my arms. Was I sprouting more hair? I even checked the sides of my neck. Were those goose bumps or *gills*? Everything felt like plain old Phoebe.

But then I noticed the hem of my loose sheath dress, which had inched several inches up my legs since yesterday.

Oh.

"Has your . . . mother abandoned you?" Marsh asked.

"No," I said, tugging my dress down as far as it would go. "She would never."

"You are . . . fortunate not to bear the same curses she does."

He was talking about my looks, of course. And for the first time in my life, I thought maybe I agreed with him.

• • •

When we exited the highway, I pushed up and over the seat, awkwardly sliding over the top and into the back, my dress catching up to my rear while Marsh averted his eyes.

"*What are you doing?*" he asked, alarmed.

"It's my time of the month," I said. "I need some room."

That stopped his questions.

It felt better in the back with all that space to stretch out, but I also needed to hide. We were pulling back into Pennybrooke, and I couldn't let Officers Shelley or Graham see me. It wasn't smart coming back to town, but what else could I do? Have Marsh leave me in the desert and hope a door magically appeared in the rocks? If the coast was clear at the motel, I'd grab the cash out of the suitcase and then hire a cab to another town. I'd figure out how to find Ma from there.

We were halfway down Main Street when Marsh pulled the car over.

"Why are we stopping?" I asked, keeping low in the backseat.

Marsh rolled down the window and said, "Excuse me. Officer. I just wanted to let you know I have a young girl in my backseat. There's no funny business happening. I'm just giving her a ride back to her motel."

My skin turned clammy. Why hadn't I told Marsh not to talk to the police? Because that's the first thing he would've done, that's why.

"Well, isn't that funny?" I heard Officer Shelley say. "It just so happens I'm searching for a young girl. Her name wouldn't happen to be Phoebe, would it?"

"It is," Marsh said.

As heavy boots approached the car, I made myself into a ball, pressing my face into the vinyl of the seat as if that would camouflage me somehow. Shelley had overcome Hal and killed him. And now he had me. My shoulders tensed in anticipation of the door popping open and a hand seizing my arm.

"Afternoon, Reverend," Shelley said at the window.

I heard panting and dared a peek. Officer Shelley held up Pan-Cake, legs dangling, tongue lolling. For the first time, she wasn't growling at him.

"Found this little lady running free in the fairgrounds," he said, scratching behind her ears. "Figured Phoebe would be mighty heartbroken if she was lost. Hello, Phoebe."

I sat upright and studied Officer Shelley. He had the same large frame, the same pale mustache, the same gunmetal eyes, but . . . something was different.

"Here you are." Shelley set Pan-Cake in Marsh's lap. Marsh spluttered like she was a king cobra until she leapt over the backseat and frantically licked the sweat off my neck.

Shelley reached into his holster, and my heart skipped a beat. But instead of pulling out a gun, he pulled out a rubber bone and squeaked it. Pan-Cake stopped licking and stood at attention on my lap.

"Hope you don't mind," Shelley said. "I stopped by the store and bought her this so I could get her to come to me." He handed the bone to Pan-Cake, who folded her paws around it and started squeaking gratefully.

Officer Shelley tipped his hat to us and winked. "Reverend Marsh. Phoebe. You two have yourselves a lovely day now."

He hooked his thumbs in his belt and then ambled down the street whistling.

• • •

We continued to the motel in silence, save the *squeak squeak squeak* of Pan-Cake's new toy. Even though I had no idea what was happening to me, my plan hadn't changed. I wanted to get as far away from this town and all of its oddities as quickly as possible. In the meantime I still felt like me. I wasn't craving blood or raw fish or anything like that. I just hoped that kept up until I found Ma.

When we pulled into the parking lot, I thanked Marsh and then went straight to the manager's office.

"Hello, Phoebe dear," Ethel said.

"Oh." I came to an abrupt stop. "Hello."

When I'd seen Ethel a few hours before, she was nearly shaking out of her skin, having just seen a man get shot through the neck and chest. But now she was grinning ear to ear. She was wearing her knee braces . . . but they were on backward. Almost like she didn't know what they were for. For some reason this sight chilled me deeper than a well-meaning Officer Shelley.

"Would you order a cab for me?" I asked the manager, my voice trembling.

The manager furrowed his bushy eyebrows. "You owe for last night and tonight."

"I'm not staying tonight," I said.

"Well, you still owe for the last. You're a nice young lady, but we're not running a shelter here."

Ethel giggled, showing gray teeth.

"Of course not," I said, hiding a shudder. "Back in a jiffy."

I ran up the motel steps, Pan-Cake squeaking alongside me.

I opened the door and then froze. The room was dank and shadowy and smelled like a dying greenhouse. Three pods lay on the beds, their tops open like half-peeled eggs. My stomach soured when I realized that whatever crawled out of those things were currently wearing officer badges and knee braces.

I might not have dared set foot in that room, but then Pan-Cake leapt up onto the bed, curled up among the pods as if they were old friends, and chewed on her squeaker toy. I took a breath and then swept inside, beelining past the bed. I threw open the closet door, hauled out the suitcase, unzipped the side pocket, and reached inside. My hand slid to the bottom. There was no money.

I flipped the suitcase upside down, dumping the clothes onto the floor. I unzipped every zipper and pulled the pocket lining inside out until the suitcase was disemboweled on the carpet.

Someone had stolen Ma's money. Hundreds of dollars. Maybe thousands. Who would do such a thing? I bit my thumb. Not only did I not have enough money to pay for the motel, I didn't have enough money to catch a cab away from Pennybrooke and its pod people. I was stuck.

My eye caught the light of the ham radio, and I snatched up the speaker.

"Hello?" I said into it. "Liz? Liz, *please*. I need your help."

There was only crackled silence.

I didn't want to spend another second near those pods, even if they were empty. I hefted the ham radio, heavy as a slab of concrete, into my suitcase and hauled it downstairs to the parking lot, determined to walk somewhere and hitch a ride before the manager caught me. But then what? I couldn't pay for a motel room. I couldn't buy food. And I was transforming into . . . something. I sat on the curb and covered my face and tried not to scream.

"Are you . . . all right?" a voice asked.

I looked up and found Reverend Marsh standing over me. He interlaced his fingers in front of his waist. Almost as quickly, he unlaced them, and then raised his hand and held it there awkwardly.

"Would you . . . like me to pat your shoulder?"

I stared at that hand, as pale as a naked mole rat.

"Sure," I said.

Marsh set his trembling hand on my shoulder. At that touch, everything I'd been holding deep in my well came gushing up: Ma, the Buried Lab, the straitjacket, Hal, Daddy's eyes, everything. As the tears fell, I pressed my cheek onto Marsh's hand. His breath intensified, but he kept it there for three seconds before pulling away.

"Perhaps I should call a psychiatrist."

I wiped my eyes. "*No.* Please. I just lost my grip for a moment. I'm . . . I'm fine now."

"Good," Marsh said, getting up and patting his pockets. "That's good. Come along."

"Where are we going?" I said, grabbing my suitcase.

"It would not be becoming to have a young lady at my house, but I have a cot at the church."

I sniffed. "Thank you," I said, and started crying again.

"It is . . . no problem."

Marsh's eyes uncomfortably searched the sky, the motel, the car, anything but me.

Marsh tried to stick me in the church's storage room at first, among the boxes of old choral books and plastic-wrapped nativity scenes for Christmastime. The ceiling was so low and the shelves so close, I felt just like a sardine in a tin can.

"Um, could I sleep in the chapel?" I asked. "So, uh, God can see me better."

The reverend gave a flat grin and nodded.

As he set up the cot in front of the pulpit, I stared at Daddy's silhouette, glowing in twilight behind a stained-glass window of Jesus and some lambs. Did I need to tell the reverend I might be a danger? That depended on what type of danger I was becoming, I supposed.

"This is a radio," Marsh said, clicking on a wooden Sears Roebuck, "but it must remain on this station. This is a house of the Lord. Not one of those hop socks."

Women's voices filled the rafters with a quiet hymn. My dress was still damp from where Marsh had instructed me to dab my fingers in a copper bowl of water and touch my forehead, stomach, and shoulders.

"The dog," he said, looking at Pan-Cake, who had abandoned her squeaker toy and was sniffing around the votive candles. "Will it be a problem?"

I remembered the odd question Hal had asked, whether she got plenty of water and sunlight.

"I don't think so," I said.

"Very well," Marsh said. "In the morning, we shall discuss what's to be done with you. "Until then, I bid you good night."

"Why are you being so nice to me?" I said.

"I am a man of God," he said. "And"—he rubbed his hands together—"I have regretted what I said about your mother. Even Jesus fraternized with whores."

"My mom is not a whore," I said.

His eyes avoided mine. "Yes. Well . . ."

He swiftly exited through the back door.

I was alone in the big, dark space with only Pan-Cake and stained-glass Jesus and his lambs to keep me company. Even though I hadn't been in many churches, this one was pretty standard I guessed. Cleaner maybe. There was an organ against the back wall, a pulpit, and six windows that faintly lit the space. The dozen or so rows of pews had been polished until they gleamed. The air was thick with the smell of Pine-Sol.

I opened my suitcase and plugged in the ham radio next to the Roebuck. I tried to make contact with the Buried Lab again. Still nothing. I covered the radio with my suitcase so Marsh wouldn't ask any questions about it, kicking myself for dumping my clothes and leaving them behind.

The cot groaned when I lay on it, threatening to snap shut and suffocate me in the night. I covered myself with one of the slimy blankets Marsh had pulled from the donations box, while Pan-Cake scratched at the space between my ankles, making herself comfortable. The women singing on the radio gave me a pearly feeling that I tried to keep inside by hugging myself while I closed my eyes.

Sleep wasn't having me. The moon beamed through the stained glass. Little shapes swarmed through the darkness of the rafters, like locusts, making the air of the room buzz.

He called Ma a whore.

A new feeling rose in my chest, as hot and urgent as molten metal. My hands felt like two vices that could tear a church pew right off its bolts. I wanted to use it as a club to smash through everything in the church—the organ, the pulpit, Jesus and his lambs, the radio, whose heavenly music sounded warbled and nauseating now. And if Pan-Cake crossed my path, I'd snatch her up, take her little head, and—

I blinked, trying to banish the locusts. Where did those thoughts come from? They didn't feel like me.

I felt dizzy, like the floor was tilting, and there came a groaning from the rafters, like I was in the hull of a ship. Wait . . . that wasn't the rafters. My stomach was grumbling. I had to eat and I had to eat *immediately*. The day had been so full of chaos I'd barely taken a bite. Except the giant lunch at school, I reminded myself. And the drugstore breakfast. But my stomach seemed to have forgotten all about those.

I leapt off the cot, throwing Pan-Cake to the floor, and strode up and down the aisle, trying to figure out how I could get some food. My hands worked, wanting to strangle whoever had stolen the money from Ma's suitcase.

That's when I saw the clasp on the donations box, gleaming in the moonlight.

• • •

"I'll take a root beer float, a grilled cheese, a cheeseburger, a chicken-fried steak with mashed potatoes, a side of fries, and"—I counted the money on the counter—"an ice cream sundae."

Joe, the owner of the malt shop, peered over my shoulder. "Where's your family?"

"It's for me," I said.

"Careful, young lady." He patted his stomach, bulging under his apron. "You don't want to end up like me."

He gave me a number, and I sat in a booth. I clutched my fork and gazed at the curdled clouds outside of the neon-washed plate glass window at Daddy's dumb face, trying to blink away the buzzing locusts and forget my grumbling stomach before I shattered every dish in the malt shop.

Some greasers gathered around the jukebox kept flashing looks my way. Their eyes slipped under the table to my legs. One of them peeled off the group and came over, running a comb through his black wave of hair, and slid across from me.

"Hey, baby."

"I'm just waiting to eat," I said. The locusts fizzed against the window.

The greaser licked his lips and drummed his fingers on the table. He had cigarette stains on his teeth, and I could see the comb soaking grease through his T-shirt pocket.

"Me and the fellas are gonna drive up to Sugarman's Pass," he said. "I'm sure we could find something for you to, heh, *eat* up there."

I felt a cramp in my hand and looked down to find that I'd bent my metal fork perfectly in half. I handed the bent fork to the greaser, and he stared at it, visibly shaken.

"On second thought . . . ," he said, and left.

He was lucky that fork didn't end up in his eye.

The food arrived, and I started stuffing my mouth with French fries as fast as I could swallow, washing them down with the shake. Then I finished the cheeseburger in five bites. It was like plugging into an electric socket. My skin started to glow. My head tingled. Suddenly, destroying the malt shop seemed like the silliest idea in the world. The clouds outside weren't curdled, they were fluffy. And Pan-Cake. How could I ever hurt that lolling ball of marshmallow? I also felt a pang of guilt about stealing from the church, but I figured it was better than smashing it to bits. I didn't feel too bad about scaring the pervy greaser.

I started in on the grilled cheese. So much had happened in the last few hours, I'd barely had time or energy to think. I tried to organize what I knew about the Buried Lab and Daddy and Hal and the pods. It was like only a couple dots were connected, but I had to guess at the whole picture.

As Liz said, there was always a scientific explanation for each disaster: radiation for the ants, a transmittable virus for werewolves, a solar flare for killer vines. Even when the Buried Lab tried to re-create these monsters, they learned the science down to the atom for times when Daddy started getting bored: *In case of emergency, release monsters on unsuspecting town.*

I borrowed a fork from a neighboring table and cut into the chicken-fried steak. But that had been the men's plan. Liz had a different idea. I remembered her in the sealed submarine room, looking at me over her teacup with her pretty lashes.

I think Father—Daddy—can't know what he wants if he's never seen it before.

Then she'd gone to get the sugar and left me alone in that sealed room with those charcoal pyramids—every one of which was pointed at me. And then I'd felt woozy, and the lights had flickered. . . .

A bite of chicken-fried steak froze halfway to my mouth.

Liz had zapped me. My half sister had *zapped me.*

She zapped me with something that made the needle on the Geiger counter climb to two k.

But with what? And why?

"Hey."

It took me a second to realize someone was talking to me. I looked up from my plate, mouth full of steak, a sheen of grease on my chin. It was the boy from the psychiatrist's office. The Shiver survivor. Lear. He stood in front of my table, awkwardly holding his arm.

I painfully swallowed my mouthful. "Hello."

Lear's eye twitched. "You mind if I, um—"

He gestured to the bench across from mine.

"Go ahead," I said, wiping my chin with a napkin while he sat.

I was grateful I'd already finished a lion's share of the food so he wouldn't know I was eating for a family of four.

I suddenly remembered the stolen file I had hidden in my sock. I could feel it crinkle against my ankle. Had that really only been that afternoon?

Lear looked nervous. He kept biting his lip, his eyes flashing to a group of seniors wearing letterman jackets. As soon as they left the shop, laughing and punching one another, Lear pinched the bridge of his nose and squeezed his eyes shut tight.

"Hey, um—"

"Yeah?"

I remembered the stares I'd drawn at school that day. I remembered the whistle like a bomb dropping. Whatever was happening to me, it was drawing boys like flies to honey. It was like I was becoming more like Ma. I tucked my hair back behind my ear and tried to look halfway presentable.

Lear opened his eyes, but he didn't look at me, just stared out the window. "Could you not tell anyone you saw me at the . . . at the office today?"

"Oh," I said, disappointed. "Sure. No problem."

He nodded and got up, stuffing his hands in his pockets.

My breath caught. I didn't want this to be over. Not that quick. Usually when I talked to a boy I thought was cute, I remembered all the parts of me that looked like Daddy, and my whole being got a tremor to it. But right then, with food in my stomach, I felt a confidence I'd never felt before.

"On one condition," I said.

Lear froze and turned around. His forehead was all wrinkled up like he was trying not to look afraid.

"You gotta walk me home," I said. "It's dark out. You never know, you know?"

Lear's mouth twitched, and he scuffed his unlaced boots. "All right, sure. I guess I could do that."

It wasn't the enthusiastic reaction I was hoping for, but it would do. He sat back down and picked at a stain on the table while I kept eating. Unlike Rhoda, Lear didn't comment on the mound of food on my plate. He didn't say much of anything.

"Don't you want to know my name?" I said, finishing my shake.

"What's your name?"

"Phoebe." Right then it sounded like a car horn to my ears. "What's yours?" I asked even though I already knew.

"Lear. Lear Finley."

Phoebe Finley, I thought. And then, *No, brain. Look what happened to the last boy you were sweet on.*

"My last name's Lane," I said a little sheepishly.

He just nodded, becoming the first boy in the history of me who didn't ask about my mom.

"Why were you at Dr. Siley's?" I asked.

Lear gave me a look. My goodness, that forehead could wrinkle.

"You can't just ask that," he said.

"Why not?" I said.

"Well, you just can't, that's all."

I was just about bursting wanting to know about the Shiver he'd survived.

"I'll tell you why I was there," I said.

Lear's eye twitched. "Okay."

I put another piece of chicken-fried steak in my mouth. "My dad was killed in a Shiver. That's what Ma and I call the monster disasters. Happened about four years ago. He tried to stop a school bus from being dragged into the ocean by a squid's tentacle and he drowned." I shrugged, chewing. "Guess the school thinks my head needs a checkup every so often."

Lear's eyes searched my face. "My dad's dead too."

My fork froze halfway to my mouth. Of course. His file had said *Father victim of vampirism*. I'd never felt guilty for inventing stories about my dad. But here I was bragging about his imaginary death to a kid who actually lost his father. Meanwhile, my daddy was fine—snoozing in the starry sky.

"What happened?" I said, setting down my fork.

Lear scratched his hair right above his ear. "I'd rather not say, if that's okay."

"Sorry," I said. *Sorry for lying.*

Lear shrugged. "I don't know how to feel about it. You finished?"

"I guess I am."

It was all I could do to stop myself from licking the plate clean.

• • •

Lear and I stood in front of St. Maria's, our shadows long and faint against the sidewalk. I wanted to ask him a hundred questions—about his dad, about therapy, about how he'd broken his nose. I wanted to ask him why he didn't ask why I was living in a church and why he didn't stare at my legs like the other boys. I wanted to smooth out the wrinkles on his forehead.

But instead I just stood there.

"Well, good night," Lear said, and headed down the walkway.

Romance wasn't what it was like in the movies, I guessed. One boy plus one girl alone on a spring night did not always equal romance. I opened the door into the dark church and felt my stomach sticking to my ribs. Even though I'd polished off half the menu at the malt shop, I could tell I'd be hungry again soon, and I'd spent every cent from the donations box.

"Will you bring me food?" I called after Lear.

He turned around on the corner.

"Please," I said. "I . . . I don't have any money. Not right now. But I can pay you back. Somehow. If you'll just please bring me food. Tomorrow. Or as soon as you can. Please."

"Where's your mom?" he said.

I hesitated, suddenly understanding Lear's not wanting to explain his past. "Please, just, bring the food. And not an amount you think would be good enough for a girl. Bring enough to feed a pro wrestler. A pro wrestling *team*. I'm not joking. And please don't ask any more questions. Just bring me food. Please."

Lear gave me a look like he wanted to ask how he could possibly dredge up that much chow, but he gave a nod, which eased my stomach a little.

"Also, will you tell Beth Graham I'm at the church?" Rhoda's candlelight eyes flickered through my mind. "No one else. Just Beth."

Lear gave another small nod and disappeared into the night.

• • •

Inside the church, I clicked on the Roebuck and tuned it to a station playing "Call Me" by Johnny Mathis. While Pan-Cake licked my long legs, I pulled off my socks, and the page from Lear's file dropped to the floor. I lit a votive candle and then unfolded the page slowly, curling its bottom toward the top to reveal a small bit of information at a time.

9/16/57—Lear Finley—First meeting
Uncle military general
Expresses interest in enlisting upon graduation

At first I felt Ma's disgust for any man in uniform. But then I thought through it a bit. Marrying a military man might just be the ticket to staying safe in a world where Daddy always had to be entertained.

If Lear was in the military, he would always have access to guns and grenades and stuff like that. If trouble ever started brewing, he'd drive a tank right through the front of our ranch-style house and pull me inside, where we'd make love until the trouble passed. In between lovemaking, he could even shoot a monster or two. I wouldn't mind.

I slid the paper down, revealing the next two items on Dr. Siley's list:

> *Obsessed with comic books and stories of "super" heroes*
> *Early prognosis: Infantile mind*

Comic books, huh? Could I love a boy with an infantile mind? So long as he remained handsome, quiet, and brooding? Yes. Yes, I could.

The song on the radio changed to "The Book of Love" by the Monotones as I unveiled the next part of my and Lear's romance.

> *Patient cares for invalid mother.*

Well, if that wasn't the sweetest . . .

> *Exhibits feelings of helplessness*
> *Feels five years old when night falls*
> *When asked why in therapy, patient is cagey, folds arms*
> *Accessed previous records and discovered—*

"This is Ant Lion to Palm Tree! Ant Lion to Palm Tree! Do you read me?"

The voice made me jump and I nearly tore Lear's paper. I looked around the church.

"This is Ant Lion to Palm Tree . . . Phoebe?"

It was the ham radio.

I switched off the Roebuck and snatched up the speaker. "I'm here! Hello?"

There came a popping sound, like a gun going off, and then screaming. At first I thought something terrible was happening in the Buried Lab. The monsters had escaped their rooms, and everyone in the lab was being murdered under the desert.

"Hello?" I whispered.

"Phoebe!" Liz said. *"Thank goodness."*

"Are you okay?" I said. "What's happening?"

"Of course we're okay! We're celebrating!"

Among the pops and screams in the background, I made out a word: *"Huzzah!"*

They weren't screams. They were cheers. Glasses clinked together. The pop must have been a bottle of champagne.

"I'm sorry I've been unavailable," Liz said. *"Things have been touch and go here. I had to explain to the men what I'd done. At first they were upset that I'd turned you loose from the lab, but then I calmly pointed out the value in having a rational being with whom we could communicate. You know, as opposed to releasing some monstrosity on an unsuspecting town to run amok like a bull in a china shop."*

My head flooded with so many questions, they all got caught in my throat.

"Oh, Phoebe, I wish you were here to celebrate with us," Liz said. *"We've made a cake bigger than your head! Well . . . maybe not bigger than* your *head. Not now, anyway. Oh, how I wish I were there to see you!"*

I ran my fingers through my hair, trying to get a sense of my head's size. "Why are you celebrating?"

*"Father—*Daddy *has lowered his remote!"* Liz said. *"It's the lowest it's been in years. He even set it in his lap! We don't have a measurement that low on the Doomsday Dial."*

This *was* good news, I guessed. But then the day's events came flooding back to me.

"Hal got shot," I said.

"Oh, darling, that's sweet of you to worry," Liz said. *"Hal is perfectly fine. He's in the sunroom now. He'll have a couple of scars, but he's otherwise none the worse for wear. He said you were very brave and asked if you'd take care of Lucky-13 for a while."*

I'd never heard of anyone being "perfectly fine" after they were shot in the throat and chest, but I'd never seen a man bleed clear goo, either. Pan-Cake licked my hand, and the dam in my throat finally broke. I leapt to my feet.

"Where did the lab go? Why wasn't there a door in the rock? Where's Ma? And—and what happened to Officer Shelley and Graham and the motel owner's wife?"

"You needn't worry about them," Liz said with some metal in her voice. *"We handled it."*

My stomach sank. "What did you do to them?"

"Phoebe, when I tell you we've handled something, you must believe me, okay? We wouldn't do anything to harm someone unless it was absolutely necessary to keep the world safe."

I wanted to ask what she meant, but something told me it wouldn't get me anywhere. Instead I collapsed back on the cot and asked the question I'd been dreading.

"Liz . . . what's happening to me?"

"Why, my dear," Liz said, *"haven't you figured it out?"*

A thought rose, like water in a basement. Of course I knew.

A part of me had known since Principal Toll had pointed to the hem of my dress hovering inches above my knees.

I opened my hand slowly, my fingers stretching out long. It was just like Liz had said. Something Daddy had never seen before.

"Will you be able to change me back?" I said, then remembered the looks the boys gave me at school. "Or . . . leave me like I am right now?"

"Oh, shoot," Liz said. *"We're having some trouble hearing you on this end. Phoebe? Am I coming through okay?"*

"Clear as a bell," I said.

She was ignoring my question. I could tell.

"Can you change me back?" I said more slowly this time. My heart was starting up something fierce. The locusts were closing in.

Another pause from Liz. *"Oh! Yes! Yes. Of course. You needn't worry on that front. All it takes is a combination of radiation and insecticide if you can believe it. For now, just enjoy the power you wield. Honestly, I'm jealous. I'd have zapped myself, you know . . . if I weren't currently indisposed."*

Someone cleared his throat in the background. *"I don't know a soul who'd be entertained by a fifty-foot broad."* It was Mr. Peak. Droopy Dog. He sounded drunk. *"Especially if she's his daughter.* Horrified *maybe."*

"Not even if she cooked you a fifty-foot meat loaf?" the British scientist said.

Mr. Peak scoffed. *"We didn't zap any cows."*

"That's not a bad idea, actually," Liz said. *"We could make Phoebe a barbecue the size of a basketball court."*

Liz and the British man laughed.

"Hello?" I said, wondering if they knew I was still listening.

"We're not in the clear yet, Phoebe," Liz said. *"Father setting down his remote is a victory, but it's only temporary. He will get bored again. That's why we need you to keep things interesting. We'll have assignments for you soon."*

Assignments? Headlines flashed through my head. Monster attacks. People screaming.

"You want me to . . . terrorize Pennybrooke?"

Liz hesitated. *"I wouldn't use that term, no. I would say we want you to act as a diversion to the man in the sky so he doesn't turn off the entire world. I do hope you understand. I worry sometimes that I'm not getting through to you because our mothers gave us different modes of communication."*

Yeah, Ma always said things plain while Liz's ma kept things hidden.

"Phoebe?" Liz said. *"We need to know where you are so we can bring you food. You must be starving, poor thing."*

My stomach ignored my racing thoughts and grumbled. I folded over, trying to silence it.

"Why would I tell you where I am?" I said. "After what you did to me?"

"Phoebe . . . ," Liz said calmly, like I was a rabid dog. *"Consider your position a moment. You're growing at an alarming rate. You can't afford food. Whatever money your mother left behind will not be enough to sustain you."*

Whatever Ma left behind? So the Buried Lab didn't steal the money.

"We can feed you," Liz said. *"More food than you could possibly eat. We'll give you a few assignments to do around town to*

keep things interesting. Once they are executed successfully, Hal will deliver a grocery store right to your doorstep. You just have to tell us where you are."

She paused, waiting for me to respond.

"Phoebe, are you there? Do you understand what I'm telling you? Once this is all over and this little rascal is out of my system, you and I can raise a glass to two half sisters saving the world the way only women could."

I yanked the cord out of the wall, and Liz and the rest of the Buried Lab fizzled out. My stomach growled again, louder this time. I knew it would only be a matter of time before I plugged the ham radio back in and *begged* for that grocery store. I was at Liz's mercy. Unless Lear came through and brought me food, that was.

I looked at his file crumpled in my hand, his dark past waiting to be revealed. I suddenly felt dirty going through his business, like I was trying to learn about him so I could control him, make him mine. Just like Liz was doing to me.

I touched the corner of Lear's file to the votive candle and watched it go up in flames.

"If you are going to rest your head in a house of the Lord," Marsh said the next morning, "I need you to tell me precisely what you did to become like . . . *this*."

He gestured from my head to my feet, lying across half of a church pew.

There was no hiding it now. No blaming my growth on shrunken dresses. Overnight, I had shot up a whole choral book's length—the only thing I had to measure myself. That put me at about seven feet tall.

This would have upset me, *should* have upset me, but I found it hard to be mad about anything when I was eating. I tore open the plastic wrapping of another loaf of bread meant for sacrament and stuffed an entire slice in my mouth. "What do you mean what I did?"

Marsh placed his hands together so it looked like he was praying and pleading at the same time. "God's punishment . . . can be forgiven. This *curse* can be reversed. By revealing all to Him, you will directly offset the growing. Or slow it down, at least. You just have to give me a full, um, *confession*."

I gave my new airplane-print dress a tug down to my knees so Marsh couldn't see any of "God's punishment." My old dress lay torn in half on the cot.

You're wrong, I thought, eating another slice of bread. Only the Buried Lab could save me. And I had no clue where it had gone off to. Still, if Marsh was going to keep me housed in his church and feed me bread while I figured out what to do, I'd sing church hymns if he asked.

"What do I have to do?"

"It's simple," he said, wiping a bit of sweat from his forehead. "You just tell me what sins you committed to bring you to your, em, *current state.*" He glanced over his shoulder. "Normally we would meet in the confessional booth, but . . ."

"I can't fit," I finished for him.

I stuffed another piece of bread in my mouth. The loaf was half gone. What could I tell the reverend made me this way? That a bunch of mad scientists, including my half sister, had zapped me with charcoal pyramids so I could terrorize Pennybrooke—all for the entertainment of some pervy shlub in the sky that I called Dad?

I swallowed the bread and shrugged. "I don't know what I did."

Marsh shifted in his suit, as if trying to wriggle out of a snakeskin. "I . . . have been told . . . I can come across as . . . cold."

Someone should have also told him that warmth came in the delivery, but it wouldn't be me.

"But I want you to know that I . . . *care* about all God's children."

"Okay," I said.

He straightened his horned-rim glasses, seeming relieved that the niceties were through. "Do you know about our Lord and savior?"

Right then God's light was blinding me through a chip in the stained-glass lamb's butt. Some believed God was a big invisible man in the sky who wore white robes and punished people for getting out and living a little. Meanwhile, I could actually *see* a big man in the sky who wore a bathrobe and wanted to see people punished for living at all. Ma might have called me her immaculate conception, but if there was a God, he most certainly wasn't Daddy.

"Not really," I said.

"Have you attended church?"

I once caught a piece of a sermon on TV that talked about the punishment God had in store for all unmarried women. Ma came home and found me crying and switched the TV off.

Now listen to me, Phoebe. You forget every word of that sermon, you hear? It isn't God who decides what's wrong with people and punishes them. It's people, all right? They decide what makes them comfortable, then say it was God's idea, and they punish you until you start looking and acting just the way they want you to. And if you don't, they lock you up or kill you or, or abandon you. I'd rather deal with a dozen Shivers than be beholden to a man in power. At least you know you can't reason with a Shiver.

I stuffed another piece of bread in my mouth. "You mean besides the coven?"

Marsh's eyes flashed, then calmed. "I can sense you're kidding. But I would encourage you to resist that sort of humor. Even joking about these topics can tempt you into flirting with, em, unsafe experimentation."

I tried to smile. I hadn't had this much fun since Ma last plucked my eyebrows.

I crumpled up the empty bread bag. "I smoke cigarettes."

"Yes?"

"And I eat a lot, obviously."

"Yes."

"And . . ." My mind drew a blank, a little disappointed with all the sinning I hadn't done yet. "Oh," I said, staring at the last slice of bread. "I took money out of the donations box. I'm sorry."

Marsh gave a grim expression. "I suppose that is what it's there for. Charitable cases such as yourself."

That wasn't the reaction I'd been expecting. "Thank you."

Marsh nodded, then rubbed his hands together. "Perhaps you are . . . obsessed with dresses? Makeup, jewelry, things of that sort? Perhaps this *growth spurt* is God's punishment for desiring . . . *material things*. He has seen to it that you cannot, em, wear anything pretty."

I ran my hand along the airplane-print dress. It was made for a larger woman, but it fit my new body like the skimpy dresses banned from late-night television because they showed the women's legs moving.

"Well, God doesn't have to worry about that anymore," I said. "Soon, nothing will fit me."

Marsh's cheeks paled.

I remembered that he had worried that Ma's wantonness would destroy the town. And in a twisted way he was right. If Ma wasn't such a firecracker, Daddy's eyes wouldn't have followed her, and there wouldn't be any problems. But that wasn't her fault, was it? It was the man in the sky who leered at her. It was the men in the lab who concocted Shivers to keep things interesting. People like Marsh blamed women like Ma because they had no idea Daddy and those men existed.

Marsh swallowed deeply and examined his folded hands. "Just because you do not bear your mother's curse does not mean you cannot fall into the same traps. Tell me about the boy who walked you here last night."

My cheeks grew hot. So that was the kind of confession he was looking for. The dirty kind about sins that preachers claimed drew Shivers to a town like ants to a picnic. If only something *had* happened with Lear last night. It might've almost been worth blowing up to the size of a baby giraffe if I'd had the chance to roll around in sin a little first.

I sighed and picked at my fingernails like confessing was going to be rough on me. "Me and Lear went out to the drive-in. He was *real* sweaty from running in track that day, but I didn't mind so much. . . ."

While Marsh remained as unflinching as a wax statue, I proceeded to "confess" every dirty thing I wanted to do to Lear. Ma told me all about the priests who liked to hear dirty stories in confessionals because it was the only thrill of their week. But that wasn't Marsh by a mile. The man was as sexless as a cornhusk. While I talked about all the things I'd never done with Lear, Marsh grimaced like I was torturing his mother. I must've been the first girl in history who tried not to giggle throughout her confession.

I was about to get to the really juicy bits when Marsh raised a trembling hand. "That's . . . enough. Quite enough."

After he taught me how to perform Hail Marys, I knelt before the pulpit and performed all one hundred.

"*There,*" Marsh said, straightening his lapels. "God will shrink you back to normal in no time."

He busied himself with polishing the organ keys and didn't say another word to me that afternoon.

• • •

"Holy. *Crap.*"

Beth stood in the church's foyer, her jaw practically hanging to the floor. I was stretching my aching legs on the pulpit and froze, expecting Beth to run screaming out of the church.

But instead she came sweeping toward me while Pan-Cake romped down the aisle to greet her.

"Pan-Cake," Beth said, "I can't even look at you right now because I've only got eyes for your momma." She held out her hands to me. "May I?"

I set my giant hand in hers. Beth ran her thumbs along my long fingers and stared up at all seven feet of me.

"You're . . ."

"Yeah."

"Just like something out of . . ."

"Pretty much."

"And you're still—?" Beth's eyes drifted toward the ceiling.

"I think so," I said. "Isn't it awful?"

"Are you kidding?" She hadn't so much as blinked. "This is the coolest thing I've ever seen! You could eat a stack of pancakes the length of your arm without worrying about gaining an ounce! And if you could poke a pervy police officer in the eye at your regular size, just imagine what you could do like this!"

I snorted. There was something about being around Beth that made me feel as warm and cozy as a Betty Crocker commercial.

"What *happened*?" Beth said, still wide-eyed. "You get too much sun when you took off into the desert?"

"It's a long story," I said.

"All right. I can't say I'm not curious, but all right." She gave my hand a squeeze. "I guess now I know."

"Know what?" I said.

"Every time I watched one of those old movies, I always wondered if the monster wasn't just misunderstood in some way."

"What old movies?" I said.

"Sorry." She shook her head. "I meant read the paper. About the attacks." She ran her fingers through the ends of my long hair. "You don't look like you're about to go gobbling up innocents."

I remembered the assignments Liz had promised, and the locusts briefly swarmed among the rafters.

"No innocents for me." At my size, it was harder to gulp quietly now. "You won't tell anyone, will you?"

"And share you with this town? I wouldn't dream of it!" Beth's gaze fell to my knees. "Boy, you're becoming a real bombshell."

"Really?"

I felt my hips. Sure enough, my walls were narrowing to raise the ceiling.

Beth pinched the hem of my dress, which was now almost up to my underwear. "This length is getting *mighty* dangerous."

"It's only going to get worse."

"She requires a new gown immediately," Marsh said, appearing in the back door. "She is not in church dress, and I cannot risk scandalizing my congregation . . . or myself."

He and I had had a close call that morning. When I'd woken up on the cot, I couldn't breathe. My dress was strangling me. My eyes bulged as I hooked my finger in the collar to give me breathing room, rolled off the cot, and then tore the dress straight down the middle with my bare hands, coughing and gagging. I was about to tear off my too-tight bra, too, when I looked up and saw Marsh, hand over his eyes.

"I can make you something to wear!" Beth said.

"You can?"

My heart lifted. I'd never had a dress tailor-made. Ma had dozens.

"Sure!" Beth said. "I've got my badge in sewing and everything. I'm no master seamstress, but it beats having a naked giantess filling the church. Reverend, do you have measuring tape?"

He fetched some while she reached into her handbag and pulled out a notebook and pencil.

"Loosen up," Beth said, giving my arm a shake. "I'm not taking pictures."

I relaxed my arms as she reached under my armpits with the measuring tape and made little notes.

"Will you stand for me?"

I did, and she measured more parts of me, including my legs, which were about as bristly as Brillo pads.

"Could you bring me a razor and some Burma-Shave?" I said.

"Why?" Beth asked, jotting measurements. "You got a date with the Jolly Green Giant?"

"No . . ." My cheeks grew hot. "Lear Finley?"

Beth's eyes went wide. "Don't tell Rhoda."

"What do you mean?"

"She's *obsessed* with Lear Finley, and she can be a bit—what's the word—*possessive.*"

A part of me clenched, wishing I was the only one who found Lear's quiet brutishness attractive. "Well, can't say I blame her."

"Uh-huh." Beth was adjusting her glasses at my limbs, lost in measurements. "You're lucky I have two little sisters who grew in opposite directions. One went straight up like a bamboo shoot, while the other went out like a turnip, shoulders wider than she was tall. You're doing a whole lot of both."

I remembered Beth's brother, weaselly Officer Graham, and the third pod in the motel room.

"How's your brother doing, Beth?" I said.

"Brian? He's fine. Only . . . he's been colder lately. He just kind of stares and smiles. Like a fish at an aquarium. I can't quite explain it."

She hefted my arm. What could I tell her? That her brother wasn't really her brother and had vegetable juice coursing through his veins?

Beth clicked her tongue. "And you say you aren't finished growing?"

I remembered Peak's words: *a fifty-foot broad . . .*

"Not by a long shot," I said.

"We'll need stretchy material then," Beth said. "I wonder if the carnival has some extra tents. . . ."

I winced. "Could you make it flattering at all?" I said, still thinking of Lear.

Beth jotted down one last thing and then flipped the notebook shut. "I'm not promising Ralph Lauren—er, um, *Christian Dior*, but we'll make you look hot enough."

"Could you make it cool instead?" I said, wiping sweat from my throat. "It's *sweltering* in this church."

"Right. Of course. That's what I meant."

"*And* respectable in the eyes of the lord," Marsh said.

"Sure," Beth said. "That too."

She gave me a wink, and I felt more saved than I had all morning.

• • •

At dusk, a knock came at the door, quiet as a mouse.

I crept down the aisle, the floorboards groaning under my feet, and cracked the door open, hunching to hide my height. Lear looked so dreamy in his flannel shirt and Levi's that my heart just about fluttered out the top of my head. He took a step back and blinked as if his eyes had been playing tricks on him the first few times we met.

I stood up straight. Sheesh.

It was about time I caught his attention.

Lear caught himself staring and he held up two grocery bags full of food. "I, um, borrowed some stuff from my mom's fallout shelter. You just gotta promise me the world isn't gonna end before you pay me back."

"Uh . . . I promise," I said.

He was just in time. I'd polished off every loaf of bread in the church and was still hungry enough to eat a horse. I'd told Beth that before, but I honestly wouldn't have trusted myself at a stable right then.

"I've been cooped up in this church all day," I said. "You wanna go for a walk?"

We crossed a bumpy field to the water tower standing behind the screen at the drive-in and climbed the ladder toward a chalky, fading sky. Daddy stared at me, a smile tugging on the corner of his lips, threatening to develop into a God's honest grin.

From way up there, Lear and I could see all of Main Street and the Levitt ranches, but more important, we could see Mitzi Gaynor, larger than life and dressed as a sailor in *South Pacific*. We didn't have a speaker like the cars below, but Ma and I had seen the picture so many times I had it memorized.

Lear and I quietly emptied the grocery bags along the water tower's metal walkway and then tore the seams of the bags to make a poor excuse for a picnic blanket. He helped himself to an apple while I ate six cans of tuna fish, five cans of fruit cocktail, four bars of Hershey's chocolate, and then washed it all down with a mixture of sweetened condensed milk and rehydrated Tang.

Normally I'd feel gross about eating that much food, but my body felt like it had run six marathons that day.

My stomach made a sound that would put a diesel truck to shame.

"Sorry," I said. "It has a mind all its own these days."

"No problem." Lear craned his neck, daring a glance at my face. "Um, how are you doing it? By eating?"

I snorted and opened my second can of pork and beans, which felt small in my hand. "Other way around. I eat because I'm growing."

"Oh. Right. Yeah. Of course. But . . ." Lear leaned in so he could get a better look at me in the moonlight. My skin prickled with attention. "How?"

I stopped stuffing my mouth and watched a fly circle the empty can of fruit cocktail. Where could I even begin?

"Will you tell me what happened with your dad?" I said.

Lear sat back and picked at some rust on the guardrail. I guessed neither of us were getting questions answered that night.

The sounds of the field came alive in our silence. Crickets sang away the sunset. The wind flattened the grass. Bats made little screeks. The taillights of a Chrysler flashed over us as a couple pulled into the drive-in. A minute later the car started to rock back and forth. Lear stared at his hands. At least somebody was seeing some action that night.

How did girls get boys to kiss them in moments like this? Now that I had eaten, I felt capable of almost anything—climbing the Chrysler Building would be a cinch so long as the top floor was made of cake—and yet romantic stuff still made me watery in the knees. I wanted Lear to kiss me so I could feel normal, just for tonight. But he just kept picking at rust.

"Phoebe?" Marsh's pinched voice shouted from the bottom of the ladder. "You must return to the church now. You are in my care."

Lear looked at me. We smiled at each other, silently agreeing to pretend like we weren't there. He handed me the rest of his apple, and then watched while I ate it, seeds and all. I wiped my mouth on the torn grocery bags and resisted the temptation to belch.

"Phoebe!" Marsh called. "You must not undo your Hail Marys!"

Lear and I leaned back on our elbows and watched Rossano Brazzi's "Some Enchanted Evening" number. I set my hand close to his, and our pinkies touched. I tried not to focus on the fact that my hand was bigger than his now.

If I was going to keep growing at this rate—a foot a day—then this might be my last chance to have contact like this. Once I grew to ten feet, or twelve, or *fifty*, I couldn't imagine the physics of being with another person. Just like I never could figure out how Ma and Daddy did their business. Liz may have said she had a way to change me back, but my heart didn't quite believe it.

The pinkie contact didn't last long. I bent my elbow to brush his side, and Lear's hand shrank away like a slug touched with salt. His eyes closed before he could see the disappointed expression on my face.

"*Phoebe!*" Marsh said. "I do not want to have to come up there. I am afraid of heights."

I crossed my hands over my stomach and watched Daddy doze off as the sun set on the last simple day of my life.

8 FEET

"He rocks in the tree tops all day long
Hoppin' and a-boppin' and singing his song
All the little birdies on Jaybird Street
Love to hear the robin go tweet tweet tweet

"Rockin' robin
Rock rock, rockin' robin,
Blow rockin' robin
'Cause we're really gonna rock tonight"

My days started to get a rhythm to them.

In the morning, I listened to Marsh practice his sermons for the Sunday following while I ate the replenished communion bread and chased Pan-Cake around the church, feeling my limbs groan and stretch like bamboo shoots.

In the afternoon, Beth would haul in materials of all types and try to stretch and contort them in such a way to fit my expanding body.

And in the evening, Lear brought all the food he could carry and watched me devour it while I tried to hold a normal conversation with him.

After Marsh left for the night, I tuned the radio to the "evil" rock-'n'-roll station and danced the aches out of my limbs while Pan-Cake ran circles around me.

The DJ had a soft spot for Bobby Day.

9 FEET

"Every little swallow, every chick-a-dee
Every little bird in the tall oak tree
The wise old owl, the big black crow
Flappin' their wings singing go bird go"

"This morning I would like to remind the congregation that your salvation is not contingent on the occasional church visit after you hear about a terrible attack on the radio. Rather it is based on *weekly attendance* and *daily dedication* to the Lord."

• • •

"How does that feel?"

"Like I'm being strangled by an anaconda."

"Back to the drawing board, I guess."

• • •

"Want some onion soup dip? I don't want to be the only one with dragon breath."

"Nah, I'm okay."

"You sure? It's delicious."

"Yeah, I'm okay."

10 FEET

"Rockin' robin
Rock rock, rockin' robin

Blow rockin' robin
'Cause we're really gonna rock tonight"

"In these times of trial, we must ask ourselves what's really wrong with today's society that God should choose for a *moon robot* to tear apart New York City? For a towering mantis to attack Washington, DC? For our neighbors in Santa Mira to be carpet-bombed by our own military to stop those . . . *frothing seed pods*?"

• • •

"How do your boobs feel?"

"Heavy."

"I sympathize. Really. I'll see what I can do."

• • •

"Are there any foods you hate?"

"Not really."

"I can't stand canned pineapple. Makes my tongue feel like it's bleeding."

"Huh."

11 FEET

"Pretty little raven at the bird-band stand
Told them how to do the bob and it was grand
They started going steady and bless my soul
He out-bopped the buzzard and the oriole"

"I'm talking about *sin*, ladies and gentlemen. Not just on an individual level, but as a *society*."

• • •

"The material's too thick. I'm sweating buckets! Honest-to-goodness buckets!"

"You look refreshed, like you just walked out of the ocean!"

"Really?"

"Well, maybe I can cut some sections out. . . ."

• • •

"You have a good time at school today?"

"It was all right, I guess."

"Excited for summer vacation?"

"I guess."

12 FEET

"He rocks in the tree tops all day long
Hoppin' and a-boppin' and singing his song
All the little birdies on Jaybird Street
Love to hear the robin go tweet tweet tweet"

"If one woman lies with a man outside of wedlock, we *all* take responsibility. If we allow one child to fall prey to the allure of alcohol, we all take responsibility. If we see a pentagram glowing on the palm of our neighbor and we don't report it, then God Himself will repay us, all of us, one hundredfold."

• • •

"I finally found an elastic big enough for your waist!"

"Good, because the airplane dress didn't survive the night. My chest burst right through it. A button hit the ceiling. No joke."

"Shut *up!* And I thought *I* had a problem. Hmm. We'll need to find a temporary solution. . . ."

• • •

"How's your ma doing? Good?"

"Yeah, she's good."

"Good."

13 FEET

"Rockin' robin,
Rock rock, rockin' robin
Blow rockin' robin
'Cause we're really gonna rock tonight"

"God has shown that it isn't enough for us to find Him in ourselves, in our families, in our friends. He is showing us that *every last soul counts*—from the president of the United States to the soda jerk on the corner to the lady of the night."

• • •

"I call it . . . *The Creation*!"

"It's hideous!"

"Well, so was the Creation. He was sewn together with dead body parts. This was sewn together with donated blankets."

"Beats being naked as the day Ma bore me, I guess. I'll call it . . . *Frank*."

"After the doctor?"

"The very same."

• • •

"I broke a pew today. Snapped it right in half. Without even thinking, just sat right on it and *bam*."

"Oh."

"I thought it was funny."

"Oh. Right. Yeah. Funny."

14 FEET

"Pretty little raven at the bird-band stand
Told them how to do the bob and it was grand
They started going steady and bless my soul
He out-bopped the buzzard and the oriole"

"God cares about us as a society. He loves us. And He is guiding us to the truth by punishing one town at a time. How, ladies and gentlemen of Pennybrooke, can we save *our* town?"

• • •

"Your feet! I didn't even think about your feet. Do they hurt at all?"

"Nah. I pulled a splinter out the other day and barely felt it."

"Well, that's a relief. I don't know where I could find enough leather to cover these. They're huge."

"Tell me about it. Pretty soon I could just strap a couple of cows to my feet."

"Ha!"

• • •

"Nice night tonight."

"Yeah."

". . ."

". . ."

15 FEET

"He rocks in the tree tops all day long
Hoppin' and a-boppin' and singing his song

All the little birdies on Jaybird Street
Love to hear the robin go tweet tweet tweet"

"It is our job to *rise up*, to become larger than ourselves, and find a way to stop *sinfulness* in its tracks once and for all."

• • •

"Here. I sewed you a, um, lady's hygienic belt."

"You did *what*?"

"You're gonna need one, aren't you?"

". . . Thank you, Beth."

• • •

"Well, see ya tomorrow, I guess."

"Yeah, see ya tomorrow."

• • •

Every night, after Lear left, Reverend Marsh would lock up the church while Pan-Cake curled up on my stomach and my eyes fluttered shut beneath Frank, my comforter Creation, belly full, skin tingling, and my growth not slowing an inch.

"Rockin' robin,
Rock rock, rockin' robin
Blow rockin' robin
'Cause we're really gonna rock tonight"

One crisp February afternoon when I was thirteen, I was walking back to the motel from the pictures in Sunrise Valley when I passed two girls who whispered, "Daughter of Ook," and started giggling.

I continued, eyes on shoes, until I heard a grunting ahead. A boy was struggling in front of the barbershop. He was bundled up for winter, and his left arm was in a sling. He was pressed up against the plate glass window, trying to get his textbooks situated in his right arm.

"Push any harder, the glass'll shatter and you'll be a bloody mess on the tile." I caught his American history book before it fell in the snow. "Maybe they'd give you a free haircut though."

The boy looked at me in surprise. He was an Indian. I hadn't noticed until now because he was all bundled up. Down the sidewalk, the girls stared. I could get a reputation for helping a kid like this.

The boy's arm trembled. I took the rest of his books.

"You don't have to do that," he said.

I glanced back at the girls. "It's my pleasure."

I hefted the books up to my chest with a grunt and started walking. The boy followed.

"I only live three blocks from here," he said, trying to keep up.

"You do?"

I hadn't meant to sound rude—I just didn't think Indians

were allowed to live in this town. It was even illegal to marry someone with darker skin.

The boy didn't take my question poorly. "My dad works at the base," he said. "He's a Navajo code talker. Helped win the war against the Japs in Iwo Jima."

The girls whispered behind us. From then on in that town, I'd be "Daughter of Ook," the girl who carried books for Indian boys.

"What's your name?" the boy asked.

"Phoebe. But it doesn't matter."

"No," he said, looking over his shoulder at the girls. "I guess it doesn't."

I winced. I'd said it didn't matter because I'd most likely be gone soon, but he took it a different way. I didn't know how to clear it up.

As we walked, I stole a couple glances to the side to size up his profile. He was handsome. His shoulders were broad, and his hair was short and shiny black. Maybe we could spend the next week or so hanging out at the sock hop together. Two outcasts. We could clear out a whole corner just for ourselves.

"How'd that happen?" I asked, nodding at his arm in the sling.

He held it up like a bird wing. "Helping build hogans for the Diné reservation. Axe came off the handle and snapped my ulna in two."

My heart awoke—maybe thinking about the pain, or maybe thinking about his muscular arms chopping.

He gave a little chuckle. "Lucky it wasn't two-sided or you'd have to carry my books until I graduated."

"You're lucky to get three blocks," I said, smirking. I glanced at him out of the corner of my eye. His smile was so sweet I had to look away. "Ulna. That's a smart word. You a whiz at school or something?"

"Oh, no, nothing like that." He scratched the back of his head in such a way that let me know he really was. "Doctor said it at the hospital, and I just remembered."

We looked left and right down an unpaved road, and then crossed along the driest hump of mud we could find. The girls were still shadowing us.

"Uh-huh," I said. "What's that other bone in your arm called?"

"Uh, radius? Humerus?"

"See?" I said, giggling. "Smarty-pan—"

My feet came to an abrupt stop. The textbooks slid out of my hands and plopped into a mud puddle. My eyes rose up up up up up. I wanted to scream, but I didn't have the breath. I barely noticed the kid scrambling around my feet, rescuing his books from the mud with his one good arm.

There was a man.

A man was filling the sky.

Ma had tried to describe Daddy to me before. She'd told me the crown of his head stretched above the clouds and his shins faded in the haze of the horizon. But seeing him tower before me—the bulging stomach, the nostrils, the slowly waving wisps of hair on a bald head—it was too much to fit in my brain.

I blinked and helped the boy rescue his textbooks.

"This is what I get—" he said, half smiling, wiping the cover of *Advanced Algebra* with his sleeve—"letting a girl carry my books for me."

He was joking, but I decided not to take it that way. I handed him the rest of his books and ran home, hoping he'd believe I left because of his comment and not because I was in a state of shock.

I practically knocked the motel door down.

Ma was painting her toenails. "Hiya, Beefy!"

That had been Ma's nickname for me ever since she'd accidentally switched the halves of my name when I was eight, making me laugh till I couldn't breathe. After this conversation, she would never use it again.

"Why didn't you *tell* me?"

"Tell you what, honey?"

"He's *ugly!*"

I screamed this. I screamed it so loud, Ma whisked across the room in her slippers to shut the motel door. "What are you talking about?"

I grabbed the string for the blinds, yanked them open, and pointed. "Daddy. He's fat and bald and he looks about as savvy as a cow on slaughter day."

"You saw him? Why, honey, that's *wonderful!* That means you're a real woman n—"

My look silenced her.

Ma chewed her fingernail, considering the sky. "Well, no one would call him a looker, that's for sure." She clicked her tongue. "Guess I was so busy raising you, I just came to think of him as Daddy."

I sat on the edge of the bed and squeezed my arms between my legs so my body didn't feel so exposed.

"Oh, Phoebe," Ma said. She came and sat beside me and tucked my hair behind my ear. "Sweetie, you're beautiful. You're gorgeous. You won the jackpot. You got your momma's looks or I'm as blind as a mole rat." She lifted my chin with her fingernail so I could see myself in the motel mirror. "See?"

I didn't see. Looking at my body then, at my face and doughy torso, I knew exactly where I got my looks. I'd *lost* the jackpot. Lost it big time. Ma may as well call me Beefy for the rest of my life.

Ma went back to the window. "If you did get anything from your father, it's his full lips and delicate hands. And I gotta disagree with you on one point, Phoebe." She gestured to Daddy through the window like he was a fabulous prize on a game show. "I think he looks intelligent. Bright as a copper kettle."

My expression told her I wasn't buying it.

She put her hands on her hips. "How else would your father know where the next bad thing was gonna happen and warn us to get out, huh? Answer me that."

My scowl deepened.

Ma relented. "It must be such a strange thing having no clue what your daddy looked like for thirteen years, then all of a sudden *boom*, there he is." She sat on the bed and took my hands. "Think of it this way. You wouldn't be here if it weren't for that big galook, and no one's gladder about that than me. For better or worse, he's your daddy and my main squeeze till the end of time. Daniel Framsky."

"Daniel *Framsky?*"

"I never told you?" Ma squinted at the window. "It was the first name that popped into my head when I saw him. Maybe 'cause he looked like such a shlub." She laughed and held my chin. "Good thing you didn't inherit one iota of his shlubbishness."

I turned my head to break free. I studied myself in the mirror and then finally looked out the window, where I could see

Daddy's gigantic hairy arm resting on an armrest across the western hemisphere.

Ma patted my knee. "You'll always be a Lane, honey. Now, I'm gonna hop in the shower and we're gonna go out and celebrate with a steak dinner and ice cream. Two women of the world eating whatever they want. I'll even sneak you some of my beer in honor of your father." She stood and de-robed. "And if intelligence is so important to you, maybe you should spend less time at the movies and more time at the library."

She closed the bathroom door and I heard the water run while she sang, "If I Had a Talking Picture of You."

I kept staring at that gigantic arm out the window. A gigantic ulna. And I couldn't stop thinking about how nice the boy with a sling had been to me . . . even when I looked like this.

• • •

I saw the boy, same time, same place the next day. He was walking slow, hitching his books into his armpits every few steps. My hand reached out to help, but then I stopped.

I now knew for certain that Daddy wasn't just a story Ma made up, and that we'd be running from town to town for the rest of our lives. I also knew what my father looked like now and that the apple hadn't fallen far from the tree.

I forced my hand back around my books from the library and walked straight past the boy. He didn't say a word.

Daddy's eyes wandered to the town a few days later. Once Ma and me were safely away from Sunrise Valley, we heard Jimmy Jamboney on the radio. *"From my helicopter view, I can see the whole town is crawling with plants, sprung to life from the solar flare. These are not the sort of plants your grandma grows in her backyard, ladies and gentlemen. They're like worms! Writhing, crawling, circling round unsuspecting ankles. Brr. This is one reporter who's got the heebie-jeebies."*

I was grateful the reporter wasn't too graphic about it. But when me and Ma stopped at a diner, we overheard two men talking about how the vines made shish kebabs of their victims, twining in one end and out the other. The men noticed my mother sitting at the end of the counter and apologized for using such indelicate language in front of a lady.

I went to the bathroom to throw up.

It's strange having dinner with a boy when you're naked and twenty feet tall.

I lay across the floor in front of the pulpit, as long as a pew but too wide to lie on one. Heck, my hips were so big, I couldn't even fit between the pews to sit in the aisle anymore. Lear was sitting on the floor, eating a sandwich, Pan-Cake curled up in his lap. Beth was still working on my gown, so all I had was Frank, the comforter Creation, draped over my body like a bath towel.

My long limbs shifted around, trying to look as appealing as I could with my new proportions. But I kept banging my shin on the altar and nearly knocking over the pulpit. Growing up, I'd always felt like I was only allowed to take up a certain amount of space. And that my body was always betraying that. It didn't help that I compared myself to Ma, whose voluptuous form seemed to take up the exact right amount of space at all times.

But this new body of mine . . . well, it was just ridiculous. Comical even. If Lear didn't like me as I was, what was I going to do? Go on a diet and grow as skeletal as Ook? Lear could even call me by my old nickname "Beefy" and I wouldn't bat an eyelash.

My limbs shifted again, more carefully this time. I kept waiting for him to sneak a peek at my shape under the comforter, but his eyes remained fixed on his sandwich. We were having our usual engaging conversation of slurps, sighs, and silent pauses when Marsh came in the back door sweating and carrying a shovel. He didn't see Lear sitting behind my giant hips.

"The community garden has never been healthier," Marsh said, pulling off his work gloves. "I have been telling people the fertilizer came from the elephants at the carnival."

Now that I was a giantess, my stomach had much farther to fall. I cleared my throat so loud it rattled the stained glass and got Marsh's attention. With my eyes I promised to throw him over the church if he breathed another word about the fertilizer.

"You have a guest." Marsh's nostrils flared at Lear like he was a skunk that may or may not have had its sacs removed. "You are Lear Finley, correct?"

"Yes, sir."

"I have not seen you in my congregation."

"I can't leave Mother alone too long," Lear said.

"What is the matter with her?" Marsh asked

Lear flinched and studied the ground. "When I was young, she—my dad, he—"

"She saved Lear from a fire when he was little," I interrupted, spinning a story from nothing at all. "Lear's dad didn't make it out, and her lungs haven't been right since. If Lear doesn't keep a close eye on her, she could choke."

Lear kept his eyes on the ground.

"I see," Marsh said. He took out his keys and headed toward the front door. "I must purchase some pipe cleaner for the organ." He paused at the entrance. "I do not imagine you can get up to any, em, *fornicating* in your current state?"

My face practically caught fire. I could see actual heat waves wafting off my cheeks. I didn't dare look at Lear.

"I did not think so," Marsh said.

The church door shut behind him.

If the reverend couldn't think up any sins between me and Lear, what chance did I have?

I lifted a fruit can to my lips and nearly knocked the pulpit over with my elbow, barely managing to catch it. My limbs were so long now, they were starting to feel like they didn't belong to me. My body felt like a tractor that could bring down the entire church if I didn't navigate it right.

"This is the last of the food," Lear said.

"Oh."

I looked over the rest of the food, half the amount he'd brought on other nights. My stomach suddenly felt so hollow I feared there was no bottom. I emptied a box of uncooked Kraft Macaroni & Cheese into my mouth, hoping the crunch would hide my panic.

Lear rubbed his eye with the palm of his hand. "My mom's gonna have a stroke if she finds out it's all gone. This was supposed to last us a year. She's terrified the world could end any minute."

I wished I could promise him it wasn't. But with me hiding in this church, Daddy's eyes were probably starting to glaze over again.

"I'm sorry," I said. "I'm still gonna pay you back. Promise."

Lear sighed, frustrated. "Why won't you tell me how you got big?"

"I don't know. It's all so confusing and scary. I don't want to put you in any danger."

Lear lifted Pan-Cake off his lap and set her aside. "I better go."

I sat up, pinning Frank to my chest. "Will you still visit me tomorrow night? We could take another trip to the water tower after everyone's asleep. Bet I could climb that ladder in three steps now."

"Maybe," he said.

The locusts hummed at the edge of my vision. It seemed the bigger I grew the more often they visited. That afternoon Beth had brought another gown, and just by bending forward, I had sent a rift straight up the back, mooning stained-glass Jesus. I was so frustrated I wanted to kick a hole right through the side of the church and keep on kicking until all of Pennybrooke was nothing more than rubble.

"It's fine," Beth had said, touching my knee, her fingers scabbed over from sewing. "I didn't like the cut of this one anyway."

Beth wasn't here to calm me now. And I didn't want Lear to leave. The bigger I got, the lonelier I became. It already felt like an eternity of waiting between Marsh in the morning, Beth in the afternoon, and Lear at night.

And time was growing short for my first kiss.

What would keep him around? What would get him to open up? What could I do to make him look not so terrified all the time?

"Wait,"I told Lear. "Don't leave yet."

To gain some courage, I grabbed a pudding cup, the size of a thimble in my fingers, peeled off the tin lid, and squeezed the tapioca in a single drip onto my tongue.

"I think I like you, Lear," I said. "I've never really liked someone before, and it scares me something fierce just saying this out loud, especially because I'm so big now and not that great to look at, but there you have it."

Lear's forehead unwrinkled a bit. My heart sped up. Now that I'd finished talking, all that was left was a dusty silence. Lear stared at his feet.

"Anyway," I said, "I wouldn't blame you if you ran right out of this church and never looked back. But I also wouldn't blame you if you decided to kiss me before my lips are much too big for kissing."

Lear wavered. My heart leapt. And then he was gone. Down the aisle, out the door, and into the night.

The church creaked in his absence. "When I said I wouldn't blame you for running, I didn't think you'd take it so seriously," I said to nobody. Then I sighed. "Guess I'd run too."

The church door fell shut, and fear overtook my body. I tried to drown it with a bucket of rehydrated milk.

• • •

That night, I paced up and down the aisle in the fading light of the stained glass. My footsteps thundered, making Pan-Cake tremble in the corner. It was hard to breathe. My skin was covered in sweat. My insides felt hollow, like my body could collapse in on itself if I didn't eat in the next five minutes.

I considered venturing out to the grocery store, breaking the doors down, and stuffing myself silly. But people didn't take kindly to things my size. What if I was caught? What if the people of Pennybrooke tied me down and locked me up? What if they shot me?

My feet traversed the length of the church in three strides and back again as my thoughts alternated between food and Lear. Locusts swarmed around Jesus's eyes. I wasn't like one of those silly girls on TV who got all loosey-goosey about love. But maybe now that my heart was five times its size, it was easier for romance to slip inside. I could sure go for a dozen Salisbury steak TV dinners right about then. I'd finally admitted to someone that I liked him, truly liked him, and he couldn't get away from me fast enough. Then again, what did I expect when I could eat twice his body weight in food? If those stained-glass lambs were real, I'd cut open their throats and eat them raw.

Spinning to head back down the aisle, I banged my ankle against a pew. I collapsed to the floor and sucked through my teeth so hard it made a couple of choral books fly open, pages fluttering.

"ARG!" I said in a voice I barely recognized as my own.

Outside, dogs barked. I clamped my hands over my giant mouth.

Pain throbbed through my leg. I closed my eyes. Instead of screaming loud enough to shatter the stained glass, instead of leaping up and putting my fist through the ceiling, instead of eating Pan-Cake, I calmly plugged in the ham radio and held the speaker, as tiny as a quail's egg between my trembling thumb and finger.

"Um . . . Palm Tree to . . . Ant Lion." My voice shook. "This is Palm Tree to Ant Lion."

There were a few moments of static before Liz's voice came over the speaker. *"Phoebe? Oh, thank goodness. I thought we'd lost you."*

"I need food."

"Of course you do, darling," Liz said. *"You must be as skinny as a telephone pole by now. Where are you?"*

I glanced around the church, my sanctuary, the place that had kept me hidden and protected from the world these last two weeks while I grew. Could I trust that Liz really was just trying to help? My stomach turned over like an avalanche and I clamped my trembling lips shut.

"Phoebe," Liz said in her delicate voice, *"Hal can deliver more*

food than you could possibly eat. He'll drive fast and be there in thirty minutes. You just have to complete an assignment for us and tell us where you are."

The thought of food made the locusts break up a bit.

"What do I need to do?"

"We need you to cause a scene. Something big enough to make it in tomorrow's paper and raise Daddy's eyebrows a bit."

My stomach thundered, and I leaned forward, trying to quiet it.

"Like what?"

"You could . . . destroy something. A public building—the school perhaps. Or the police station. It's your choice."

My nails dug into my palms. I had enough rage built up inside me that I was confident I could flatten both. I unclenched my hands. I'd never much cared for suburban towns like Pennybrooke, but I never wanted to be the terror in one either. Not for girls like Katie. Or the boy with his arm in a sling. Not for anybody.

"Have you ever been in a Shiver?" I asked Liz.

"Of course I have. Probably more than anyone other than you."

"Then you know what they're like. You know the fear that freezes up your bone marrow, making you believe the whole world's coming to a close." I breathed in then out. "How can you ask me to do that to people?"

"Because, Phoebe, it's all we have right now. We have to keep Daddy entertained until we find a better solution. You know this."

"Yeah," I said in a voice so quiet I didn't know if Liz heard me. "I guess I do."

Mr. Peak spoke up in the background. *"Tell her she needs to act now."*

"Phoebe?" Liz said. *"Daddy's eyes are dulling a bit. He hasn't picked up the remote again, but we're growing concerned."*

It had been a relief not seeing Daddy's eyes these past weeks. I'd even taken my hose baths on the far side of the church so I wouldn't have to see him.

"Phoebe?"

"St. Maria's Church."

"Excellent," Liz said. *"And you're going to . . ."*

"Yes."

"Hal is standing by with food," she said.

I clicked off the speaker and regretted not requesting a cigarette the size of a fence post.

((((BONG))))

As the clock tower began to strike midnight, I stood before the church doorway, holding the Creation against my body. A little voice told me that if I didn't make it outside before the final strike, then I would chicken out and starve to death in the church while drowning in the shadows of my thoughts.

((((BONG))))

I did have a slight problem, but Ma had it solved for me when I was little.

"Phoebe, honey, I'm gonna teach you how to wrap a towel around your body so it won't fall off, not even if a fleet of fighter jets passes overhead. I've seen too many women exposed in all their glory before God and country, and I won't have that happen to my daughter. Ready?"

"Ready!"

Ready.

((((BONG))))

Ma faced away from me, holding the towel out so it stretched along her back. "First, you're going to fold the right side over your body, and tuck it under your armpit like this. You use your strong hand to make sure the bottom layer is tighter."

I did as she'd instructed with my Frankenstein comforter.

((((BONG BONG BONG))))

Ma turned around. "Then you're going to fold the other half over that bottom layer. Now pay attention—this is where women get it wrong and lose their towel and their dignity the moment they bend over to get the morning paper. Instead of just tucking, you're going to tuck and *roll*. Like so."

I tucked Frank's opposite corner to the side of my cleavage and then rolled the tops of the two halves together, creating a lump of towel above my breasts.

((((BONG BONG BONG))))

"Then you can do whatever you want, see?" Ma did a twirl around the room, made a couple of jumps, knocked a book off the nightstand, and bent over to pick it up without even holding the towel to her body. "Try to avoid cartwheels."

I gave Frank a wiggle to make sure it was secure—

((((BONG))))

—I turned the church's door handle, the size of a shooter marble between my fingers—

((((BONG))))

—and I peeked outside at the empty street.

((((BONG))))

Crouching, I stepped through the door just as the bell struck its final note.

((((BONG))))

I wavered on the church lawn. Inside, I always had a wall boxing me in and lending support while I did my laps. Out here, my feet felt unnervingly far from my head, giving me vertigo. Everything felt wide open and tiny. I could peek down the chimneys of the houses, like Santa's Elf Village at the mall, with their miniature cellophane windows and plastic gingerbread walls.

Daddy grinned down at me as if we'd been playing hide-and-seek and he'd finally found me.

"Wish me luck," I said to him even though I may as well have been talking to the sky.

• • •

After the thing was done, I lay back in the church, doubled over with hunger pangs, eyes so full of locusts, I thought I might go blind.

A firm knock came at the door. I crawled on my belly to open it and almost slammed it again when I saw Officers Shelley and Graham. But then I noticed the grocery bags in their arms and started devouring the food like it was oxygen.

As Officer Shelley closed the door, I caught a glimpse of Officer Graham's dead-fish eyes. I tried to see past them to that heart of gold beneath, but it was nowhere to be found.

The door clicked shut, and I heard a whimpering in the corner.

"Here, Pan-Cake," I said, holding out my hand. "It's okay. Momma's nice again."

She leapt into my palm. I lay down so she could curl up in the hollow of my throat.

And that was how Marsh found me the next morning, lying in a sea of food wrappers and snoring loud as the bugle on Judgment Day, making the stained glass of Jesus and his lambs tremble in its frame.

"You are forbidden from having any more visitors," Marsh said in the faint dawn light. "Not until you start living by God's commandments."

"Beth is supposed to bring my dress any day now!" I looked at Frank. "You want me to stay naked under this thing?"

Marsh flinched like I'd struck him across the face. "I shall collect the garment for you."

I had no argument for that. But who would ease my nerves in my moments of rage? Not Marsh, that was for sure.

"Is it any surprise that you're still growing?" Marsh said, gesturing to the empty food wrappers. "Stealing food? Eating yourself into a stupor? And *this*!"

He flipped on the radio and "Maybe" by the Chantels filled the church.

Marsh switched it off in disgust. I'd forgotten to tune the radio back.

"I didn't steal this food," I said.

He crossed his arms. "Then where did you get it?"

I sighed. It was odd being talked down to by a man whose head barely reached my hip. From up here, I could gaze down his perfect, shining part, as neat and deliberate as Moses's own parting sea.

Marsh crossed his arms. "I also know that you have been . . . *fornicating* with that boy."

"I have *not*," I said.

"Then why has he been coming to the church at night, sneaking around like a, like a *rat*?"

"He's been bringing me food."

Marsh picked up a wrapper, different from the food storage cans Lear had brought. "From the grocery store? How is he affording it?"

I wiped my face with my giant hands.

"This ends now," Marsh said. "How can the Lord diminish your size if you insist on consuming every morsel you find? From now on, you will start eating sensible meals three times a day."

Locusts flooded the church. Marsh may have given me shelter, but if he got between me and food, there would be hell to pay.

I stood up full. "You're just trying to make an example of me so you can fill your pews!" My voice thundered through the rafters.

Marsh calmly and carefully adjusted his lapels, glasses, and hair, and then walked to the back entrance. It was only then that I noticed he was shaking. "I must go prepare my statement about the pitfalls of attending the carnival. Apparently, they are to have a *rock and roll* band." Before he closed the door, he said, "Eyes to heaven, Phoebe. God only gives us challenges we cannot handle so we can grow into someone who can handle anything."

• • •

A few days later, I stood up to stretch and bumped my head on the church's ceiling.

"Ow," I said, rubbing my head. Then, "*Oh.*"

I was twenty-five feet tall. Soon there wouldn't be enough

food in Pennybrooke to keep me alive, and I'd die here. Mass would be held around my bones.

I could hear Marsh's low voice speaking to one of the members of his congregation over the phone. "I am terribly sick, I'm afraid," he said. "And I could not secure a replacement."

He was coming up with excuses for why there would be no service that Sunday. The Sunday before we had just been able to squeeze me into the storage room, but now my hips couldn't fit through the single doorframe. I could still fit through the double-door entrance to complete Liz's assignments, but there was nowhere for me to hide outside on a bright Sunday morning.

I could only marvel at my height for so long, staring from the ceiling all the way down to my feet, before my stomach informed me it was time for breakfast. Officers Graham and Shelley had started delivering groceries twice a day now, and they were a mile better than Lear's preserves. In the morning came chilled milk bottles and pancakes and melons and cheeses and berries and bananas and bacon and steaming omelets and premixed orange juice concentrate. In the evening came baskets of hams and roasted chickens and hamburgers and potato salad and Jell-O and pudding and cakes and pies and tomato juice. Liz told me I'd earned every crumb.

At her request I had performed three more "events" that week. I spread them out and did them at odd hours so as not to be too predictable and get caught. The people of Pennybrooke were starting to panic, so the police established a night watch. Of course, the pod versions of Officers Shelley and Graham volunteered and then kept an eye out while I did what I had to do.

I stomped down the aisle, stomach grumbling, and opened the door handle with my fingernails. There was no food on the front doorstep. My stomach twitched, but I didn't let it worry me yet. Crouching, I picked up the ham radio's speaker, like a grain of rice between my fingers.

"Palm Tree to Ant Lion. Palm Tree to Ant Lion." Even though I was whispering, my huge voice still wafted small breezes around the church.

"Hello, Phoebe," Liz said. *"I'm guessing you're calling about the food."*

"Yeah. I caused another, um, *event* last night, but there was no delivery this morning."

This event had been my favorite so far. I broke into the record store, collected vinyl of white singers doing terrible renditions of black singers' music, and threw them like Frisbees into the desert.

"Yes, it was very cute," Liz said. *"But I'm reading boredom in the lines on Father's face."*

Funny. On last night's venture out, the remote was nowhere to be seen over the mountaintops.

"Phoebe," Liz said, *"this time we need you to give an actual person a good scare."*

My heart started to beat so heavy, I could practically hear the air around me resonate. This was where things changed. This was where I turned into the kind of Shiver Ma and I always tried to escape.

"What happens if I don't?" I held my legs, as big as buckled trees.

"Well, then we can't deliver any more food."

My pounding heart was drowned out by my gurgling stomach.

I heard Peak clear his throat over the speaker. *"And we'll take more drastic measures."*

"If you please, Mr. Peak," Liz said. *"I have this under control."* There was some grumbling and then a door slamming.

"You mean release more monsters?" I said, my voice rising. "I thought that's why you did this to me. So you wouldn't have to do something worse."

Liz sighed. *"I know I'm asking for a lot, Phoebe. But we don't want to take any chances. A little fear goes a long way with Father. Panic is very interesting to him. Men screaming and women shooting guns and things of that sort."* She paused. *"I just made a little joke, Phoebe. You can laugh."*

"Ha," I said.

"With a little more panic, Daddy is more likely to remain tuned in to see what happens next. We can tease him along like this for months."

"But what comes after panic?" I said.

"We aren't asking you to hurt anyone."

"Not yet you aren't," I said.

"We will only resort to violence if it becomes absolutely necessary."

How could it not eventually? The more familiar you become with something, the more boring it seems, just like Liz had said. Daddy would only be able to watch people worrying for so long before he'd want more. Before he'd want blood.

Liz's voice suddenly brightened. *"This baby sure is taking his sweet time. But you'll be an auntie soon enough. What do you think of that?"*

I scoffed. "I'm over the moon."

"Please complete this event within the next three days," Liz said. *"We do not want to have to resort to Peak's . . . drastic measures. This is Ant Lion signing off."*

The speaker fell silent.

I was just setting down the radio speaker when a knock came at the door. *Shave and a haircut*. Beth. Fortunately, Marsh was still busy in the back room, calling members of the congregation.

"Come in," I said.

Beth entered the church like a ray of sunshine, carrying a duffel bag stuffed to bursting.

But there she saw my face. "What's wrong?"

"Nothing. Just"—I put my hand on my stomach—"a bit of indigestion is all. Too much eating maybe."

Or not enough.

"Well, I've got *great* news."

I hoped it was a swimming pool full of food, but I didn't think Beth could fit that in a duffel bag.

She plopped the bag down on the ground. "I finally finished."

"Oh. Good," I said, trying to look relieved. I smoothed out the comforter Creation. "Frank is starting to smell like his namesake."

Beth knelt and unzipped the duffel bag slowly like she was making a big reveal. "I realized I'd been thinking about this all wrong. We can't make you fit in a dress. Your body rejects it like a bad kidney. Besides, it's springtime outside!"

She reached in and pulled out a large white piece of vinyl and held her arms out wide to display it. It was a strapless bikini top. I smiled. This was just about the only thing that could cheer me up right then.

"Do you like it?" Beth said from behind the material. "I can't see your face."

"Oh, Beth," I said in all sincerity. "It's *perfect.*"

Beth let the top droop and beamed. "Try it on!"

I did, turning toward the wall with Frank draped over my shoulders. I felt a weird blend of excitement about getting a new article of clothing and trying to forget that this clothing could fit a small whale.

"Well?" Beth said. "Stand up so I can get a look at ya."

I spun from crossed legs to standing in one move.

"You look . . . ," Beth said, "*ravishing.*"

"You really think so?"

It felt so good being able to stand without having to press a comforter to my body that I flicked on the radio. I tuned it back to my station, and started an impromptu dance right there in the church. I'd never been any sort of a dancer, but I sashayed down the aisle, then turned and put in a couple spins, even tossed in some Little Richard, running my ringers along the tops of the pews like they were piano keys. I did this all before the stained-glass eyes of Jesus, and to me, he seemed as happy as any rock-'n'-roll audience could be.

Beth laughed. "How's it feel?"

I did a little wiggle. The two-piece felt a little saggy in the bottom and droopy in the chest, but the ache in my bones told me they still weren't done growing.

"It's just nice not to be hanging out all over the place," I said.

"Boy," Beth said, staring up at me with admiring eyes, "you look so pretty I could just about kiss you."

She must've seen the blood rush to my cheeks because she followed it up with, "Don't worry! I won't do it. Ha-ha. It's not such a big deal where I come from."

"You don't come from Pennybrooke?"

She knelt beside the duffel bag again. "No, I was kinda adopted, remember? But that's a conversation for another time. Besides, I've got another surprise for you." She pulled out a can of paint. "After you're fitted, we can paint your nails!"

I squinted at the label. It was my favorite shade.

"Thanks, Beth."

She stuck a couple safety pins in her mouth and pointed to the floor. I sat in front of the pulpit, my back to her. I felt her tug the strap tight and fold it over.

"Lear's in for a treat," she said.

"Sure he is," I said, twirling my hair four feet in the air.

I tried not to think about him too much these days. On the officers' last delivery, I had asked them to bring me money to replace Mrs. Finley's food, but they refused, worried I'd get someone to buy me groceries. I didn't think Lear was going to visit again anyway. His absence made me feel my size.

"Turn," Beth said, and then fastened more safety pins in the front. "When I got here, you had such a storm cloud over you, I was afraid of getting struck. It wouldn't have anything to do with today's headline, would it?"

I'd seen the newspaper on the church's front step that morning: MYSTERY VANDAL STRIKES AGAIN! The picture showed Freeman High's flagpole tied in a pretzel shape. I'd eaten the paper before Marsh could see it.

"That was me," I said. "I did that."

Beth snorted. "Well, I thought it was freaking awesome. The drama team's been desperately trying to figure out what did it for the drills. But if you don't mind me asking . . . *why?*"

"Someone is making me."

Beth eyed the ham radio. "Do you want to be doing these things?"

"I have no choice. It's how I get food."

Beth put away her safety pins and then gave me that smile like something sweet was cooking. "What if I started a charity drive at the school, just for you?"

"And what?" I said, doubtful. "Say it's for the Gray Rock reservation or something?"

"I'll be vague about it. I'll have a sign that reads 'You can save a life.'"

More than one, I thought. If I had enough to eat, I wouldn't have to keep following Liz's orders until she eventually made me hurt someone.

"But what do we do when that food runs out?" I asked.

"I dunno." Beth smiled. "We'll start a rumor that there's another bacteria scare in the TV dinners and then raid the trash cans."

I laughed, the fear melting right out of my face.

"Speaking of school," Beth said. "Rhoda's been asking after you."

"Ugh," I said. "Did she ask about Queenie?"

"Who's Queenie?"

"Never mind."

"She keeps wondering if you got gobbled up by the monster everyone's talking about. Calvin predicted that Emperor Ook's bones have been coming to life at night and are taking revenge on Pennybrooke, starting with you, his damsel's daughter."

Right. Calvin. The ham. I'd forgotten all about him.

"Well, he certainly has an imagination," I said. "Is it true what you said about Rhoda? Did her ma really try to kill her with sleeping pills and shoot herself? Was she really struck by lightning?"

Beth shrugged. "Wish I could tell ya."

Adjustments finished, she took out the paint can and a brush and made big swaths across my fingernails.

Marsh cleared his throat, making us both jump.

"This is not what I had in mind when I requested a dress, Beth," he said at the back entrance. His eyes were fixed firmly on the ceiling, avoiding me in my bikini.

Beth smirked. "I'd like to see you make something that would cover this gorgeous girl with the amount of material that it takes to make four normal-size dresses. No offense, Phoebe." I gave my head a shake, hair whipping.

"Besides, Reverend, you aren't the one who's going to be wearing it."

Marsh crossed his arms and dared a glance in my direction. "Perhaps you can staple some of the church's curtains around the bottom."

"Perhaps," Beth said, and flashed me a look that said she'd sooner set the two-piece on fire.

"I think it best if you leave now, Ms. Graham," Marsh said.

Beth threw the duffel bag over her shoulder. "I'll be back to make the final adjustments, but for now I'm off to start a charity drive. Lates."

I smiled and waved goodbye with my newly painted nails.

Beth spoke so strangely sometimes.

When the clock tower struck midnight, I squeezed my hips through the church's double-door entrance. I almost lost the top to my two-piece, but it was late and Pennybrooke was quiet, so no one noticed. Well, almost no one.

Daddy was too much in sight, glowing bright as the moon. The corners of his giant lips, wide as a constellation, were flat, as if he was waiting for me to entertain him with something other than small pranks. He was in for a surprise.

I crept through the moonlit streets, keeping low behind fences and hedges. A dog barked. A window light went on. I curled into a ball and froze, holding as still as a parked car while a sewer grate breathed cold on my toes. When the light turned off, I crept past the drive-in. The lot was dark and empty. A cat shined its eyes at me before bounding across the field and slipping under a fence. A bottle broke. Somewhere, the wind played chimes.

The grocery store's door was locked, but I gave the door a good shove, and it came open with a pop. I found a kiddie pool and filled it with food that could open without a can opener and then left money on the register for the food and the broken doorframe. I propped it under my arm and was about to sneak away when I saw a figure at the end of the lawn.

It was Officer Shelley. Or what used to be Officer Shelley.

"I can't let you do that," he said, nodding to the kiddie pool full of food. "It's cheating."

He didn't have his gun drawn, but he stood in my path, arms crossed, no taller than my knee.

"How are you going to stop me?" I said.

"We have our ways." He stepped aside. "Don't let it happen again."

Even though I could punt Shelley across the entire town, he still gave me a chill. As I walked out of Pennybrooke and down the highway, I wondered how the Buried Lab would feel if they knew this food wasn't for me.

• • •

The desert earth crunched beneath my feet as I walked along the lonely stretch of highway, leaving Hula-Hoop-size craters in my wake. The stars were putting on a real show that night: hot and bright as neon lights. The Joshua trees looked like frozen dancers. Coyotes cried through the dry air.

The locusts scattered through the wide-open sky, no longer buzzing around my head in a thick cloud. Some Shivers, when they get angry, snatch up a beautiful woman and haul her to the top of the Chrysler Building. But I wanted to separate myself from the gorilla—even if his anger did make him see locusts like mine. I refused to do what Daddy and Liz wanted me to do. I wanted to put some balance back in the world for the missions Liz had sent me on. And for all the times I'd had to leave a friend behind.

The walk took longer than I thought. After Pennybrooke disappeared behind me, my stomach told me if I didn't eat, I was going to gobble up the Navajo people instead of surprising them with a gift. I started nibbling at the food in the kiddie pool, leaving a trail of wrappers and boxes by the side of the road.

When I arrived at Gray Rock, I set the kiddie pool, half full of food now, next to one of the hogans. I was about to head back when I heard a tiny gasp.

I looked down and found a Navajo girl, no older than five, staring with her mouth hanging open. Her head barely cleared my ankle, but she didn't run away screaming.

"Hello," I said in the least threatening voice I could muster.

"Are you here to kill us?" she asked.

"No," I said. "I brought you food."

She looked at the kiddie pool and then wrinkled her nose up at me. "Are you Wonder Woman?"

I gave a little laugh, which didn't come out little. "No."

"What *are* you?"

"Just a girl," I said, kneeling in front of her. "Like you."

The girl giggled. "*Nooooooooo.*"

The door of the hogan opened and Eugene, Gray Rock's chairman, came out in a bathrobe. He pulled the girl to his side and stared up at me.

I held up my hands. "I come in peace."

He nodded. "I've heard that line before."

I nudged the kiddie pool closer. "I brought food."

The girl crouched down and pulled out a Twinkie.

The man smiled at her then quirked an eyebrow at me. "You're Phoebe," he said. "The Girl Scout."

"Kind of," I said, meaning I wasn't really a Girl Scout, and I didn't really feel like Phoebe anymore.

"Why did you bring this?" he said, nodding to the food.

My giant shoulders deflated. "What do you mean?"

Eugene stroked his chin. "Well, are you doing it to make you feel good about yourself? Or are you doing it because you think we actually need it?"

"Neither." I looked up at Daddy, who stared dully down at me. "I—I mean *both*. I mean . . . I was just trying to help. I figured it'd be better than Bibles."

Eugene nodded. "Okay. All right."

The girl tugged on Eugene's sleeve and held up the Twinkie, asking if she could eat it.

"Go ahead," he said. Then he bent down and grabbed a can of SPAM and waggled it at me. "My favorite."

He and the girl went back into the hogan. I was so confused about the interaction that I was tempted to bring the rest of the food for the long walk back, but then I thought better of it and left it behind.

I was wrong about the locusts. There were enough of them to flood a desert sky. And here I thought I'd done something good. My feet crunched back along the highway, and I felt confused about what was right or wrong and whether any of it mattered. The sun started to rise, leaving me feeling just as helpless as when it had set.

• • •

The morning sprinklers were on by the time I got back to the church. Marsh was waiting outside, wringing his hands like a worried father. Or what I imagined one to look like, at least.

He grabbed my pinkie and led me up the walkway. "Did anyone see you?"

"I don't think so."

"*In*," Marsh said, opening both church doors and throwing them wide.

"You first," I said, tugging at the bottom of my two-piece. "If I go first I'll scandalize you."

Marsh entered, and I lay down belly-flat and followed.

That is, I tried to follow.

I could fit my head and torso through the double frame just fine, but when it came to my hips, I had to squeeze and wiggle like I was thirteen again, trying to fit into a tight new dress. Only this time, I had outgrown an entire church.

I just barely managed to make it through, the fat of my butt expanding in relief as I lay on the aisle, out of breath.

"Where have you been?" Marsh asked.

"I took food down to Gray Rock."

"Where?"

"The, um, Navajo Reservation."

Marsh's expression loosened a bit, as if he hadn't expected me to do something charitable, but it hardened twice as quick. "You are lying to me."

I stayed on my belly, worn out. "I'm not lying."

"And where did you get this . . . *food*?"

I didn't answer. Here I finally did something good with my size, or tried to do something good, at least, and I was still being punished.

Marsh stepped up to the pulpit and placed his waxen fingers on the open Bible as if to draw strength from its pages. "I am wary about allowing you to remain in this church. In that outfit and with the"—he cleared his throat—"*happenings* around town. I will not house someone whose every action is dictated by Satan."

What about half sisters? I thought.

I pushed up to my knees. "You didn't seem wary about these *happenings* when it brought all those extra people to church last Sunday while I was stuffed in the storage."

Marsh steepled his fingers. "I am not averse to having the

opportunity to save more souls, no." He looked up into my eyes. "But at what cost to the immortal souls of this town?"

I fumed. I was in no mood for this. The reverend liked to talk about sin, but he hadn't spent much time thinking about the terrible conditions people were put in before they committed it.

"And where will I go?" I asked him, heat building behind my eyes. "Huh? You want to send me out there where everyone will scream the moment they set eyes on me and shoot me or lock me up?"

Marsh's mouth set. "No, I do not. But I will if I must. We must each of us take responsibility for God's wrath."

I stood up full, crouching so my head didn't crack the ceiling. It only took one step down the aisle to make my shadow fall over him.

"And what if I am God's wrath?" I screamed.

Marsh's hand leapt to his heart. In the silence that followed, the ham radio crackled and Liz's voice came through.

"Phoebe. Phoebe, I must speak to you immediately."

I took a deep breath, and moving my suitcase, picked up the hidden speaker. "I'm here."

"Phoebe, what have you done?" Liz asked.

"What do you mean?"

"Father looks ready to pass out, he's so bored."

I caught Marsh's eye. "I brought food to the Navajo people."

"Oh, Phoebe," Liz said, not hiding her disappointment. *"Father isn't interested in watching a feel-good scene. You may have undone all of the fear you've created this week."*

Marsh's face twitched, like the radio was receiving communication from the devil herself. I looked away from him.

Liz sighed. *"I didn't want to have to resort to this, but your latest action has left me no choice. You need to hurt someone. Tonight. Do you understand?"*

Marsh's face twitched, like the radio was receiving communication from the devil herself.

"What if I refuse?" I said. "I got food tonight all by myself. I could get more."

Liz's voice changed then. It was subtle, but wrung of the usual sisterly warmth. *"Phoebe, your mother is not on a special mission,"* she said. *"We have her locked in a cell. Right here in the lab. We tried to get her to do an assignment, but she refused to cooperate."*

My fingernails squeezed the speaker so tight the plastic crackled. My voice grew quiet and dangerous. "You didn't let me see her?"

I'd rip that goatee off the British scientist's chin. I'd bite Droopy Dog's head off. I'd tear Liz in half. Maybe the baby would survive, like a party popper.

"Now, don't be rash, Phoebe. It's good that your mother is in our custody. She was putting a lot of people in danger by moving you around as often as she did. Think about it. Your mother knew that whenever you moved to another motel, our father's eyes would follow and people would die. . . . And yet instead of remaining in the hospital, she chose the selfish route."

I could barely understand what Liz was saying. My head steamed with rage. Lava coursed through my veins. I wanted to go and get Ma immediately. Scoop her up like Emperor Ook had, cradle her to my breast, and carry her to safety. But how? The Buried Lab had moved. . . .

Or had it? No. Of course it hadn't. It was so simple. They

couldn't possibly move an entire lab, but they could move a door. Replace it with another rock maybe. The Buried Lab was probably right where I'd left it.

I looked at my hands. They were big as tractor shovels, big enough to dig up a desert. . . .

"I'm coming for you," I said into the speaker.

"Phoebe," Liz said. *"I don't think I need to tell you that if we sense the slightest tremor above the lab, then we will hurt Loretta."*

My whole body started to shake. "What kind of sister are you?"

"The kind that cares about you and your mother and every other person in this world."

"Every person?" I said.

Liz sighed. *"I'm sorry to say this, Phoebe, but if you don't acquiesce to our demands within the next twenty-four hours, you will receive a package with your mother's fingers instead of the usual food. Here."*

There was a fumbling, and I heard a tinny sobbing, as if coming through a second speaker.

"Ma?"

I suddenly felt as tiny and helpless as a little girl.

The sobs cut short.

"I look forward to reading about your exploits in the paper," Liz said. *"Over and out."*

The line fell silent. I sat in shock. I realized that back in the buried lab, Liz had let me hear Ma crying in order to lead me out of my room and down the halls toward the charcoal pyramids . . .

The thought brought me to my feet, and I stomped toward the church's doors. I didn't know what I was going to do, but it wasn't going to be pretty. Liz wanted someone to die? She'd get her wish.

Before I could reach the door, Marsh stepped in my path. He held up his hands, even though they only came halfway up my thigh.

"You cannot go out there. People will see you."

"What do you care?" I said, wiping my eyes. "You were gonna kick me out anyway."

He kept his hands raised. "I said that in order to get you to behave."

"Yeah, well, how'd that work out for you?"

I tried to step around him, but he pressed himself against the door, so I'd have to physically grab him if I wanted to leave.

"Don't say anything about God changing me back," I said. "I've been good. I haven't done any fornicating and I haven't hurt anyone. All I'm guilty of is being hungry and liking rock 'n' roll music. So far your prayers and your confessions have done *nothing*. If anything, it's a bunch of hot air that's making me bloated."

"Phoebe," Marsh said, dropping his hands.

It was the first time he'd said my name. The moment he said it I realized I was wound tight as a tightrope. Air huffed in and out of my nose like a rabid bull. My hands were in fists. Marsh watched as I unclenched them. My breathing stuttered, just a little. I leaned against a pew for support and I let out a sob.

Ma's fingers . . .

A bucket-size tear splattered across the carpet.

Marsh ran a hand through his greasy hair. "It is easy to forget that it is the devil who does not want us to have choices. It is God who gave us free will. I don't know what I just heard over that . . . radio. But I must admit it sounds as if someone else's sin is making you this way."

"That doesn't do me any good," I said. "I need to eat. Who's going to feed me? *You*?"

Marsh had no answer for that.

A knock came at the door, *shave and a haircut*, and Beth came in with her duffel bag. My stomach revved like a chainsaw.

"*Beth*," I said, flooding with relief. "You're saving my life."

Then I saw her face. She didn't say a word as she unzipped the bag and turned it upside down. Three cans rolled out: creamed corn, corned beef hash, and green beans.

"Sorry, Phoebe," she said. "I guess people aren't feeling too charitable these days. They're putting all their food in storage for the Shiver they think is on the way."

It was the first time I didn't have fuzzy feelings toward her, even though I knew it wasn't her fault. I opened the cans and poured them on my tongue, finishing them all in a swallow. They only made me hungrier.

Now, in order to eat, I'd have to hurt someone.

I lifted my foot and then brought it crashing down, splintering a pew in two. Marsh and Beth pressed against the front door. I brought up my other foot and smashed another pew, trembling the ceiling. Then I fell to the ground and curled up in a ball.

"Phoebe?" Beth said. She couldn't hide the fear in her voice.

"*Get out*," I said. "Both of you."

They left the church without another word.

As dusk darkened the stained glass that night, the locusts slipped through the cracks of the church and made shapes between the rafters: *Rhoda licking Lear's face at the drive-in. Ma screaming and clawing at the walls of her concrete cell. Liz's pretty lips telling me to kill Beth.*

I was a monster. Lear knew it, and that's why he wasn't coming back. Now Beth and Marsh, the only people who were there for me, knew it too. I was a monster all alone.

I wrapped Frank around myself like a blanket and tried to fall asleep so my thoughts would leave me be. But my heart wouldn't stop pounding, as big and loud as a war drum. My stomach wrenched like it was devouring me from the inside. I writhed on the floor. There came a hollow whistle through the frames of the stained glass. How could a church make such an ungodly sound?

I turned on the radio just as "It's Only Make Believe" was ending.

"Hello, all you swinging cats out there in radioland," the DJ said. *"I hope you're having a lovely evening filled with good music. Make sure to get on down to the carnival that's happening in Pennybrooke's fair field. Although, folks will be in for a slight disappointment. The famous Loretta Lane, the one kidnapped by Emperor Ook himself and hauled to the top of the Chrysler Building, is still MIA. I for one will sure miss seeing her in that nice little torn number."*

I sat up. They would have food at the carnival. Hot dogs and cotton candy and caramel apples and popcorn—food enough to feed people from three counties . . . or one giant girl.

• • •

The carnival was lit up like a galaxy, giving the stars a run for their money. Sounds wormed into my ear—screams and smashing bumper cars and warbled merry-go-round music—making my fists want to silence every last one of them. Spotlights shone on the big top tent that held Ook's bones.

I peeked over the concrete barrier that separated the town from the dusty field. My heart pounded something awful. The closer I got to the bright carnival, the more exposed I'd be. The problem was getting there unnoticed. If I could make it to Emperor Ook's tent, I could hide behind it while I sniffed out where the food was kept.

When I stepped over the wall, a cigarette fell to the asphalt, bounced a few inches, and then smoldered next to my foot.

A tiny voice below said, "Mother Mary, have mercy."

Leaning against the opposite side of the wall was Calvin Marple. He'd dropped his cigarette and was looking up and up and up until he met my eyes.

"It's *you,*" Calvin said, bracing the wall. "You're the one who's been . . . Oh God. Look, I'm sorry I took the money, all right? You just weren't at the motel, and . . . and I thought that was a real lousy trick to pull on a guy, and—and I still have plenty left, I swear. I—oh God." He couldn't stop shaking.

Calvin stole the money?

I imagined him showing up to the motel, finding the room empty, and then digging through Ma's suitcase.

The locusts fluttered from my eyes to my fingertips. It was one thing to stand someone up for a make-out date. It was another thing entirely to rob a person blind out of revenge.

"You little *rat*," I said.

Calvin's pants darkened with urine.

"*You* put me in this position," I said. "If it weren't for you, I would have had plenty of money to feed myself."

Shaking, Calvin tried on a smile and gestured to my large form. "M-m-maybe I did you a favor?" My giant face crumpled into a scowl, and Calvin fell to his knees. "It was a joke! I swear! I'm sorry. Oh God. I'm sorry."

I realized then that Calvin just might be my saving grace.

I rose to my full height, towering over his trembling form. "If you don't return every last cent of the money and promise to never breathe a word about me, I am going to eat you whole."

Calvin's jaw started to shake. Instead of running to get the money like I thought he would, he screamed. And not just any scream. It was so high-pitched and terrified it put the women in the pictures to shame.

I panicked and looked toward the carnival. "Shh! You're gonna get me caught!"

Calvin sucked in a breath and tore another hole through the night.

In order to shut him up, I flicked his forehead. Problem was, I was thinking with my old brain—the one that controlled small, pudgy Phoebe fingers. I shut him up all right. My giant fingernail connected with his forehead like a bat to a softball. His head whipped back, his skull thudding dully against the wall. His limp body slid down to the concrete.

The locusts evaporated. My hands flew to my mouth.

"Calvin?" I said, crouching over him. "Calvin, are you okay?"

He let out a groan. Blood spread across the concrete.

Someone called out from the carnival. "It came from over here!"

I watched, horrified, as carnival-goers gathered at the edge of the lot and then leapt over the concrete barrier. Hopefully, their attention would be on the boy on the ground and not the girl giant careening down the street.

Voices shouted behind me. "There she is!"

At first I thought they meant me, but then someone else said, "That isn't a her! That's Calvin Marple!"

"He's bleeding!"

"Calvin? Calvin! Can you hear us?"

Then someone gasped. "Look! There!"

"My God! What is it?"

I didn't have to look back to know they were talking about me.

• • •

My fifteen-foot legs left the people of Pennybrooke in the dust, and I managed to make it back to the church without anyone seeing where I went. I barely managed to wriggle and squeeze my way through the entrance, splintering the frame, before slamming the doors and catching my breath.

"Oh God," I whispered. "Please let Calvin be all right."

Stained-glass Jesus gave me an accusing look. For once I deserved it.

The ham radio crackled and Liz's voice came through. *"Phoebe? Are you there? I don't know what you did, but Daddy looks more pleased than ever! Well done!"*

I crossed the church and brought my fist down on the radio, smashing it. I didn't stop until it was in a thousand pieces.

I couldn't stop crying. Not even after I consumed the mountain of food the officers delivered to the church's doorstep. Pan-Cake was hiding under the pews from her monster mother. I couldn't blame her. I'd smashed Marsh's Roebuck radio after it reported that a boy *"got his head bashed in"* at the carnival by a mysterious figure *"as tall as a skyscraper."*

Well, Calvin, it wasn't television, but you sure made it on the radio.

When the food was finished, I knelt at the pulpit and put my hands together and tried to perform the act of contrition Marsh had taught me. But I couldn't remember the words.

At eleven, a knock came on the church door. My heart started to pound. The carnival-goers had found me. They were going to tie me up and drag me away. And I wasn't about to stop them.

The knock came again. Soft as mouse feet. *Lear.*

"Hey," he said when I opened the door. "Sorry I disappeared."

I wiped the tears from my cheeks and the food from my lips. My knees were shaking from kneeling so long. Had he heard about Calvin? Had he come to ask me what I'd done?

He held up a plastic-wrapped basket tied with ribbon. "This was sitting on the stoop. I'm guessing it's for you?"

It was a basket full of jams and fruits. A special gift from the Buried Lab, I assumed, for entertaining Daddy. I let it fall to the floor.

"It's dark in here," Lear said.

I didn't answer, just crawled back to the pulpit and drew my knees to my chest, trying not to look too big. I never wanted to be scary again.

Lear lit votive candles until the stained glass flickered with soft light. Then he came down the aisle, carrying a booklet. "I went away for a while because I've been, um, working on something. It was the only way I knew how to . . . um, explain stuff." He stared at the booklet. "Kids aren't allowed to read these things anymore. Most have been burned up."

I wiped my eyes, suddenly curious. I reached my arm down the aisle and opened my hand, which was almost big enough for Lear to crawl into. Lear gave the booklet one last look, then set it in my palm. It felt as tiny as a matchbook between my fingers. I had to squint to read the title.

TALES OF THE UNSPEAKABLE

It was a comic book—homemade on plain white eight-by-ten paper, folded in half and tied with string in the middle. The drawings weren't as high quality as the ones I'd seen at the drugstore, but they weren't too shabby, either.

"Did you make this?" I said.

Lear nodded.

A number in the corner of the cover of the comic caught my eye.

10¢!

"Do I have to pay you ten cents to read it?"

"Nah," Lear said, sticking his hands in his pockets. "I just drew that on there because all comics have that."

Our eyes met briefly. He didn't ask about the tears, of course. I was grateful.

"I'm gonna sit in the corner while you read that," he said.

"Okay," I said.

I hadn't forgotten about Calvin or Ma. Not for a second.

But this was a chance to get my mind off things for a bit while I figured out what to do. I lay on my back, and by flickering candlelight, I read Lear's comic book.

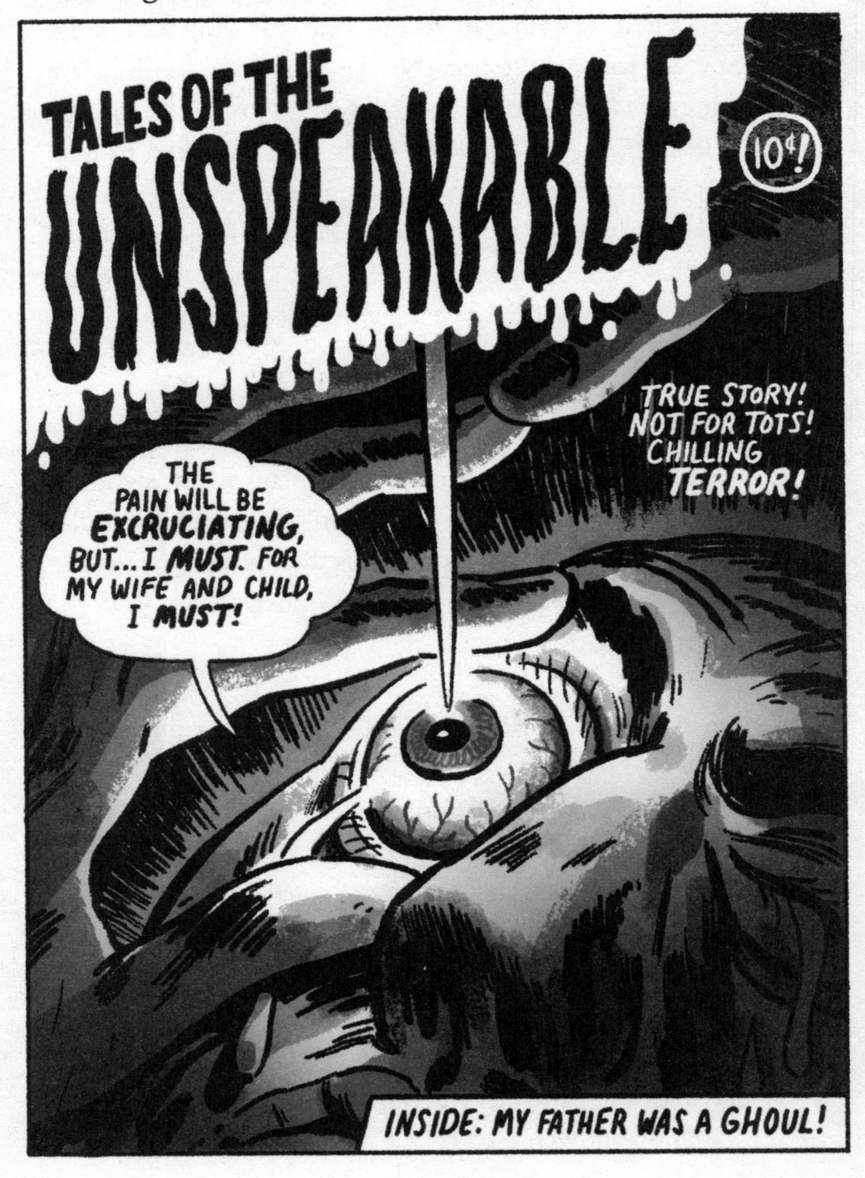

I'M SORRY! I DON'T WANT TO HURT YOU!
BUT I... HAVE... NO... CHOICE!
MY FATHER WAS A GHOUL!
THREE DAYS EARLIER... LIFE WAS SIMPLER.
WHIPPLE ST
♫
GOOD MORNING, FAMILY! GREAT NEWS! AFTER BEING LAID OFF FROM THE MUNITIONS FACTORY LAST MONTH, I FINALLY FOUND A NEW JOB!
OH, DARLING, THAT'S WONDERFUL!
WAY TO GO, DAD!
WELL, DON'T KEEP US IN SUSPENSE!
IT'S CALLED THE DUVAL PROJECT!
DUVAL? WHY, THAT SOUNDS FOREIGN!
IT IS! SOME ITALIAN OUTFIT. ALL I GOT TO DO IS SHOW UP TO THE LAB, RECEIVE SOME INJECTIONS, AND REPORT BACK ON THE EFFECTS! EASIEST JOB I EVER HAD!
DOES THIS MEAN WE CAN AFFORD TO BUY COMICS AGAIN, DAD?
I'M ONE STEP AHEAD OF YOU, SON!
GEE! THIS STACK OF COMICS IS BIGGER THAN ME!
LOOKS LIKE OUR TROUBLES ARE FINALLY OVER.
DON'T GET TOO COZY YET, DEAR READERS!

THE NEXT MORNING...
FATHER AND SON SET OFF ON SOME BRAND-NEW ADVENTURES!
SAY, HOW DO YOU THINK THE U.S. ARMY WILL FIND ITS WAY OUTTA THIS ONE, SON?
GEE, I DON'T KNOW, DAD! TURN THE PAGE AND LET'S FIND OUT!
THE UNITED STATES AT WAR
MY G*D. THE SMELL OF MY SON'S HEAD IS MAKING ME SALIVATE! THE FEEL OF HIS HEARTBEAT AGAINST MY CHEST MAKES MY STOMACH GROWL AS IF IT HAD A MIND OF ITS OWN!
GRRGGL
POW! BANG! CRASH! JUST LIKE UNCLE SPILLANE! CHK-CHK-CHK CHK-CHK!!
GULP FANGS!
ARTHUR SAW HIS SON IN A WHOLE NEW WAY... AS A SOURCE OF NUTRITION!
SAY, DAD YOUR STOMACH SURE IS GROWLING UP A STORM! YOU HUNGRY OR SOMETHIN'?
GRRGGLL
SORRY, SON! I JUST REMEMBERED SOMETHING I NEED TO TAKE CARE OF UPSTAIRS!
OOP!
ARTHUR GIVES ONE LOOK BACK AND FINDS TO HIS HORROR THAT HIS SON LOOKS JUST LIKE A JUICY STEAK!
ER, THAT'S OK, DAD! CAN WE FINISH THIS COMIC LATER?
YOU BET, SON!
AT LEAST, I HOPE W CAN!

ARTHUR GOES TO SPLASH SOME WATER ON HIS FACE, BUT WAITING IN THE MIRROR IS A NASTY SURPRISE! AN UNRECOGNIZABLE CREATURE OF MUSCLE AND BONE GLARES BACK AT HIM. ITS EYES POP OUT ALARMINGLY!
CHOKE GOOD G*D! MY SKIN! IT'S... IT'S GONE!
BUT WAIT... WHEN I TOUCH MY CHEEK, I CAN FEEL IT'S STILL THERE! MY EYES ARE TELLING ME NOTHING BUT LIES!
THEY'RE SAYING I HAVE NO SKIN! THEY'RE MAKING ME THINK MY SON IS NOTHING BUT A STEAK COOKED MY FAVORITE WAY- MEDIUM-RARE!
I WONDER IF THIS STRANGENESS HAS ANYTHING TO DO WITH THOSE INJECTIONS THEY GAVE ME AT THE LAB!
SAY, DAD! CAN WE FINISH THAT COMIC NOW? I'M JUST DYING TO KNOW HOW THE AMERICANS SMOKE THE ENEMY OUT OF THOSE CAVES!
AT THE SOUND OF HIS SON'S VOICE, ARTHUR'S STOMACH ONCE AGAIN STARTS TO GURGLE!
GRRGLLL
ARTHUR RECALLS AN OLD PHRASE FROM THE BIBLE: "AND IF THINE EYE OFFENDS THEE, PLUCK IT OUT." -MARK 9:47
WELL, THAT SEEMS A BIT EXTREME. BESIDES, THIS CONDITION OF MINE MAY ONLY BE TEMPORARY!
STILL, I CAN'T TAKE ANY RISKS!
AND SO... ARTHUR FINLEY PROCEEDS WITH THE GRUESOME TASK OF SEWING HIS OWN EYES SHUT!
OUCH! THIS SMARTS! BUT IT SURE BEATS TRYING TO EAT MY SON--MY VERY OWN FLESH AND BLOOD!
LATER...
YOU'RE JUST IN TIME, DAD! OUR BOYS IN GRAY ARE RUNNING UP THE SLOPE!
OKAY, SON, BUT, UM, YOU'LL HAVE TO BE THE READER NOW. I'M AFRAID I CAN'T... SNIFF SNIFF
BUT EVEN THIS DRASTIC MEASURE DID NOT SOLVE ARTHUR'S PROBLEM!

HE COULD STILL SMELL HIS SON! HE COULD STILL HEAR HIM! THE SOUND OF HIS SON'S VOICE MADE HIS STOMACH GROWL!
MY G*D, NO!
ER, DAD?
WITHIN MOMENTS, ARTHURS HUNGER GOT THE BEST OF HIM!
SON, WHY DON'T YOU... COME CLOSER?
GEE, DAD, WHAT'S WRONG WITH YOUR TEETH?
AAAUUGH!!
HSSSS!!
ARTHUR! WHAT'S GOTTEN INTO YOU?!
YOUR... YOUR EYES! WHAT'S HAPPENED TO YOUR EYES?!
RUN, LEAR! GO TO THE NEIGHBORS! GET HELP!!
BUT LEAR COULD NOT FIND IT IN HIM TO LEAVE HIS MOTHER BEHIND WITH THE GRUESOME CREATURE THAT WAS ONCE HIS FATHER.

AND SO...
ARTHUR FINLEY KEEPS HIS FAMILY LOCKED IN THE BASEMENT AS RESERVES FOR HIS UNGODLY APPETITE! MOTHER AND SON CLING TO EACH OTHER TIGHTLY, DREADING THE FOOTSTEPS AND THE CLICK OF THE LOCK!
SOON, THE BASEMENT DOOR FLIES OPEN WITH A BANG!
BANG!
EVERY NIGHT, THE MAN WHO WAS ONCE A LOVING FATHER AND HUSBAND VISITS THEM TO FEAST!
YOU MUSTN'T BLAME ME. I DON'T WANT TO KILL YOU! YOU, MY ONLY WIFE AND SON!
WHERE CAN I... DRINK THAT NO ONE WILL EVER NOTICE? THE NECK WILL BE TOO OBVIOUS AND SCAR YOU FOR LIFE!
AH, YES. I KNOW...
SSLLURP SSLURP
AND EVERY NIGHT, ARTHUR LEAVES, UNABLE TO SQUEEZE TEARS THROUGH HIS SEWN-UP EYES!
I LOVE YOU.
I'M SORRY.

YES, HELLO? IS THIS GENERAL SPILLANE? SOMETHING VERY STRANGE IS HAPPENING AT YOUR SISTER'S HOUSE!
I THINK YOU'D BETTER COME QUICK!
ONE NIGHT, ARTHUR IS FEASTING, WHEN AGAIN THE DOOR FLIES OPEN WITH A BANG!
BANG!
STEP AWAY FROM THE BOY—
MY G*D!
ARTHUR HAS TRANSFORMED INTO A GHOUL!
I DIDN'T WANT TO HURT THEM, I SWEAR!
TAKE THAT, CREATURE OF THE NIGHT! BACK FROM WHENCE YOU CAME!
AAARRRGH!!
AARRGH!!

DID THAT FOUL BEAST HURT YOU ANY, SON?
ER, NO. NO, HE DIDN'T.
MY G*D, IT'S JUST TOO TERRIBLE!
WHAT BEGINS AS CRIES OF TERROR SOON TURN INTO HIGH-PITCHED PEALS OF LAUGHTER! MRS. FINLEY'S HAIR TURNS WHITE FROM FRIGHT!
HE— HE DRANK US LIKE— LIKE MILKSHAKES! I CAN'T— I CAN'T HANDLE IT— I...
AHAHAHA!!
YOUR MOTHER WILL NEVER BE THE SAME AFTER WHAT SHE'S SEEN. AND WHO CAN BLAME HER?
YOU'VE GOT TO REMAIN STRONG, LEAR. YOU'RE THE MAN OF THE HOUSE, NOW!
OH.
WELL, IT WASN'T PRETTY, BUT WHAT WE HAVE HERE IS A HAPPY ENDING.
ANOTHER VICTORY FOR THE AMERICAN MILITARY!

I pressed Lear's comic to my chest. A story like that should've turned on the waterworks—even with the cheesy dialogue. But for me it had the opposite effect. Finally, a boy with a history more tragic than mine. Running from motel to motel, escaping Shivers my whole life, even slowly transforming into a giant felt like a breeze compared to Lear's story.

He made sense now. The wrinkly forehead. The quietness. If my dad drank blood from my side, I don't know how I'd function, let alone look a person in the eye.

I flipped back through the comic's pages. "You mind if I ask you a question?"

"Go ahead," Lear said from the darkness of the corner, Pan-Cake curled up in his lap.

"You're not a . . . are you?"

"No, I would have had to drink my dad's blood to become one too." Lear felt his side. "I'm just, um, deformed."

I wanted to see the bite marks, but I figured we could take this one small step at a time. I flipped the pages backward, playing the horrifying images in reverse until Lear's dad was right as rain again.

"Why is it called *My Father Was a Ghoul*?"

"What do you mean?"

"Well . . . ," I said carefully. Lear was opening up so much, I didn't want to say something that would scare the secrets back to their hiding places. "The story is from the perspective of the dad, but the title of the comic sounds like it's from you."

The corner of the church was silent a moment. "I guess I wanted to figure out what it must have been like for him. Transforming. Seeing his own son as something to . . . eat." Lear took a breath. "My uncle decided my dad was a bad guy and deserved to die. But he wasn't the bad one. It's whoever transformed him into that . . . that *thing*. Those are the real bad guys."

It felt like someone punched me in the stomach. What if the Buried Lab had done this? If I hadn't smashed the ham radio, I would have contacted Liz right then and demanded answers.

I flipped to General Spillane on the last page, glowing with morning light and grinning in victory. I remembered the part of Lear's file that said he wanted to join the army.

"Is that why you wanted to join the reserves?" I asked. "To . . . feel stronger?"

My heart skipped a beat when I realized I'd given away that I'd read his file, but Lear didn't seem to notice.

"It's more complicated than that," he said. "I just want to be in a position where I get to make the decisions, you know? Even though it's tough to figure out what the right thing is. My uncle killed my dad. But he also saved my life. I just wish I could've found my voice and told him that my dad wasn't bad. That he just . . ."

Lear made a pathetic sound—like the wheeze at the end of a deflating balloon. He rubbed his eyes with the palms of his hands.

"Sorry," he said, sniffing.

"Don't apologize."

I slid my giant hand across the floor until it was right next to him. He rested his head on my pinkie, like it was a big pillow.

"I just—" Lear began. "I just never knew what my dad was thinking is all," he said. "And I wanted to know. That's why I like to be around girls. It's easier to tell what's going on in their heads. When my mom, um, lost her mind, that felt like an appropriate response to what was happening. I think I might have lost mine, too, but I'm a boy, so I'm not supposed to let it show. And that's the thing. I don't ever—I don't ever know what's going on in guys' minds. It scares me."

Boy, he wasn't the only one. The police. The men at the lab. Daddy.

I could tell Lear didn't want me staring at him, so I flipped through the pages and looked at a drawing of little Lear's face instead. One where he was happy.

"How did you break your nose?" I asked.

Lear rubbed his face. "I accidentally walked into a wall when I was eleven."

My little snort came out as a big snort.

"Thank you for sharing this with me," I said, touching the comic to my lips. "It's beautiful. You know, in a terrifying way."

"Promise you'll never tell anyone?"

"Promise." I looked at the comic. "Did you make this just for me?"

Lear nodded and hugged himself. "It feels weird being on the outside like that. It doesn't feel good. If the guys at school found out . . ."

I wanted to keep the comic, reread it over and over, but . . .

"Grab a candle," I said.

He brought one over, and I handed him the comic. He looked at it a moment and then touched its corner to the flame. We watched Lear's story burn. After it was nothing but ash, I lay on my side in front of the pulpit and patted the floor between my breast and my arm. Lear stared at that space for a few seconds, not budging. Then he sniffed and lay beside me, and I bent my arm around him, careful not to touch his side.

It felt strange at first, like I was cradling a baby. But then he wrapped his arm around my forearm, and I felt his cheek against my skin, and I felt his back against my chest. We both breathed in and out, my breath ruffling his hair.

I remembered Calvin, and the spot on my finger where my nail had connected with his skull started to throb.

We lay in silence a while, the darkness of the chapel dancing around us. I tried to imagine we were just two regular-size kids snuggling in candlelight without a worry in the world. It wasn't easy.

"Will you tell me now?" Lear said.

"Tell you what?"

He looked into my eyes and did that thing where his eyes moved from one of mine to the other and back again. But my eyes were so far apart, he had to turn his head to do it. "Tell me how I can become like you."

"You don't want this," I said. "Besides, the people who did this to me would kill us if we went there."

Lear sank into my arm in disappointment.

But then I realized there was something I could tell him. A secret for a secret. I opened my mouth to begin, but then swallowed it. I'd never told anyone about this before. Not even Katie.

I sat up and grabbed the little ribbon-wrapped basket from the corner. I slurped the jams out of their jars to give myself courage.

"The world might be ending," I said.

He gazed up at me, eyes fearful with belief. "What do you mean?"

"*Hoo, boy,*" I said. "I know I told you my dad died in a Shiver, but that was a lie. I'm sorry. Really, my dad is the size of a mountain. He, um, fills the sky and watches the world, and wherever he looks, monsters appear."

Lear didn't say anything. Only listened.

I snuggled back up to him and told him everything. From

my innocent eyes playing peek-a-boo with Daddy among the clouds, to seeing him for the first time, to the fact that he was staring at Pennybrooke now. Staring at me.

As he listened, Lear drew invisible things on my arm, as if he was re-creating the story on my skin. After I was finished, I noticed the locusts had fled. Just telling someone else everything lessened the weight a little. With Lear in my arms, I was starting to feel drowsy and nice.

"Anyway," I said, "if I don't keep things interesting, Daddy will use his remote control and turn the whole world off—ending everything once and for all."

Lear rolled onto his side and sighed, contented. This was the last reaction I was expecting.

"What is it?" I said, my eyelids drooping.

"If there is a man in the sky who makes disasters with his eyes," Lear said, "then maybe a lot of the lousy stuff that happens isn't our fault. Or anyone's."

I touched his hair with my pinkie, delicately dragging it from his forehead to the top of his neck, then lifting and doing it again. Just having him around almost made me forget what I had become. Almost.

"You'd better pay me back for all that food before the world ends," Lear said. "Otherwise, my mom's going to kill me."

A laugh burst out of me, whipping Lear's hair.

He curled up in my arm. "I guess I should have asked this before, but is it safe to cuddle like this? Are you radioactive?"

"I have no idea," I said.

We giggled together for the first time. That was the last thing I remembered.

I woke to the sound of paper tearing.

My eyelids were heavy, almost like they were glued shut. I barely managed to peel them open, one and then the other. Lear was gone, my arms delicately wrapped around nothing at all. At the end of the church's aisle, something confusing was happening. Rhoda was holding Pan-Cake in the crook of her arm while tearing pages out of choral books and dropping them into a large pile in front of the double-door entrance.

As if sensing that I was awake, Rhoda spoke. "It's funny to me that you would try and make yourself look decent when you're the size of an elephant. Three elephants, really."

She kept tearing pages while I tried to sit up. The whole church started to spin and my head thunked painfully back to the floor.

Rhoda continued. "I mean, Lear only visited you so he could get a look at how obscenely big you are. Like going to a circus to see the fat lady."

I tried pushing myself up, but my arms were like cooked noodles. The whole church seemed to tilt at an angle so steep I could barely tell which way was up. Through my bleary eyes I saw the remains of the basket of jams and fruits left on the stoop the night before.

Rhoda tore more pages and added them to the pile. "It was your shade of nail polish that gave you away. It was all over poor Calvin's forehead when I visited him in the hospital. I remembered it from the first time I met you. The kind of shade I wouldn't put on a chimpanzee." She sighed and tore another page from the choral book and delicately released it like a tumbling flower petal. "When Marsh canceled church, I knew something fishy was going on. He'd hold service around his deathbed. I hadn't seen you at school or around town, and then when people at the carnival said they saw a girl taller than a telephone pole, I put two and two together."

And she had brought me a special basket full of jams and sleeping pills.

I managed to push up onto one of my trembling elbows. "Is Calvin okay?"

"Wouldn't you like to know?" Rhoda said. "He got such a knock to the noggin, he may never flirt with another girl again."

Locusts dripped in the corners of my vision. Rhoda continued to tear up choral books as if it was the most normal thing in the world.

"What are you doing?" I asked, holding up my heavy head.

She ignored my question. "First you tried to seduce Calvin, which I thought was pathetic but harmless enough. But that just wasn't enough for you, was it? When he stood you up at the motel, you had to hurt him because you couldn't stand the rejection. And then you tried to steal another girl's beau."

"That isn't what happened," I said thickly.

Rhoda clicked her tongue. "You are greedy greedy, Phoebe Lane. Trying to take all the boys for yourself. It's no wonder you blew up to the size you are."

I squeezed my eyes shut, hoping to stop the church from spinning.

Pan-Cake started to whimper in Rhoda's arms. "There, there. Did she hurt you, you poor thing? Mommy's got a basket of kisses all for you."

I opened my bleary eyes. "Did you drug me just to get a dog?"

Rhoda stopped tearing pages and flashed a smile down the aisle. "That's not what people will think. I'll be a town hero. The girl who stopped the creature who hurt poor, innocent Calvin."

She reached into her skirt waistband and pulled out a matchbook. The sight made me want to leap up, but my legs were useless.

Rhoda struck a match and watched it flicker. All of a sudden, I didn't see a girl at the end of the aisle. I saw something much different. People may have thought that Rhoda's mom was the monster for feeding her all those sleeping pills, but maybe her mom was really just trying to rid the world of one. Not all monsters had fur or scales or tentacles. Some of them wore pigtails.

Before I could cry out, Rhoda tossed the match on the pile of scattered choir pages. As the paper started to smolder, I tried clawing my way down the aisle, but my hips wouldn't fit between the pews.

"Toodle-loo," Rhoda said. She stepped around the fire and out of the church, the cleats of her shoes clicking.

I pushed myself back and dragged my body the long way around the edge of the church toward the entrance. The choral pages blackened. Flames leapt. The church doors started to crackle as smoke licked ash up the wall and slithered along the ceiling. In ten seconds flat, the whole entrance was in flames. I was trapped.

My lungs burned and went into a panic, telling me to escape, flee, get out, flatten everything that stood between me and fresh air. I scanned the chapel through the haze. I couldn't fit out the single-door back exit. There was only one thing I could try.

By this point my heart was pounding with enough adrenaline to push to my feet. Wavering, I just managed to heft a pew over my shoulder and throw it with all my might through Jesus and his lambs, making a great outward explosion. Smoke rushed toward the morning sky.

I did my best to high step onto the sill, punching out the leftover shards of glass, shoving my body into the frame. I didn't fit. Any way I squeezed myself, there was no way my hips were getting through. I kept my head out the window for a few breaths of fresh air, took one last gasp, and then leapt off the windowsill back into the fire.

The chapel had transformed into a hellscape. The air was filled with soot and flames; the heat roasted my skin. The front entrance was a devilish waterfall, black and roaring upward. I started kicking at the side wall, hoping my giant leg would serve as a ramming rod, but I was too weak from the sleeping pills.

The front entrance popped and splintered, and there came a gasping sound as the oxygen sucked the fire and smoke outside. There was only one exit. And it was through the flames.

I grabbed Frank and wrapped it around as much of my body as I could. I ran down the church aisle toward the fire, which crackled and howled, daring me to enter. I dove through it, headfirst. My head broke through the doors, and I landed on coals and embers, burning through the comforter to my stomach. I was stuck. I screamed and kicked against the floor, my stomach sizzling, my mouth screaming and gulping lungfuls of smoke. My hips finally broke through the charred frame, and I lay beneath the wide white sky, coughing, sputtering, and smoldering until darkness overtook me.

• • •

"Dear *God.*"

"What *is* it?"

"Say, isn't it that Lane girl?"

"No, it's the monster!"

"It's both!"

I blinked tears from my eyes and looked left and right at a crowd of shocked faces, flickering with firelight. It seemed every citizen in Pennybrooke was there, holding buckets of water to help put out the church . . . and here they found a burned giantess instead.

In the crowd, I saw the greasers smoking and smirking. I saw Dr. Siley, his arms folded, the church fire reflected in his glasses. I saw Rhoda grinning, a worried-looking Pan-Cake in her arms. I saw Officers Graham and Shelley and their dead vegetable eyes. I saw Lear, pale and terrified. I reached out to him, but he looked helplessly at the mob and ran.

A man screamed, "She hurt my Calvin! She must pay!"

The shocked faces sprang into action. They tossed the still-smoking Frank over my chest, and the men sat on its edges to keep me pinned to the ground. Pan-Cake wriggled free from Rhoda's grasp and latched onto the comforter's corner, tugging to free me. But her tiny strength was no match for the population of Pennybrooke.

"I didn't mean to hurt Calvin!" I croaked, and then painfully coughed up smoke. "It was an accident!"

"That didn't look like any accident I've seen!"

I couldn't argue. Not only because it was hard to breathe with my chest constricted by the comforter and the weight of the men, but because I *had* flicked Calvin on purpose.

"Let her *go*, you *dicks!*"

It was Beth. I couldn't see her through my stinging eyes, but hearing her voice was enough to settle the panic in my heart a bit.

"Now, now, Beth," I heard Principal Toll say. "They won't harm her. This is America, where everyone is given fair trial."

"Fight them, Phoebe!" Beth cried. "Throw them off! Escape!"

But all the fight was out of me. The wings of the locusts burned up with the church. All I wanted was sleep, and maybe more than that. I let my stinging eyes flutter shut.

The people of Pennybrooke started to grope and pinch me through the comforter. They slapped at my bare thighs. A small hand touched my breast and jiggled it. "Just like a water bed! Ha-ha!"

Maybe the fight wasn't out of me after all. I sat upright, throwing off the comforter and sending a dozen men sprawling. I clenched my fists, ready to swing them like a club, but then the burns on my stomach screamed to life, and I fell back, whimpering. Before I could so much as curl my legs into my chest, they threw the comforter back over me and even more people sat on its edges.

"Boy, she's a lively one, isn't she?"

Someone touched my thigh. "Fuzzy too! Never again will I have to wonder what it's like to hunt a woolly mammoth!"

"Come on, Davey! Hop aboard her foot! It's like a bucking bronco!"

I thrashed, but they just laughed at my helplessness.

"Well, what do we do with her?"

"She almost burned up in the church. I say we finish the job!"

There was a wave of agreement.

"Stop!" a new voice screamed. "She must be forgiven! She has given full confession!"

It was Marsh.

"You've been hiding this monstrosity?" Mr. Marple said.

"I have been trying to save her, yes."

"The reverend cares more about the monster than his own church!" someone cried.

"Forgive thine enemy!" Marsh screamed in an impromptu sermon. "Jesus forgave even the women who sold their bodies—" There was a meaty sound, like a fist connecting with a jaw, and Marsh's voice fell silent.

"Here's a Bible quote for ya!" someone screamed. "Hell hath no fury like a woman scorned."

"That is not in the Bible!" Marsh said through what sounded like a bloodied mouth. "If you kill this girl, then you are no better than the beasts that crawl out of the earth as God's punishment for our sins. Nay, your actions will only make the monsters multiply." He stepped around my hair and set a small hand on the unburnt part of my shoulder. "Though she may be a giant, this girl has earned God's forgiveness and has not sinned since! To this I can attest!"

I rolled my head awkwardly, painfully to the side.

"I did it," I told Marsh. "I hurt Calvin."

The look on his face broke my heart. I'd cursed his sermons for good. He'd failed to cast out the biggest demon of all.

Someone seized Marsh's arm and yanked him into the crowd. The people of Pennybrooke started screaming for my death.

I thought of Liz. This was the part where I was supposed to let my rage pick me up off the ground and fight until either I or the entire town was dead. But I was never meant to be a Shiver.

"I'm done!" I said. "I won't fight anymore." I found Daddy's disappointed eyes through the clearing smoke as I addressed the crowd. "Do what you want to me."

The mob grew quiet as something slow and heavy rumbled down the road. There came the squeal of a metal door opening, followed by a sharp voice. "Jesus in his knickers! They don't grow 'em like this where I come from. What do you all eat for breakfast down here? Uranium?"

A shadow stepped into my periphery. A general, decorated with stripes and shiny stars on his epaulets, removed his hat. "Blanket sitters, you are relieved!"

Everyone jumped off me, dragging Frank with them, leaving me in my bikini.

"I'm General Spillane. I'll be handling things from here."

My skin turned cold. Lear had called his uncle.

The general marched circles around me and sniffed deeply.

"Whoo, boy." He wafted his hand in front of his nose. "No wonder my boot camp boys have been so restless. They can probably smell you sixty miles away. Do me a favor, miss, and don't spread your legs, or else we might have a full-on exodus from the base. Why do you folks have her restrained?"

"She hurt my boy, sir," Mr. Marple said.

"That true, giantess?" the general said.

My body tensed from my hair all the way down to my toenails. I wanted to tell him I hadn't meant to hurt anybody. But I remembered all the monsters who had come in peace, like the alien Klaatu. Even Emperor Ook himself. They still got killed in the end.

"Cat got your tongue, huh?" the general said. "Or is it a tiger? Heh-heh. Does anyone know if she bleeds?"

"Um," Mr. Marple said, "what do you mean, sir?"

"Get your mind out of the gutter." The general pinched my side. "I mean does she have impenetrable skin? I guess it's questions like these that got me where I am today. Private Mangum, hand me your weapon."

"Sir!"

Boots came squishing across the church's lawn.

"No!" Beth screamed.

The general cocked his eyebrows toward her. "Somebody do me a favor and restrain that girl."

"There, there, Beth," Principal Toll said. "The general knows what he's doing."

A gun cocked and I flinched.

"Don't!" I screamed. "Don't shoot me! Please!"

"She speaks!" the general said, wiggling his finger in his ear. "Boy, does she speak. Heck, those pipes would put my old lady's to shame. Do you bleed, giantess?"

"I . . . I don't know."

The burns on my stomach blistered and wept down my sides, but the pain had quickly dulled to a tingling.

"Ah, well, I guess I wouldn't have taken your word for it, anyhow. That's what makes us the US military and not the commies. Step back, folks."

I heard some shuffling and then felt a pinprick of cold press the top of my pinkie toe. "Controlled fire!"

There came a staccato burst of sound as bullets ripped through my toe. I screamed.

"She bleeds!" the general cried. "Hoo, boy, does she ever!

Medic! Look at that gusher. I've seen men lose half that much blood and pass out cold."

I stifled a sob.

"Ah, come now, giantess," the general said, patting my shoulder. "To a girl your size that's nothing more than a paper cut." He put his face up to my ear and spoke real quiet. "But at least you know we can hurt ya if you try anything. Men! Please point your weapons at the giantess's head." He tapped the center of his forehead. "Give her a third eye if she so much as winks at you."

I could sense a dozen guns pointed in my direction, a dry wind whistling down their barrels. Rope was tossed over my torso and then tossed again. In less than a minute, they had me bound and gagged.

"Wait!" Lear screamed, sprinting down the street. "She's not the bad guy!" He pointed to the mob. "They are. They were going to burn her for no reason."

"That so?" General Spillane said.

My whole being started to glow, but it didn't last long. Lear still didn't know what I'd done to Calvin. Before I could set Lear straight, a garbled voice came out of the general's walkie-talkie, so loud and staticky I couldn't understand a word. The general lifted it to his cheek. "Spillane here."

The screaming over the walkie-talkie continued, indecipherable.

"If this is a joke I will use your tongue to plug your other end," he said, stomping off.

I met Lear's eyes. The people of Pennybrooke were frozen around us, waiting for the general's next command.

"I hurt Calvin, Lear," I said. "I flicked his forehead."

Lear's eyes didn't leave mine. His forehead wrinkled up. "Did you mean to?"

Tears flooded my eyes. My chest shook. "I was just trying to stop him from screaming."

He placed his small hand on my cheek. "I believe you, Phoebe."

The general marched back in as quickly as he had exited. His mouth was set as tight as a sprung bear trap. He shook his head at me. "And here I am with a G. D. giantess who can't get a toe scrape without turning on the waterworks."

"What's happening?" Mr. Marple said.

The general glanced around at the crowd. "We might need to evacuate the town."

Everyone gasped.

"Why?" someone asked.

"Ants," he muttered. "Big ones. Whole army of 'em, headed from the north."

Everyone started to panic. I'd have leapt up myself if it weren't for all the guns pointed at my head. In the sky, Daddy's eyes weren't looking at me anymore. They were fixed on a wall of dust slowly rising on the horizon.

"Now, now," General Spillane said, calmly holding up his hands. He gestured to his soldiers. "Just so happens you have one of the best platoons from the best army on God's gray earth right here. We dealt with these ants in '54. We'll keep you safe."

My mind raced. The ants were coming from the north. . . . That meant the Buried Lab had released them. But why? *Because they heard me say I wasn't going to terrorize Pennybrooke and they grew impatient.* I remembered that single monsters no longer kept Daddy entertained. The giant ants might not be all the lab released.

"Let Phoebe go!" Lear said. "She can help fight the ants."

No, I thought. *Anything but that.*

The thought gave me a crawly feeling under my skin. I had an image of a silhouette in the distance, struggling in an ant's pincers. *Katie.*

"Ha!" the general said. "She may have arms the size of tree trunks, but I can tell she's never fought a day in her life. That being said"—he gave my thigh a jiggle—"she does have a lot of meat on her. I might have a better idea."

Lear turned pale. "What are you going to do?"

General Spillane laughed. "You're keen on this girl, aren't you, son? I guess her size makes you rethink the old myth that no one woman can satisfy a man. But trust me, this broad's useless. Weeps at a paper cut. Hell, she can't even fit in a kitchen anymore. Although, I guess with a broad that size, every outfit is going to be skimpy, eh? Heh-heh."

Lear curled his fists. "This isn't a time for jokes!"

The general stuck his nose to Lear's like he was one of his soldiers. "You're right. It isn't. I've got an entire town to save, and I'm not going to send some girl who blew up like a balloon and could pop just as easy out to battle." He turned to Mr. Marple. "You say she killed a kid?"

"Hurt him bad."

"Well, that's a monster in my book. In times of war you don't have time for trials. You have to be judge, jury, *and* executioner. Only today the executioners have six legs and pincers." The walkie-talkie started blathering again, and the general held it to his ear. "Well, that's *excellent* news. Yes, thank you.

Over and out." He clipped the walkie-talkie back to his belt and clapped Lear on the shoulder. "Good news. The ants are headed straight toward the Indian reservation. That should slow 'em up for the evening, give us time to erect a barricade."

"Bastard!" I heard Beth cry. "Those are people!"

The general thumbed his nose. "Wasn't someone going to restrain that girl?"

"What do we do with this thing, sir?" a soldier called, holding up Frank.

"How's it smell?" the general asked.

The soldier knelt and gave my comforter a sniff. "Like a fishnet left out in the sun, sir!"

"I'll make the jokes around here, Sergeant. Toss it on the truck bed. The stench alone will draw the ants." General Spillane jabbed me in the side. "Stand up, giantess. No need to waste my boys' muscle with those tree-trunk gams of yours."

I pushed myself up, wavered a bit on my feet, and coughed, but then found my balance. My pinkie toe throbbed, but the general was right, it wasn't much worse than a paper cut.

"Look at that, boys!" the general said. "She don't even need a leash! Let's haul out!"

They loaded me onto a rig big enough to transport a house and threw a tarp over my face. The last thing I saw was Lear, drooping like a wet flower and gazing helplessly after me. As the truck pulled away, Pan-Cake barked, while the people of Pennybrooke remained oddly quiet, having avoided one giant disaster only to be met by the swarm of another.

When the soldiers whipped off the tarp, I found myself in an airplane hangar. The ceiling had large windows that looked out over an open sky. The moon cast squares of light across my body.

"Tell me, Phoebe," the general said, stroking his chin, "how we gonna keep you from trying to escape tonight?"

My teeth chattered, thinking about the guns. "I—I won't—"

"Hush now, I'm thinking. You're going to try to get away once those ants start nibbling your earlobes, and there's no telling how many bullets it would take to stop something your size." He paced back and forth. "Hmm. Those arms are big enough they could rip a chain mount right out of concrete, and those legs are big enough to buckle that hangar door. . . ." He stopped walking and snapped. "Driggs, Foer, figure out a way to staple her hair to the floor. No better way to make a female behave. Get some rest, giantess. And don't go growing any more on me, hear?"

• • •

And that's how he left me: dressed in my two-piece on the cold concrete, wrists and ankles in chains, hair stapled to the floor. The scent of the desert and the occasional shriek of a bat came through the garage door, where a guard paced, throwing his long shadow across the garage.

I could barely move my fingertips. My blood felt frozen in my veins. It wasn't just the cold. I was in shock. The impossible thing that happened to Ma was happening to me. I was locked up with nothing to do but stare at the ceiling and wait to die. My scalp hurt so bad I almost wished for a straitjacket instead.

Tears trickled down the sides of my cheeks and pooled in my ears. I couldn't keep crying like this. I had to escape. I had to rip out my own hair.

I lifted my head, scalp stinging as I strained against the staples. I pulled so hard I saw white. The staples didn't budge.

"Stop moving!" the guard yelled.

I let my head fall back on the concrete and continued to weep. It was only a matter of time before the ants reached the hangar. I could hear them rumbling like thunder on the horizon. I imagined their manic pincers going at my legs like chainsaws, their rolling eyes and scrabbling legs and twitching antennae wriggling higher and higher and higher on my body until . . .

In the corner of my eye I saw Frank, the comforter Creation, twitch then bend upward like a slug. I tried to turn my head, but felt a sharp tug behind my ear from the staples. A figure freed itself from the comforter and then crawled on all fours across the hangar and slipped under my hair.

My breath quickened. I didn't know what I was waiting for: a comforting voice or a bullet to the brain. Then, small warm hands pressed against my neck.

"Phoebe," a voice whispered.

I nearly sobbed in relief. *Beth.*

"Don't talk," she said. "And hold still." *Snip . . . snip . . . snip* . . . I felt a slice through my hair. "I only have my sewing scissors, so this is gonna take a while. . . ."

I gave a slight nod. Just so long as she freed me before the army of ants arrived.

Snip . . . snip . . . snip . . .

Beth cut and whispered, "As soon as Principal Toll heard the general say he was judge, jury, and executioner, he let me go. Guess he learned a thing or two about the military today. They find any excuse to do what they want, when they want." *Snip . . . snip . . . snip . . .* "Once the soldiers tossed Frank onto the truck bed, I hid inside it."

I wanted to sob in relief, but I didn't want to draw the guard's attention.

"Phoebe," Beth whispered. "Listen to me. Once you're free, we're going to go help the people of Gray Rock."

"We're *what*?" I whispered.

"Quiet!" the guard at the garage door said.

Beth's snipping fell silent.

"It was just a cough," I said to the guard.

He grunted and continued to pace.

Beth kept cutting, speaking more softly. "You heard what the general said. He's going to let them die. The ants will tear right through their homes and then through the Navajo people."

My pulse pounded in my ears so loud, I could barely hear her words. When we escaped, we were going to move *toward* the ants? That went against every instinct I had. I'd only ever run away from Shivers.

"I can't," I said, barely lending breath to my moving lips.

"Who else is going to help them?" Beth said. "Not the army."

Snip . . . snip . . . snip . . .

All of a sudden that snipping didn't sound like my freedom. It sounded like my death.

"But . . . but . . ."

"Just pretend you're in a movie," Beth said.

Through the hangar ceiling I could see Daddy had returned to his La-Z-Boy and was cracking open a beer. It was eerie how on the nose Beth was.

"What do you mean?" I mouthed.

"You ever been in a theater and felt like yelling at the people on the screen? 'Kiss her! Punch him! Don't go in there!'"

I'd had lots of thoughts like that while reading Lear's comic. *Run! He isn't your dad anymore! Get out of the house while you still can!* Why was it when you're in a real-life emergency situation, you do all the things that would make you yell at the screen?

Snip . . . snip . . . snip . . .

Because we don't want to believe that evil exists—that there is no monster actually lurking in the shadows. We check the basement to calm our beating hearts. We want to believe that the people in our lives are good so we trust them, even if all signs say they've transformed into a vampire. We want to believe our moms would never lie to us, that our half sisters would never zap us with gamma rays.

Snip . . . snip . . . snip . . .

"Whatever you would yell at yourself if you were in a movie right now," Beth said, "that's what you should do."

Here's what I wanted to do: I wanted to run out into the desert and dig up Ma. I wanted to use the room of charcoal pyramids to shrink myself back to normal size. And then I wanted to return to life the way it was before. Moving from motel to motel felt like a breeze compared to the last couple weeks.

But as for what I would yell at myself if I was watching this, what I *should* do . . . I didn't know. I'd spent my life on the edge of a horror story. I'd always made it out before the darkness closed in, before the Shiver descended, and then I read about the aftermath in the news. But now I was inside a horror story that I could not run away from. I couldn't turn off the TV, couldn't close the comic book, I wouldn't suddenly sit up with a gasp in bed, covered in sweat, and realize the whole thing had been a bad dream. The horror story had me. There was no getting out.

Tears spilled down my cheeks. "But what if it never ends?"

Beth squeezed my earlobe. "You have to believe it might someday."

She didn't understand. She didn't know what it was like to have a dad who loved blood and guts and helpless women more than anything in the world and who held the remote control that could turn off the entire universe if life wasn't horrifying enough.

"After we save the Navajo people," Beth said, "we're going to help save Pennybrooke."

My head jerked up, and I felt hairs rip out of the back of my neck. I just managed not to grunt in pain. Why would I save the people of *Pennybrooke*? I remembered the women leering while the men poked and jiggled me. The Pennybrooke police were useless at best and perverted at worst, Marsh was willfully ignorant of how the world really worked, Calvin was a thief, Rhoda was a psychopath, Lear put his trust in his uncle and got me in this terrible position, and Beth was trying to get me to go on a suicide mission by attacking an army of giant *ants*.

Snip . . . snip . . . snip . . .

"What if I told you to stop cutting right now?" I whispered. "What if I told you I had no interest in saving the Navajo people? Or anyone?"

The snipping stopped. I could feel the heat coming off Beth's face on the back of my neck.

"Do you mean it, Phoebe?"

I sniffed as if I did.

Did I?

I had to admit that my thoughts kept turning to what I hated about the people of Pennybrooke because I was terrified. No part of me believed that I could escape a platoon of soldiers, traverse a desert without a kiddie pool of food, and then defeat an army of giant ants. Like the general said, I'd never fought a day in my life. If I believed the people of Pennybrooke were truly despicable, I wouldn't have to feel too bad about letting them die.

Beth opened and closed the scissors hesitantly, wondering if she should continue.

Whenever Ma and I reached a new town, she always trimmed my hair. And every time, she reminded me of the same thing. "Hair is power, Phoebe. It directs the eyes of men to wherever you want them to look, sure. But it also holds memories. Anytime you want to forget something, snip off a few inches. Your head will feel light as a feather, and you'll swear it's far too light to just be the hair missing. That's how"—*snip*—"we leave"—*snip*—"our worries behind." *Snip snip.* "Now how about bangs? This seems like a bangs sort of town, doesn't it?"

Beth had cut straight down to my scalp. So many memories had been in that hair. Both bad and good. The flirtatious carny. Ma's spattered nail polish. Officer Shelley touching my clavicle. Gladys mispronouncing "Nava-Joe." Liz's deceptive smile. Calvin's head striking the pavement. Daddy's eyes fixed right on me.

But that hair also held Katie singing "Diamonds Are a Girl's Best Friend." It held the boy with the sling accidentally touching my hand when we were picking up textbooks. It held Beth holding up my new top and Marsh laying a trembling hand on my shoulder and Lear curling up in my arms.

"Finish cutting," I mouthed to Beth.

"Really?"

"Yes. Before I change my mind."

The snipping redoubled.

Snip. Snip. Snip. Snip. Snip.

My head grew lighter and soon I could move my neck back and forth, releasing the muscles. The feeling terrified me.

Snip. Snip. Snip. Snip. Snip.

I wasn't ready.

Snip. Snip. Snip. Snip. Snip.

I didn't care if my head was free or not. I wouldn't have the courage to stand.

Snip. Snip. Snip. Snip.

The lighter my head felt, the more I pushed it into the floor. I couldn't do this.

Snip. Snip. Sssssssnip!

"That's it," Beth whispered.

My hair wasn't stapled to the floor anymore. I was free. I lifted my head a few inches off the ground and gave it a little shake.

"What now?" Beth whispered, out of breath.

Now she was the one who sounded terrified.

"Come where I can see you," I whispered.

She crawled out from under my neck, away from the guard. I turned my head, and I smooched Beth right on the lips. Well, her whole face, really. She wiped away my saliva with her sleeve.

"Sorry," I said.

"It's okay," she said, smiling. "If this were a movie, I probably would have yelled for you to do that."

I didn't know if it was the happy memories of Pennybrooke or the prospect of being free or the promise of raiding food from the base's mess hall, but I suddenly felt the opposite of terrified. A feeling surged from my bone marrow straight up through my skin.

"Crawl into my hand," I whispered.

Beth did.

I closed my hand around Beth, like she was a doll, head sticking out the top, feet sticking out the bottom. She was a lot squishier than a doll though, so I kept my grip loose.

Still lying flat, I tilted my head so I could see the window on the far end of the hangar, opposite the wall with the door and the soldier. The window was open. And why wouldn't it be? With my hair stapled to the floor, General Spillane thought he had me under control.

"Is the guard watching?" I mouthed toward Beth.

She squirmed around in my palm so she could see the garage door. "He's looking down the hallway."

Maybe if I slowly pulled up on the chains, I could work them out of the concrete. Then, if I quietly pushed my body along the floor, I could make it most of the way to the window before the soldier noticed.

I turned my wrist in circles to get a good grip on the chain. The soldier in the doorway heard the clinking and whirled around.

"What are you doing?" he called across the hangar.

I clenched my fingers and swallowed.

"I was just scratching an itch," I said.

He started the long walk toward me. "Coughing, scratching. You sure do squirm around a lot. What the *hell?*" He saw Beth in my hand. And my cut hair. He raised his gun. "She's—she's—she's free! Code butterfly! CODE BUTTERFLY!"

I leapt up so suddenly that my chains popped out of the

concrete in explosions of dust. The soldier's eyes grew as big as dinner plates, and he fired a warning shot at the ceiling. A skylight exploded, and shards of glass rained around us.

I froze. *That would've been me.* My blood splattering on the floor.

The soldier lowered his gun at my chest, then quickly pointed it at the ground and back up again. "Lie down. Now!"

My legs shook. I looked at the ground where my hair was still fastened to the floor, the bolts of my chains peeled up like Band-Aids. Now that I didn't have any hair left, they would go to even more extreme measures to subdue me. Like staple my skin.

"I can't do that," I said.

"I said *lie down!*" the soldier screamed.

I could feel Beth trembling in my hand. This must have been what it was like . . . when Emperor Ook held Ma. When all he wanted was to keep her and himself safe. I put my other hand over Beth's head so that all of her was covered.

"She has a hostage!" the soldier screamed over his shoulder.

None of the other soldiers were coming, and he started to panic.

"Lie down!" he screamed at me. "LIE DOWN NOW!"

He was acting big and mean, but to me, he seemed like a little army toy. Of course, this soldier came with a gun that really fired.

I stood tall, trying to act less afraid than he was. I clutched Beth tight to my chest.

"I'm going to walk out of here," I said, meeting his eyes, just over the gun barrel. "I know you don't want to die. So I'm just going to—"

The gun erupted with light. Beth screamed. The bullets struck me in the stomach, and I folded in half, my breath forced out of me in a grunt. I fell to my knees, shielding Beth with my hands. I caught my breath in painful gasps and then looked at my stomach in the moonlight. There was no blood. Only bruises in a little dark constellation. From point blank range, the bullets would make me bleed. But from afar, they couldn't break the skin.

I lifted my head, scowling. The soldier started to back up. I put Beth behind my back, and I went at him. He fired, and it hurt, it hurt worse than anything I'd felt before, but instead of slowing down, I broke into a run and screamed, my voice booming throughout the hangar, trembling the remaining windows.

When I reached the soldier, I lashed out, slapping his arms and sending his gun skittering. He scrambled to escape, but I caught him by the waist of his pants with my finger and thumb. I lifted him up so he dangled in front of my eyes.

"Please," he said. "P-please."

"Look at me," I said.

He did, face quivering.

"Go sit in the corner," I told him.

I set him down, and he dutifully did as he was told.

I placed Beth on her feet. She was beaming.

"That was amazing! How do you feel?"

I pressed a fist into my stomach. "Like I belly-flopped on a bed of nails."

"But you're still cracking jokes!"

I grunted and picked up the gun from the ground. I was about to crumple it like a paper clip when Beth said, "Wait."

She held out her hands.

"Really?" I said.

"I'll only use it in an emergency. And I'll only shoot them in the legs."

I handed her the gun, which she strapped over her arm. I picked her up and set her on my shoulder. She threw her leg around my neck and held tight to handfuls of my stubby hair.

Crouching, I exited the hangar and walked down the long hallway, Beth swaying on my shoulders, protected behind my head. A few soldiers came around the corner and started shooting, but I ran forward, covering my head and Beth with my arms. When I reached them, I made big sweeping kicks until I felt my feet connect with their bodies and their gunfire fell silent.

Beth squeezed the back of my head, saying, "Oh Jesus, oh Jesus," which is what I wanted to be saying, but I figured one of us had to play the hero. I crouched and let the angry swarm of bruises die down a little. I gave a little cough. No blood. I kept on.

At the end of the hallway, I came to another industrial garage door. It was bolted, so I brought my fist down hard on the handle, breaking it off easy as a bottle top. I lifted the door a couple feet with my pointer finger and peeked outside. A wall of soldiers stood before the half-built barricade, their guns pointed at the door.

"She's got a civilian on her shoulders!" one of them shouted. "Aim low!"

"Ready?" I whispered to Beth.

"I think so," she said, squeezing my head.

I breathed, nodded, and threw open the garage door.

The world exploded. Machine guns burst to life in blinding sparklers, striking my middle like I'd run into a power line. I lunged forward and lashed out at every flare of light, swatting soldiers to the ground left and right and getting so caught up in the mix that some soldiers stopped shooting to keep from hitting each other.

I continued to bat soldiers to the ground and off their feet like rag dolls. Some grunted. Some whimpered. And some started begging for me to stop when they saw me bearing down on them. I'd nearly batted away every gun, when the general's voice came booming through the chaos.

"Stand down, men! STAND DOWN, I SAID!"

The soldiers who were still standing saluted. Some of them couldn't stand very straight. Some couldn't stand at all.

Spillane paced around his men, face bright as a cherry tomato, nearly chuckling. "Hoo-whee!" He surveyed the scene. "Looks like someone woke up on the wrong side of the airplane hangar!"

A thousand points on my body bloomed to life in sickly pain. I was out of breath, and my ribs felt like they were ready to collapse on my lungs. I couldn't let the general see that I was a couple dozen bullets away from being finished. So I stood tall and made my voice as big as possible.

"You have to let us out of here," I said.

The general put his hands on his hips. He didn't seem to notice Beth, who was still behind my head, holding tight to my ears.

"I have to admit you put on a much better show than I anticipated." He turned in a circle, appreciating the destruction around him. "But now I'd be a fool to let you go. Especially after this, heh, *breathtaking* demonstration of force and sheer willpower. This was my best platoon, and you snapped some of 'em easy as Popsicle sticks." He kicked a soldier who hadn't been able to stand when called to attention. "Why, with proper training you could be worth a whole army."

I had to catch my breath again. Something was wrong. Like I might be bleeding on the inside. But it was hard to tell. I'd just been shot a thousand times and survived.

"People are in trouble," I said. "I need to go save them."

The general squinted. "Who?"

"The Navajo people," I said.

The general gave a little laugh. "I gotta tell ya"—he carelessly scratched the back of his neck—"those people are as done as crumbs at a picnic, pardon the expression. Besides, the Indians will help divert the herd away from Pennybrooke. Save a lot more people that way."

"You could save them all," Beth said. "You just refuse to try."

"What's that you got up there?" the general said, peering around my ear. "A passenger? I'm guessing by your tone, little miss, that you aren't the giantess's prisoner."

"No, I am not," Beth said, squeezing my ears.

It took just about every last iota of strength left in me to push past the pain and stand up straight. "We're going to Gray Rock."

The general gave me an admonishing look, like his daughter had just told him she was going to the dance even though he'd forbidden it. "Most powerful human weapon in the world, and she's got a soft spot for Indians. All right, Phoebe. Have it your way." He turned to his soldiers. "If she comes at you again, shoot her in the eyeballs."

The soldiers raised their guns and formed a new wall.

I didn't need a test to know that if a bullet hit me in the eye, it would probably pop and ooze down my face.

"Beth," I whispered.

She squeezed my head.

"I need you to tell me where to kick."

"Okay, yeah," she said. "I'll pretend they're on a clock."

I covered my eyes with both arms and ran forward, my hands peppered with bullets.

"Eleven o'clock!" Beth screamed.

I kicked to my left and felt a soldier buckle around my foot.

"One o'clock!"

Another soldier went flying.

"Nine!"

I kicked out with my other foot, but it whooshed through air.

"Sorry! Ten!"

I rebounded and realigned, kicking farther to the right. I felt the sick crunch of someone's jaw against my toe.

"Three o'clock! Fast!"

I pivoted and back-kicked, sending a soldier flying, then rounded to face the wall of soldiers again, huffing.

"Stand down!" the general said. "You made a big mistake, little passenger! By holding that gun, you can officially be considered hostile."

I peeked between my fingers just as the general unholstered his gun and aimed at my head. There was a bang, and I flinched, but the bullet whizzed past my ear.

Beth made a sound like *"Uk!"* and I felt her tumble down my back.

"No!" I cried.

I rounded and crouched over Beth's body. She pressed her hands into her stomach, blood spurting between her fingers.

"Medic!" the general screamed.

"I'm sorry," I said, petting Beth's hair. "I'm so so sorry."

Beth groaned and said a word I'd never heard before. *"Shit."* And then . . . and then she *laughed*. "This hurts so much worse than I ever thought it would. Hold me, Phoebe, would ya?"

I picked her up and cradled her in my hands.

"No need for the long face," she said, unable to breathe full. "I'm not really dying."

She was shuddering and pale. Her blood had soaked through her shirt.

"Oh, Beth."

"I just wanted to give a shot to the little guy, you know? Or the big girl."

"What do you mean?"

"I wanted to live in a world of black and white—where you could always tell right from wrong."

"Beth, I . . . I don't understand."

"Look around. Isn't it obvious?"

I looked at the barricade. The desert. The sky. "No."

"That's not your fault." She reached up and touched my chin with her wet fingers. "Do the right thing and don't die. Give it a good ending. Not a shitty one where the disobedient girls get locked up and all the Native American nations are just part of the background."

"I don't understand. Beth . . ."

"Just give it a good ending." She coughed blood into her hand and laughed again. "The gay girl dies at the end. Figures. It's the fifties." She winced and gave me a serious look.

"Channel five thirty-two. Remember that." She took in a deep, ragged breath, and then her hazy eyes looked to the sky, right at Daddy. "The colors. *The colors . . .*"

And then Beth twinkled and vanished in my hands. I rubbed my fingers together, as if I could make her reappear. The blood was gone. She was gone. I looked up into the sky. Right above Daddy's head a star sparkled.

"Lie down, Phoebe!" the general called. "It's over. You're surrounded."

I looked around, confused. The medic was no longer on his way. It was as if Beth had never existed.

I didn't have time to think about that right then. The guns were trained on my eyes. I didn't have a little passenger on my shoulder to guide me anymore. I put my hands in the air.

"On your back, Phoebe," the general said. "Close in, boys!"

I lay down as the soldiers gathered in a circle around me bringing their guns close to my skin. In one motion, I made a snow angel in the sand, sweeping my arms and my legs outward, knocking the legs out from under two dozen soldiers. A few guns went off, striking me in the sides, but I leapt to my feet. Before any soldiers could recover, I knocked them down again.

Out of the corner of my eye, I saw the general retreating, unholstering his walkie-talkie. "Backup! I need backup!"

I ran and caught him around the waist, lifting him, struggling and kicking, high into the sky. Spillane looked at the drop, thirty feet if it was an inch, and understood. If I let go, he'd have a heck of a fall and break both legs. He stopped struggling.

I put his face right up to my nose. "Tell your troops to *stand down.*"

He scowled.

I nestled my thumbs under his chin. "All I have to do is press up and your head will snap back like a Pez dispenser," I said. "*Obey me.*"

"Stand down!" the general screamed.

The soldiers rocked uncertainly, foot to foot. They lowered their guns.

I was free. I could run out to the desert any direction I chose. I could stay safely away until the army of ants swept through and then come back for Ma. I was sure that's just what the old Phoebe, the normal-size one, would have done. But that was before I met Beth. Her blood was still on the concrete.

"Tell them to get the truck ready," I said. "We're riding out to Gray Rock."

"Why?"

"Because we're going to bring as many people as we can back to Pennybrooke. You're not going to use them as a shield."

The general pressed his tiny nose into mine. "I am not your prisoner. You are under my orders, helping me stem the tide of ants. Is that understood?"

"If it makes you feel better to think of it that way, go right ahead." I set him down. "Command your soldiers to load up food, too. Every bit they can carry."

We rode out to Gray Rock, the wind blowing through my cut hair, the truck as wobbly as a giant roller skate beneath my knees, and Frank blowing off my shoulders like Superman's cape.

"It's a kind thought, Phoebe," Eugene said. "But I think we have things handled here."

A bright skull moon cast shadows along the desert terrain where hundreds of Navajo people were busy fortifying Gray Rock. Men loaded shotguns and hammered wooden planks between the hogans, while old women held their grandchildren, making comforting sounds. The wind carried a rumble like an approaching locomotive. Daddy stuffed a handful of popcorn into his face.

"But the ants will be here any minute," I said.

Eugene stared out at the horizon to the rising dust storm kicked up by thousands of giant insect legs. "Don't think we hadn't noticed."

"They'll chew right through the wood of your hogans."

"That may be." Eugene nodded and stroked his chin. "But in the past, whenever your people have offered us one thing, we've always received another. You invited us into your society when you needed our help to speak code. Then, once the war was finished, you broke every treaty because you had no use for us anymore. Not you personally, of course. But most people around here just don't trust promises from white people. We feel better relying on ourselves."

"But Pennybrooke has concrete buildings to hide in," I said. "The army is there. They have machine guns."

Eugene gave me a sad smile. "Did you know that Navajo people consider the ant to be sacred?"

I shook my head.

"We've studied them, the Willazhini," he said. "The way they move. The way they sense the world." He pointed to the sloping hillside where women scattered food between wooden rails built down the hillside. "We're going to try to corral the swarm and divert them away from the hogans. Your donation helped, by the way. We're using it as a kind of crumb trail." He chuckled. "Sorry we're wasting it on ants."

"But these aren't just normal ants," I said. "They were zapped in a lab by . . . well, people like me."

It only took an upward look from Eugene to remember I'd been zapped in the same lab. He gazed off toward the approaching rumble. "Not to mention the fact that those same people forced us to mine the uranium that grew these ants," he said. "We all played our part." He crossed his arms and shook his head. "Honestly, I feel sorry for the people of Pennybrooke tonight. Most of them have only ever looked at an ant long enough to squish it. They could probably use your help more than us. Now, if you'll excuse me, I should really get back to building."

I nodded and numbly walked back to the rig in the parking lot where the Girl Scouts had parked the station wagon what felt like ages ago, back when my biggest concern in the world was trying to find Ma. I crouched and tapped my giant fingernail on the driver's-side window. The general had a difficult time rolling down the window with his wrists handcuffed to the steering wheel.

"They don't want to come," I said.

"What did you expect?" the general said. "Ingrates."

"Can you blame them?" I said.

The general cleared his throat. "I didn't want to make the

people of Pennybrooke fill their trousers, but in '54, the army had a hell of a time bringing these ants down. Bullets ricocheted right off their exoskeletons."

The thought gave me an ache in my knuckles. "How did you do it?"

"*Fire*," he said, eyes shining. "What else? We've got flamethrowers back at the base."

"How many ants are coming?" I said.

"My people counted four hundred from the chopper. That number might have grown since the last sweep."

"Four *hundred*?"

The general shrugged. "Pretty soon you and me and everyone here are going to be nothing more than meat sandwiches." He winked. "Granted, one of us will last a little longer than the rest."

I ran my hands through my chopped-up hair. Beth had told me to help the Navajo people. To not let them be part of the background, whatever that meant. But it looked like they didn't need my help.

"You gonna stay here and argue with the Indians?" the general said casually. "Better make a decision quick. On six legs, those ants will overtake this rig like a wounded caterpillar."

"How long till they get here?" I asked.

"Your guess is as good as mine, giantess."

My arms fell to my sides, and the general gave me a pitying look.

"An hour," he said. "Tops."

A gasp rose behind us, and Eugene ushered people into their stronghold.

"Well, now," the general said casually. "This is where things get interesting."

A cloud slid off the moon, pulling a veil of shadow from the desert. The sight scared me right to my feet. The ant was as big as a bus. Bigger. Even though I was as tall as a flagpole, its mandibles reached as high as my waist. Its sleek body glowed like oil in the moonlight as it moved right around the rails on the hillside and skittered around the hogans in frantic bursts, antennae writhing.

"That's the scout!" the general called up to me.

"The what?"

"The scout! Every army has one. It travels ahead to mark the territory with scent so the rest know where the food is. It's probably marking those Indians right now, making them smell enticing as a barbecue." He cleared his throat. "If you really want to help these people, you'll stop that thing."

Eugene stood on one of the roofs and called out commands. "Don't let it scent the hogans!"

Several shotguns went off behind the barricade, but the bullets bounced harmlessly off the ant's back as its abdomen sprayed a translucent goo in its wake. Eugene clearly hadn't expected the scout this early. He watched helplessly as it lifted its giant mandibles toward the moon and emitted a chickering sound that echoed through my giant ears and itched my brain. I clamped my hands in my armpits.

"Now is not the time to clam up, giantess," the general called. "Just imagine that thing is my platoon of soldiers, and I'm sure you'll do just fine."

I couldn't move. Those things had eaten Katie and hundreds of other people in her town. Their exoskeletons deflected bullets. What chance did I have?

"Tell you what," the general said. "If you can drag that

scout to an open area, I'll run it over with this rig. That should put a dent in its side, at least."

I looked thirty feet down and the general gave me a thumbs-up. Before I could second-guess myself, I took a step across the sand toward the giant ant. I took another step and tried to remind myself that I had hands the size of tabletops. I had feet the size of baby elephants.

On my third step, the ant noticed me, and my confidence evaporated. Its body was made of three round shapes held up by six spindly, jointed legs. The antennae worked like muscular bendy straws toward my chest, as if it had never seen anything like me.

And I remembered I owed these ants something.

"This is for Katie," I said, and I ran at it, screaming.

For a moment the ant didn't seem to know what to do. It lunged forward, mashing its wet mandibles, but when my shadow overtook it, it whirled and scrabbled back the way it came.

"Don't let it get away, Phoebe!" Eugene cried.

I lunged forward and caught the ant's back leg and yanked backward as hard as I could. I had hoped the leg would rip out of its joint, but it stayed put. I leaned back and started to drag the scout toward the rig, but its five other legs scrabbled forward, and we were caught in a tug-of-war.

"You've got this, Phoebe!" Eugene called.

I raised a fist over my head and swung it downward with every bit of fear I had in me. My hand rounded off the abdomen, like I'd punched a cast-iron skillet. The feeling vibrated through my bones and I cried out. I tried to shake the pain from my hand, but this gave the ant enough time to spin round and sink its mandibles into the arm still holding its leg.

My forearm exploded with pain, like it had been caught in hedge clippers with serrated edges. Gastric juices gushed out of the ant's mouth, and my skin started to sizzle. The people behind the barricade gasped. My screams echoed across the desert. My eyes went wide, frantically searching for something, anything.

"The eye, Phoebe!" Eugene called. "Hit it in the eye!"

I brought my elbow down hard into the ant's oily orb of an eyeball, which crunched, gushing like a melon. The ant shrieked as a frothy fluid gushed between the mandibles, scalding my forearm. Its jaws loosened, but refused to let go. If I tried to pull my arm out now, I'd strip the muscle and skin from my bone.

The ant and I held our position, both badly injured. My breath heaved. Its legs twitched. Its popped eye leaked onto my feet. I started to drag the injured ant toward an open area.

"General!" I screamed toward the truck. "General, now! Run it over!"

Spillane smiled and saluted me through the windshield. And then he started the engine. The rig swept up a circle of dust as it pulled back onto the highway.

"No!" I screamed. "Please! Come back!"

I had to end this fight. I had to get my arm back. I couldn't reach the ant's other eye without losing more skin.

"Hit its petiole!"

I was dizzy with pain, but my eyes managed to locate Eugene, standing on the hogan. "The *what?*"

He pointed. "The part that connects its body to its butt!"

I searched along the ant's body, and noticed the dip

between its middle and back section. With excruciating pain I wrenched my arm to the side and brought my leg around, bringing it down full force onto the connecting tube of exoskeleton, buckling it like a tree branch. The ant's body slumped forward and fell still. I placed a foot on each mandible and pried them open, sucking through my teeth as my arm came free.

"Grab the body!" Eugene screamed to his people. "Spread the scent between the rails. The rest of you, start scrubbing that goo off the hogans!"

I ran, limping toward the highway.

"Thank you, Phoebe!" Eugene called after me, and a cry of agreement followed.

The rig was still accelerating by the time I caught up to it. I ran as quickly as my legs would carry me, my injured arm dangling at my side. The truck slowed to switch gears, and in that brief hesitation, I was just able to snag the edge of the truck bed with my good arm.

"Gotcha!" I cried.

I continued to run, lifting the truck's back end so the tires couldn't connect with the road. *Bzzzt!* My shin grazed the rotating tire, and I stumbled. The tires reconnected with the asphalt and screeched ahead. I regained my balance and sprinted faster, trying to catch the truck bed again. But the general had gained too much ground. He sped up to forty . . . fifty . . . sixty miles per hour, and before I knew it, he was impossible to catch.

I collapsed to my knees in the middle of the dark highway. "COWARD!"

The word echoed across the great empty desert as the truck's brake lights shrank to two points in the distance.

He'd waited. He'd waited until my arm was caught in the ant's pincers so I wouldn't be able to catch him.

I sat in shock, my arm trembling in my lap, burned and bleeding. The approaching cloud of dust had a wet sound now—hundreds of oily mandibles.

I had fought just one ant and nearly lost my arm. How could I fight a dozen? A hundred? *Four* hundred? I broke down and sobbed in the middle of the highway until I heard a tiny voice say, "Don't be scared! She's nice."

I lifted my face from my hands. Five Navajo children stood before me. Three boys and two girls. I recognized the girl who took the Twinkie from the kiddie pool. Her cheeks were glowing.

She stepped forward while the others kept their distance. "See? What scary thing *cries*?"

They must have slipped away during the chaos created by the scout.

"What are you guys doing here?" I said, standing up. "You have to go back home."

"We want to be with you!" the girl said.

One of the boys stepped forward and punched his hand. "Yeah! We watched you beat up that ant!"

The other three were silent.

"No!" I said. "Absolutely n—"

The chickering sound echoed down the highway a hundred fold as a wave of ants swept over the hill, between and around the railings, into Gray Rock. The night filled with gunshots. The kids watched in horror and awe.

Running them home now would be a suicide mission. If I was carrying them, I wouldn't even have my hands free to fight.

"Well?" the little girl asked, hands on hips.

"I . . ."

To the south, Pennybrooke twinkled. To the north, the moon glinted off a sea of black armor. I remembered Beth's words and wondered what I would yell at myself if I were watching all this in a movie.

Pennybrooke was empty. The houses were abandoned, doors hanging open, televisions blaring through the night. On Main Street, "In the Still of the Night" emanated from the sock hop's jukebox and echoed down the abandoned storefronts.

I set the five kids on the sidewalk. Their hair was windblown from our sprint through the desert. Two of them had tear lines running down their dusty cheeks.

"Let's find somewhere for you guys to hide," I said.

They followed me through the empty streets, running to keep up with my long strides. Soon we arrived at a barbed wire fence with armed guards. The Penmark Roller Rink had been transformed into a fortress.

"General!" one of the guards called. "She's here!"

The barricade's doors swung open and General Spillane stepped out. He dropped his cigar and stomped on it. "Bet you're real proud of yourself, giantess."

"What do you mean?" I said.

He jabbed a finger toward my injured arm. "You've got that ant scout's scent *all over you*, and you just tracked it across the desert and *straight* to this building. Any chance of that swarm sweeping past Pennybrooke without so much as wiggling an antenna in our direction was just shot by your brilliant move."

I blinked at my hands. "I—I didn't know." My fingers curled. "You *left* me."

"Yeah, I left you because if the ants filled their bellies with giantess meat, they wouldn't come here and eat all the innocents." He tapped his temple. "I'm strategic that way."

Over the barbed-wire top of the barricade, which came up to my chest, I could see into the open doors of the roller rink. The lights were off and hundreds of figures stared out, silent and listening, like an unsettling diorama.

Even if I could fit through those tight doors, these were people who hated me so much they were ready to burn me alive. A small part of me had known this would end with me out here all alone.

"A-*choo*!"

One of the Navajo kids sneezed, and the general peered around my foot.

"Well, what do we have here?" he said.

The Twinkie girl peeked out from behind my legs.

"They ran away from home," I said. "They need shelter from the ants."

Just then a tiny ball of white fluff came barking out of the roller rink. I put out my hand, and Pan-Cake leapt into it. She was no bigger than the end of a Q-tip in my palm, but I could still feel her microscopic licks. Her hair was tied with tiny bows.

"Queenie? *Queenie!* Get back here, you disobedient thing!"

Just seeing Rhoda's bouncing pigtails made the burns on my stomach flare.

"*You*," Rhoda said, marching up to me, but stopping right beside the general. "You give that dog back this *instant*."

I cupped my other hand around Pan-Cake. If I was going to die alone, I at least wanted company. If I had to, I'd hide Pan-Cake in my mouth so the ants wouldn't get her.

A man came sprinting out of the building. "Rhoda! There you are, darling. Come back inside. The monsters will be here any moment."

One of them is already here, I thought, glaring at Rhoda.

"Captain Penmark," the general said. "This concerns you. These children are seeking asylum."

"Well, they can't come in!" Rhoda said, almost delighted. "Like you said, General, they're covered in ant juice. It would lead them right to us."

"No!" I said uncertainly. "They're not. That's just me."

Rhoda scowled at Mr. Penmark, who scratched the back of his neck. He glanced back toward the open doors. "Either way, I'm not sure we have the room."

The NO COLOREDS sign was still hung in the roller rink's window.

"What do you mean?" I said. "You have plenty of space! Look, Rhoda. You can have Pan—I mean, Queenie—back. Just take these kids inside!"

I held my hand open, but Pan-Cake remained curled up in my palm, quivering at the sight of Rhoda.

Rhoda folded her arms in disgust. "I don't want her anymore. She's covered in ant juice. They're *all* covered in ant juice. You can keep the dog and the Indians. I'll take the roller rink."

Mr. Penmark shrugged his shoulders. "It's us or them, General."

I made a fist the size of a battering ram and showed it to Mr. Penmark. "I'll break your building's wall down and stick these kids in there myself."

"If you come anywhere near this building, then we'll be

forced to shoot," General Spillane said, then looked at the kids. "And you wouldn't want a bullet to catch one of your little friends here."

If it weren't for the guns trained on the kids, I would have picked up Rhoda, rubbed her all over my body, and said, *There! Now you're no better than any of us.*

But Rhoda grinned at my helplessness, flipped a white braid over her shoulder, and her clicking heels disappeared inside the rink. Mr. Penmark didn't meet my eye as he joined his daughter.

"Nothing I can do," the general said, sounding almost regretful. "It's private property. And I can't put these people in jeopardy by letting these kids track ant pheromones inside."

I looked down at the five kids, shivering in the open street. And here I thought I could offer protection to all of the Navajo people. It was just like Eugene had said. I promised one thing, and now I was delivering something much different.

Lear came striding out of the roller rink. He passed right by the general and stood before me.

"I'm going with you," he said.

The general clicked his tongue. "Boy, that girl's got you wrapped around her little pinkie, doesn't she?"

Lear faced his uncle. "You can't stop me."

"That's where you're wrong, son. I don't want to command my soldiers to take my own nephew into custody, but if you're going to try and get yourself killed, you'll be in handcuffs faster than this girlfriend of yours can finish a ham sandwich."

I felt Lear's hand on my calf. "Phoebe will stop you."

The general laughed and shook his head. "That true, giantess?"

I looked from Lear to the general to the soldiers and their guns on the barricade to the children behind me. Lucky for me I was saved from answering that question.

"Lear?"

A frail woman stood in the barricade's entrance. Her hair was white as swan feathers, and she clasped her wrist.

Lear went to her and took her thin hands in his. "I have to do this, Mom. I knew Dad wasn't a monster, but I didn't say anything before Uncle Spillane killed him. I've regretted it every day since." He looked up at me. "Phoebe isn't a monster either. She's good. And if they're going to make her and these kids stay outside, then I'm going to stay out here too."

Mrs. Finley touched her son's face and turned it toward hers, trying to understand what he was thinking.

General Spillane placed his hand on Lear's shoulder. "Come on inside, son, before you do something well and truly stupid."

In one fluid motion Lear grabbed the gun from his uncle's holster and tremblingly pointed it at the general's head while he backed up and stood between my legs. Mrs. Finley gasped.

The general held out a hand. "Think about what you're doing, Lear. This isn't like you."

"What isn't?" Lear said, unable to keep the gun or his voice from wavering. "Standing up for innocent people you'd sooner kill than listen to?"

"I suspect you think you're being heroic," the general said, nodding to the gun. "But you don't understand that saving people requires sacrifice. How do you think I got where I am today?"

"You're right," Lear said. He set the gun on the ground. "I'm not like you."

The general took a step toward the gun but stopped when

Mrs. Finley touched his arm. Everyone stared at one another in silence, waiting for someone to say something.

"Where are we supposed to go?" I asked the general.

"I'd seek out something made of metal," he said, and he started to lead Mrs. Finley inside. "Ants can't chew through it. Lock it up, boys!"

Lear and his mother watched each other until the soldiers pulled the giant doors shut, leaving him, me, Pan-Cake, and five little kids outside. A couple of the kids started to sniffle around my ankles, realizing we were being locked outside with the monsters.

Up in the sky, Daddy was grinning like a loon.

• • •

"Some of these houses have to have bomb shelters," Lear said as we walked past the Levitt ranches with the five kids. "That should keep the ants out."

Neither of us commented on the fact that I wouldn't be able to fit. I'd be left out here when the sea of mandibles swept in.

Lear suddenly stopped walking, turned to the kids, and tapped his chin. "I just realized," he said in a surprisingly chipper voice, "I don't know any of your names."

"Duane," the boy who wanted to see me fight the ants said.

"Manuelito," said another.

"Ruth," said one of the little girls.

"I'm Maria," the girl I knew said, and pointed to the last boy, who'd done the most crying. "That's Connor."

"Nice to meet you all," Lear said. "I'm Lear, and I think you guys know Phoebe. This is her dog, Pan-Cake." He stretched his arms out. "Phoebe has to use a really, *really* long leash to take her on walks."

Duane, Ruth, and Maria giggled at this.

"Do you guys like games?"

Maria and Ruth nodded. Duane rubbed his hands together excitedly.

"What are you doing?" I said, crouching. "We don't have time for this."

Lear quirked an eyebrow. "You haven't spent much time with kids, have you?"

"How could you tell?" I said.

He ruffled Connor's hair. "They're going to be a lot more likely to follow instructions if they think this is a game. They also won't cry or scream and draw attention to themselves."

"Okay, sure. That makes sense." I searched his face for traces of what just happened with his mom. "Are you okay?"

"I'm fine," he said, and turned back to the kids. "All right! This is just like hide-and-go-seek, except you have to hide for a very, *very* long time. We're going to put you inside one of these houses, and—"

"Phoebe," a croaked voice said behind me.

It was Marsh. He had a Bible under his arm and his face and collar were covered in ash, like he'd been digging through the burned remains of the church.

"What are you doing out here?" I said. "Why aren't you in the roller rink with the rest?"

Marsh wrung his hands, as if trying to warm himself against the night. "They told me if I was interested in protecting monsters like you then I could remain out here with the ants." He tremblingly reached into his collar and brought out a cross. "But I know that God will protect me against his own creatures."

A warm feeling washed through my chest. I didn't mention that these ants weren't one of God's plagues but my half sister's.

"Who are these children?" Marsh asked.

I explained how they came here and why they weren't allowed inside the rink either.

"Those *monsters*," Marsh said.

I would have hugged him if I thought he wouldn't hate it.

"Got it?" Lear asked the kids.

"Got it!" they shouted.

Lear scanned the street. "Now we just have to find a house with a shelter."

"You won't be going in any houses," a new voice said. "*He* needs to be able to watch."

Two figures stood in the middle of the street. Officers Graham and Shelley. They had their guns drawn.

"We have to hide these kids," I said. "The ants are coming."

Officer Shelley clicked his tongue. "We have word from the lab that the most interesting scenario is if you and those kids remain outside. Anything else will be too safe, and the big guy might get bored."

"What big guy?" Marsh said. "What is he talking about? Phoebe?"

I ignored him. I wanted to grab the officers' bodies and squeeze until all of their plant juice popped out of their eyeballs. But they thought just like the military. They had their guns trained on the kids instead of me.

"Where are we supposed to go?" I asked.

"Where else?" Officer Graham said.

He nodded toward the carnival.

With all of the lights turned out, with no rides rumbling and no kids screaming, the carnival felt more like a graveyard. The air smelled of popcorn and caramel apples and funnel cakes, but for the first time in weeks, I was too nervous to eat.

We walked past the empty game booths with milk bottles and balloons and checkerboard squares. Pan-Cake had stopped panting, as if she could sense the approaching evil but was too afraid to growl. Connor pressed his face into Lear's side.

"Everything is so wide open," Lear said quietly. "Where will be safe?"

Strange silhouettes rose around us against the starry night: the Ferris wheel, the merry-go-round, the big top tent holding Emperor Ook's bones . . .

"Those are the three highest points," I said, pointing to each. "The ants will have a tougher time reaching them up there."

"The Ferris wheel," Lear said. "The ants won't be able to climb it. The bars are too thin and far apart."

"Perhaps," Marsh said hesitantly. He hitched Ruth higher in his arms, momentarily forgetting his hatred of being touched. "But we must not place all of our eggs in one basket."

"They're not eggs," Lear said. "Are you guys eggs?"

"No!" Duane shouted.

"I, em, only mean that if the ants do manage to reach the top," Marsh said, "we shall lose them all."

Ruth sniffled, and he patted her back.

"But I'll have an easier time protecting them if they're all in one space," I said. "Like the barricade around the roller rink, we—"

A chickering cut through the desert air. Ruth and Connor whimpered.

"They're here," Lear said, then stared up at me. "Make a decision."

I had a flash of my arm caught in an ant's mandibles and not being able to reach the kids in time. "We'll split them up." I looked at Marsh. "I hope you're right."

Without another word, I scooped up Duane and Manuelito and ran them to the Ferris wheel, placing them in the top gondola. Manuelito's lip started to quiver.

"Shh, shh, it's okay," I whispered, trying to think of what Lear would say. "You guys ever squished bugs before?"

Duane nodded hesitantly while Manuelito quickly shook his head. Right. Eugene had told me that the Navajo people considered ants sacred.

"Er, um," I said, "I'll just make sure they don't come near you."

I felt a pat on my foot. "Put me up there!" Lear called.

He was holding a basket of baseballs from one of the carnival games.

I scooped him and the baseballs up and set him inside the gondola. Duane immediately grabbed a ball.

"Phoebe," Lear said, before I turned to go.

"Yeah?"

"Good luck."

"Yeah, right," I said. "Luck . . . Thank you."

I tried to smile and then ran back to Marsh, who was saying a prayer over Ruth, Maria, and Connor.

"There's no time for that," I said.

Marsh brushed off his knees. "I was searching for guidance. The top of the merry-go-round is slanted," he said, pointing. "You cannot put the kids up there. They will slide right off."

My heart pounded in my throat. "Where, then?"

He went to the strength tester and hefted the sledgehammer used to strike the sensor to make a weight fly up and hit the bell at the top.

"*'A curse on him who keeps his sword from bloodshed,'*" he whispered to himself. Then, "Put Ruth by the bell. I will remain down here."

The tower didn't seem as secure as the other hiding places, but it was a sight higher than anything else around. An ant would be able to reach up and pluck a kid right off the roof of any of these booths.

Next I looked at Marsh's arms, which had trouble hefting a big Bible, let alone swinging a sledgehammer.

"Are you sure you can keep her safe?" I said.

"God will work through me." He stared at the ground. "And I have no regrets. Especially when it comes to you."

I smiled at that.

I picked up Ruth and placed her on the high perch.

"Here," I said, using my pinkie to delicately organize her trembling legs around the bell.

She sniffled, and I felt guilty leaving her all alone up there.

"I need you to take care of someone very special, okay?" I said.

She nodded, and I put Pan-Cake in her arms.

"Too bad I can't zap Pan-Cake with gamma rays, huh?" I told Ruth. "She'd gobble up plenty of ants. Or lick them until they ran away, at least."

Ruth gave a smirk, and Pan-Cake gave her a tiny lick on the cheek.

"Now hold on tight," I said to the girl. "Hide-and-seek will be over before you know it."

I scooped up Maria and Connor and ran toward the towering tent that sat on the border between the desert and the carnival. The bottom was staked to the sand to prevent people from sneaking a free peek. But that didn't mean ants' mandibles wouldn't saw right through the tent's material. I ducked into the large entrance flaps.

"Hello, Ook," I said.

The skeleton of the giant gorilla had always seemed bigger than life in the past. But now here he was, only a few feet taller than me.

Connor started to wail at the sight of the grinning simian skull.

"No, no, shh, it's okay," I said. "This is an old friend of my mom's." I placed Maria in Ook's right eye socket. "He may look like a monster, but he was very gentle, like me." I placed Connor in the left. "He just wanted someone to love, but because he was so big and hairy, he couldn't help but scare people. He was very misunderstood."

The two kids stared at me out of the shadows of Ook's skull.

"He's going to keep you safe tonight," I said.

Maria patted the side of her socket. "Thank you, Ook."

I pressed my finger to my lips to tell her to keep quiet, and

I stepped outside of the tent. It was only then that I let my face crumple. *Oh, please don't let me end up like Ook's skeleton tonight—my skin and muscle stripped from my bone, my eyes chewed out of their sockets.*

The cloud of dust was covering the moon now. The ants were coming, like a black razor across the desert. I suddenly felt unequipped, like I was headed into battle naked. I wished Eugene was there to perch on my shoulder and tell me how the ants moved, how they thought, how to deter them from Pennybrooke. The only way I knew how to handle this was with violence.

Okay.

Stay away from their mandibles.

Don't grab their legs.

Punch the eyes and stomp the skinny part in the back.

There came a great pop, and the carnival lights sparkled to life. The merry-go-round started to turn, filling the night with dizzying music. The officers must have turned the power back on.

"Heaven forbid you don't see this," I said, looking up at Daddy, who could barely contain his smile. "Just know I'm not doing this for you. I'm doing this for Ma. And for Beth."

Before I was ready, the first line of the ants swept in, a wall of stabbing legs, working mandibles, and twitching antennae. When they were only a few yards away, I leapt into the air and came down with both feet onto the petioles of two ants, snapping them in half. Before the ants to either side had time to lash out, I hooked my good arm around the neck of one, swinging it up and over and crunching it onto the other. I stomped forward, left and then right, separating the abdomens of two more.

An ant lunged at me, its mandibles nearly piercing me through the stomach, but I stepped back in the nick of time, grabbed hold of its antennae, and yanked upward. They popped out of its head, and the ant scrabbled away, bumping into other ants, as senseless as an antennae-less TV. This was much easier than stomping, so as a new line rushed in, I focused on the antennae, snatching them like flower stems, sending half a dozen scrabbling.

A hill of carapaces was built up around me now, making a sort of foxhole over which I could snag antennae while keeping my legs and torso protected. Soon I found I didn't even have to pluck out both antennae. I could just rip out one and send the ant scurrying in circles.

My lungs were on fire. My feet were bruised. My palms were burning from tearing out antennae. But I felt alive. What would Ma say if she could see me then? Her daughter, Empress Ook, standing amid a pile of monster corpses. After I rescued her, I'd describe the scene, and she could tell me what she thought herself.

I had a good thing going, a wall of ant bodies to protect me and a way to defeat the ants without having to crack through their exoskeletons. But then I heard a faint cry from across the carnival.

"Phoebe!"

I peeked over my barricade of carapaces. The Ferris wheel was alight and spinning, the gondola holding Lear and two of the boys slowly descending toward the lashing mandibles. Officer Graham was working the controls, calmly, as if he were off duty, volunteering at the carnival. The ants paid him no attention.

How was I going to get through that many ants and reach them? I needed a weapon . . . I leapt over the ant barricade and, skipping along the backs of ants, slipped into Ook's tent and yanked the skeleton's lengthy humerus free from the frame.

"You guys okay?" I said to the kids in Ook's sockets. "Yes? Good."

I burst out of the tent flap, and sprinted to the Ferris wheel.

"Sorry," I said to Officer Graham, or what used to be him, as I smashed him with the humerus in a juicy splatter.

I tried to work the Ferris wheel's tiny controls, but the lever snapped off in my giant fingernails. The wheel kept turning, bringing Lear and the kids closer and closer to the shrieking, salivating ants.

Bullets may ricochet off exoskeletons, but Ook's arm bone smashed straight through their heads. *KRNCH! SKLRCH! SKSH!* I beat a path to the wheel and then seized the two rotating metallic circles and brought the whole thing to a screeching halt. An ant clamped onto my calf with its pincers. Another clamped onto my thigh. I screamed through the pain as I used every ounce of my strength to rotate the Ferris wheel upward. Finally Lear's gondola came to a swinging stop at the top.

I grabbed the nearest empty gondola, plucking it off the wheel, and brought it crashing down, caving in the head of one ant and then the other, bringing cold relief to my legs.

A baseball hit me in the forehead.

"Sorry!" Duane shouted.

I worked my way back toward the tent, swinging Ook's forearm, crunching ants, while snapping antennae with my free hand. Soon, I wasn't thinking about the killing. I was thinking about the lives behind me.

KRNCH! I saved Lear.

SKRSH! I saved Marsh.

SPTTT! I saved Calvin.

SHLLK! BLLK! PSHT! FLLP! GRRSH! I saved Maria and Duane and Manuelito and Connor and Ruth.

I was starting to get the hang of things, even almost enjoying myself, when one of the ants reared its head and caught Ook's humerus between its mandibles.

"Give it back!" I screamed, pulling as hard as I could.

But the ant's jaws were as fixed as cement. I was kicking ants off me left and right, trying to get the bone back, when I heard another scream, this one from a kid.

Without letting go of the bone, I looked over my shoulder. Near the test of strength, several ants hobbled, their legs snapped by the sledgehammer. But Marsh was nowhere in sight. Officer Shelley had the hammer now and was laughing maniacally while he brought it smashing down onto the sensor, sending the weight careening upward and striking the bell, rattling Ruth, who dangled from the top of the tower by her legs, crying and just managing to cling on to Pan-Cake.

"You've got to be kidding me," I said.

Officer Shelley had hoisted the sledgehammer over his head for the final blow when I snatched him up and squeezed him to death, plant juice popping out of his mouth and eyeballs. I heard a yipe and my hand darted out and caught Pan-Cake just as she fell from Ruth's hands. I readjusted the poor dangling child, setting her back on top of the bell.

"Wow, you're really good at following instructions!" I said

in a bright voice, like she hadn't almost died. "Where's the reverend?"

Ruth just sobbed and clung on to the bell. I handed Pan-Cake back to her, and the girl buried her face in her white fur.

"It's okay," I said, trying to sound soothing. "The bad man is dead. He won't try to knock you down anymore. Did you see what happened to the reverend?"

She pointed a shaky finger. Near the darts game was a circle of ants feasting on something. I ran and leapt. The weight of my feet crunched straight through two of their heads. I shook the gooey heads off my feet while snapping the antennae of the two others.

And then saw a sight I didn't want to see: Reverend Marsh all in pieces.

Numb, I knelt and quickly dug a hole with my hand.

"Thank you for making me feel protected despite my mom's wantonness," I said, scooping sand over his body and watering it with a giant tear. "And for taking care of all the gross stuff without ever complaining. I'm sorry I don't have more time."

I could barely catch my breath before sprinting back to Ook's tent.

The tent had been ripped open, the tattered material dangling from the wooden frame. There were no screams coming from inside. I killed the ants outside and then tore away what remained of the tent, shining moonlight onto the skeleton inside. An ant had scaled Ook's ribs like a ladder. Its two pincers were working furiously inside of the skull's eye sockets. I grabbed the ant and broke it over my knee, discarding its body.

Maria, in the right socket, held her arms out to me, lip trembling. I took her and placed her on my shoulder. The other socket was silent. I reached inside with my pointer finger and felt a small body, warm and wet.

I delicately pulled Connor out. He was alive. Barely. His stomach had been sawn open by the ant's pincer. He was having a hard time catching his breath. His glazed-over eyes twinkled with circus lights. He tried to hold his blood inside of him, but his arms were too weak. The world wavered in my tears.

This wasn't how this was supposed to happen. Why did I become a giantess if I wasn't able to save people? I had a chance to be bigger than myself, like Beth said. I could become a superhero, just like the ones in Lear's comic books. It wasn't supposed to end like this.

Maria squeezed my earlobe and whispered, "Is he dying?"

"Um—" My breath caught. "No. We're going to get him to a hospital."

But the hospital would be abandoned, and there were hundreds of ants between it and us.

"You just keep breathing," I told Connor. His eyes couldn't focus on me. "You hear me? Just keep—"

My voice caught in my throat. I held the small, bleeding child and looked around, helpless. A new wave of ants were sweeping in from the desert. So far, I had killed, what, a few dozen? If that? I was beaten and exhausted. And according to the general, hundreds more were on their way. I couldn't make myself fight to the death like Ook could. I just couldn't.

A scream tore through the night. Back at the test of strength an ant was slowly slipping its way up the narrow tower, pincers working toward the bell and Ruth, who quivered and clung to Pan-Cake.

Then came more screams. "Phoebe!" On the Ferris wheel, the ants were building a bridge out of their bodies, working their way from gondola to gondola, to feast on the three warm bodies at the top.

And then, as if this were all a joke in need of a punch line, a strange whirring emanated from the desert. A flying saucer buzzed its way toward Pennybrooke, sand spinning off its metallic sides, as if it had just unburied itself. From its base shot a blinding beam of light that sliced its way across the ground in a wave of fire, melting the sand into glass.

Of course, I thought helplessly. If it were only ants murdering people, then Daddy might get bored.

So this was it. We were dead. It didn't matter how hard I fought. In the end, the Shivers would always get the best of us.

Staring at that flying saucer, I realized I'd been doing exactly what the Buried Lab wanted me to do: kill for Daddy's pleasure. Liz had led me to believe there was no other choice.

I looked at the dying boy in my hands. Well, we would see about that.

I set Connor back in Ook's socket. I set Maria in the same socket and said, "Keep him warm. Hug him. But be careful of his stomach."

She nodded and wrapped her arms around his quivering body.

I marched through the carnival, straight toward Daddy, his eyes glowing with the light from the saucer. If an ant dared scrabble up to me, its life ended in a quick, crunchy splatter.

"HEY!" I screamed into the sky at my father. "*HEY*!"

His smile remained unflinching, as wide as a mountain range. The remote rested on his knee. I may not have had Ma's looks, but I was big enough and violent enough that he *should* be able to hear me now. He just had to.

"YOU WANT MORE?" I screamed. "HUH? THIS ISN'T ENOUGH FOR YOU?"

Right then Daddy only had eyes for the saucer, whose laser of fire was carving toward the roller rink.

"YOU HAVEN'T SEEN ENOUGH GUTS AND BLOOD AND BODIES? ANSWER ME!"

Daddy only grinned as the flying saucer's laser started to melt through the building, which filled with screams. I needed to get his attention. But how? Liz had said Daddy liked only monsters and violence and women of a certain type . . .

A thought sent a shiver right up all ten feet of my spine.

"*FINE!*" I screamed. "YOU WANT SEX AND VIOLENCE?"

I seized a nearby ant body by the antennae. I wrenched left and then right, and then with a juicy splintering, twisted and yanked, popping its head right off its body. I held the ant head high above my head.

"I GOT SOMETHING FOR YOU TO SEE!"

If the only thing Daddy responded to was violence and sex, then I would give him more than he could handle. I spun the ant head around and I kissed it. I kissed it as passionately as I had imagined kissing Lear, stroking the ant's antennae like it was luscious hair while writhing my body like the women on television, making sounds only appropriate for the bedroom.

"OH, YEAH! MMM-MM! GIVE IT TO ME, ANT! MM!"

Daddy's head slowly turned.

And something in him changed.

It wasn't his smile.

It wasn't his hand on the remote control.

It was his eyes.

Daddy's pupils shrank, like shrinking moons. They grew smaller and smaller, moving more quickly than anything on him ever had. His pupils shrank to the size of black stars as they focused on me. Our eyes connected. His smile started to fade.

That's when I slid my tongue between the ant's mandibles.

"OH YEAH! OH GOSH! YOU SURE KNOW HOW TO TURN A LADY ON, YOU BEAUTIFUL, DISGUSTING INSECT!"

Daddy's expression turned to horror. While he'd smiled every time someone died a splattery death or a town was flattened, this is what scared him. A giant girl French-kissing an ant head.

Daddy's hand leapt out of his lap in real time, moving so quickly that it made me drop the ant head. His hands fumbled with the remote control. He nearly dropped it behind the mountains, but then he recovered and quickly pointed it directly at me, his thumb trembling over the big power button.

"WAIT!" I screamed, putting my hands in the air.

This was it. The end of the world—the entirety of existence clicking off, collapsing in a line and then shrinking to a single brief blip.

Daddy's lips started to tremble. He realized I was talking to him. Was he staring at a TV screen and seeing one of the characters in the movie staring back? Or did he recognize some of himself in me?

"I'M YOUR DAUGHTER, YOU BASTARD!" I screamed.

Daddy's face turned pale.

And then he changed the channel.

⚡⚡⚡ **KSSHT!** ⚡⚡⚡

Trees swayed above me. Trees unlike anything I'd seen before. Their trunks were thin and white, and they were bushy at the top. I was lying on a forest floor.

My hands ran along my body. Besides being covered in mud, it felt . . . good. My bruises were healed, my cuts all closed up. When I stood up, I didn't stretch as high as the trees. I was normal size. I was just Phoebe.

At first, the gentle sway of the trees and fluttering of leaves was soothing. But then there came an explosion of sound from the other side of the bushes. I remembered Lear and the kids and pushed through the leaves to see if they were in trouble. I stepped out of the forest and into a war zone. Asian people were running, screaming. Men dressed in army fatigues shot at them. I was close enough that I could smell the hot oil of the guns. The bullets nearly deafened me. One of the men shooting had something standing up in his pants.

"Have at 'em, boys!" he screamed, laughing.

It was Calvin. His head was intact, but he was shooting people and getting the same sort of kick out of it as most men would get at a striptease. I wanted to shout out to him, but he looked nearly unrecognizable. He was scruffy and dirty and the humor in his eyes was replaced by the same metal Officer Shelley had before he'd become a pod person.

As Calvin advanced, shooting at the people, I looked up in

the sky. Daddy stared down, horrified. When our eyes met, he started as if he was just as surprised to see me there as I was.

"Change it!" I cried, waving my hands at the sky. *"Change it!"*

One of the soldiers pointed at me. "There!"

Calvin turned his gun in my direction and—

⚡⚡⚡ KSSHT! ⚡⚡⚡

Everything was dancing. The flowers, the butterflies, the clouds in the sky—all moving to the rhythm of a three-animal band: a pig blowing into a jug, a wolf plucking a bass made out of a cigar box and a single string, and a turtle scrubbing a brush against a washboard.

I was dancing too. I couldn't help it. The music was making me. My noodle arms were wobbling at either side. My hands were covered in white gloves and only had three fingers each. A cow pranced by on noodle legs, singing a song about the birds and the trees and the little bees' knees.

A hunter snuck out of the brush with a gun and took a shot at the cow. It struck her bell, which swung in a circle and bonked her right on the noggin. A large lump raised from the cow's head like a mountain and three birds started to fly around it. One of the birds noticed me staring, rolled up its feathered sleeves, and spit at me.

Up in the sky, the sun was beaming. I expected to see a smiling face, but instead . . . it was Daddy's.

"No!" I screamed at him. "No no no no no n—"

⚡⚡⚡ KSSHT! ⚡⚡⚡

I was standing in front of a conveyor belt. Liz stood next to me, wearing an apron and a chef's hat. Her face was covered in chocolate. I noticed the conveyor belt had stopped, and fresh-cooling chocolates were piling up at its end.

Liz put her gloved hands on her hips. "Look at the mess you've got us into this time!"

We were in a factory. I also wore gloves and an apron.

"Me?" I said.

Liz rolled her eyes at the factory wall, even though we were the only ones there.

She waved a chocolate-covered spatula in my face. "If the boss asks what happened, we'll tell him a toucan came in through that window and broke the machine."

I furrowed my brows at her.

"Huh?" I said.

Liz elbowed me. "I *said*, if Daddy asks what happened, we'll tell him a toucan broke through that window and *broke* the machine." She gave me an expectant look.

"Why a . . . toucan?" I said.

"He's hated 'em ever since he went on safari and one stole his hairpiece. Every chance he got, he blew the feathers right off one and screamed, 'Toucan play at that game!'"

The rattle of the conveyor belt almost sounded like applause.

Outside the window, I could see Daddy's same shocked expression.

This time, all I had to do was shake my head.

⚡⚡⚡ KSSHT! ⚡⚡⚡

I was in a brightly lit kitchen, pastures rolling toward a sunset outside the window. Something smelled heavenly, like cinnamon and gravy. A woman stood up from an oven and turned around.

"Ma!" I said, and threw my arms around her waist. My head

only came up to her chest. Pigtails draped over my shoulders.

Ma looked more radiant than she ever had onstage, her hair a perfect swoop over a polka-dot shirt and striped apron. She held a steaming tray.

"Looks like *someone* smelled dinner," Ma said, smiling.

She set the steaming tray on the clean kitchen counter and removed her oven mitts. She still had her fingers.

"How did you escape?" I said, grabbing hold of all ten of them and squeezing. "Did they hurt you any?"

Ma took her hands back and grabbed plates and forks, not seeming to have heard a word I said. "You know, Phoebe, you'll be a mother someday, and you'll need to learn all the tricks of the kitchen." She opened a hand attractively toward the steaming food—meat loaf and mashed potatoes and mixed peas and carrots. "Now, how long do you think this took me to cook? Five hours? Six?"

"Ma, what are you talking about?"

She answered her own question. "Ten *minutes*. Can you believe that? Two pounds of food, and all for a dollar. The advertisement for this *Indian Brave Meat Loaf* said for the modern woman on the run, and I thought, if that doesn't describe my daughter and me, then *nothing* will. Ha-ha."

I shook my head, trying to figure out where my ma had got to and how this woman was walking with no strings attached. She had Ma's voice and Ma's face . . . but she wasn't Ma.

The woman's eyes smiled straight through my horrified expression, and then she started to serve up the food. "Now, who's hungry?"

I found Daddy beyond the rolling pastures and slowly shook my head.

⚡⚡⚡ KSSHT! ⚡⚡⚡

I was in Joe's malt shop.

Sitting across from me was Rhoda. She'd lost the braided pigtails and wore a tight sweater. A part of me wanted to run, get away from her, but she didn't look like she was about to set any fires. Her ice queen expression had thawed and she smiled too big at Calvin, who sat beside her in the booth, head intact, delivering an animated anecdote.

"*Officer,* I says. You've got the wrong guy. And he says, 'You're darned tootin' I've got the wrong guy. Calvin Marple, when have you ever been *right*?"

A hand squeezed mine, and I found my fingers were interlaced with Lear's. He gave me a wink, and his eye didn't twitch or his mouth tic or anything. Every inch of him was covered in muscle, which made my knees go watery. He was wearing a letterman jacket, and he squeezed my hand so hard, I could feel his class ring. It shined like nothing I'd ever seen before. I had a brand-new word to describe what it was doing to my eyes . . . *Gold*.

Calvin continued his anecdote. "So I says to the officer, I says, 'That firecracker may have been a doozy, but it's nothing compared to the firecracker you've got at home.' The officer laughed so hard he let me go!"

Rhoda burst into giggles, a strange sound coming from her. I stared around the malt shop, more words springing to mind. The squeeze bottles next to Lear's elbow were *yellow* and *red*. The window shone with the neon light: *pink* and *blue.* My trapeze dress was *Sherwood green*.

"Ah, c'mon," Calvin said, opening his hands toward me and Lear. "That was a killer comeback."

"Sure," Lear said all cool-like, "Jack Paar will be calling any minute now."

Calvin waved him away. "Ah, go jump off a bridge."

So much was happening. Too much to wrap my head around. But they were all good things . . . My size: check. No noodley arms: check. Calvin wasn't murdering people: check. Rhoda had kindness in her eyes.

And the *colors* . . .

I found Daddy's eyes through the plate glass window. He looked more bewildered now than frightened. I gave my head a little shake, and he lowered the remote slightly.

"I thought it was *hilarious*, Daddy," Rhoda said to Calvin, a little too eagerly.

Daddy?

"Of course you did," Calvin said, "but you crack up reading a postage stamp."

Rhoda blushed, her cheeks a vibrant pink.

Had that other life been a dream? Had my mind borrowed faces from the real world and mixed them up in a nightmare involving ants and a flying saucer and a giantess and all the rest? Was it all over now? My insides warmed at the thought, but then turned cold twice as quick. A dream was a break from life. I didn't remember living this colorful life before the nightmare. If anything, this was the dream. My fingertips squeaked along the purple vinyl of the booth. It felt so real.

"You need some water, Phoebe?" Rhoda said, looking at me concerned. "You look like you've seen a ghost."

"I'm . . . I'm okay," I said, still wary of her.

"You gonna finish your fries?" she asked.

I looked down at the plate in front of me. Apparently, I'd

taken only one bite of my hamburger. But I felt famished. Not the giant hunger I'd experienced before—I wasn't about to put my fist through the plate glass or anything. But everybody else's plates were empty, and I'd barely touched mine. Strange.

I put my hand to my stomach and found it was tight as a drum. Here I was, regular-size Phoebe, *only less so*. I was thin for the first time in my life. This channel was getting better and better.

"You mind?" Rhoda said, reaching over to my plate.

"Oh," I said. "Go right ahead."

Rhoda took a fry, and that's when I noticed her pudgy cheeks. However many pounds I was missing, she had gained.

I picked up my blue milk shake with red cherries on top and took a sip, hoping it would help me think.

"Whoa," Lear said, "careful now. You don't want to end up like Joe over there."

Joe was wiping down the counter, his belly ballooning his apron, so grease-stained it was almost yellow.

"Yeah, or old Rhoda," Calvin said, giving her chubby cheek two little slaps.

Rhoda set down the unfinished fry. Now that I was getting a better look at her, I noticed one of her eyes seemed to have gone lopsided. The line of her mouth was drawn taut.

"Don't mind her," Calvin said. "She's just broken up about the bug that got the Indians."

"The . . . bug?" I said. "Just one?"

"Yeah," Calvin said, "flu wiped out half the tribe."

"You mean . . . it wasn't giant ants?" I said.

The table fell silent a moment, and then Calvin started

cracking up. "Giant ants! That's a good one, Pheebs. I gotta write that one down."

I wasn't laughing. Half of the Navajo people had died.

Rhoda sighed. "I just wonder how many we could've saved if we had baptized more."

Calvin pointed a thumb at her. "Rhoda thinks she's Laura Ingalls or something."

Lear snorted.

"What do you mean?" I said.

"The flu didn't touch Pennybrooke," Rhoda said. "Well, except that Graham girl. She was always going out to the reservation to tend to the sick without wearing a mask, but that was her own fault."

My heart squeezed. Beth was gone in this world too.

Rhoda got a self-important look on her face. "Reverend Marsh said Pennybrooke was saved because we're a God-fearing people. The Navajo are plagued by sin and drink, so they were struck down."

I swallowed deep. Marsh was alive on this channel. I was surprised by how excited I was to see him. Even if he hadn't developed into the person he'd died as in my world.

Calvin snickered. "I keep asking Rhoda if the church is so special, then why did lightning strike the clock tower and burn the whole thing down?"

Rhoda cleared her throat and answered simply. "The reverend said God was providing us the opportunity to build a church that could hold more souls, to rebuild stronger than ever."

"Sure," Calvin said, smirking. "God plays favorites in mysterious ways."

Flustered, Rhoda reached for a napkin and accidentally knocked over a Coke. Brown soda frothed across the table, spilling all over Calvin's pants. Rhoda's hands leapt to her mouth.

"Ah, jeez!" Calvin said. "Look what ya did, clumsy!"

Rhoda grabbed a napkin and started dabbing at his pants.

"Just . . . don't touch me," Calvin said.

Rhoda stood and grabbed her purse. "I'll replace them, Daddy. I *promise*."

Calvin got up and brushed at his clothes. "It's all over my leather jacket, too. You gonna replace that?"

Rhoda's shoulders deflated, and I actually felt a touch of sympathy for her.

"Didn't think so," Calvin said. "I'll be in the car."

She turned back to me and Lear, her cheeks flushed.

"Sorry about that," she said. "I can be such a klutz sometimes."

"That wasn't your fault," I said. "Accidents happen."

Lear gave another snort, but I didn't look at him.

"Yeah," Rhoda said. "Accidents happen to disasters like me." She waved and headed toward the door. "Well, see you at prom tomorrow."

Prom? I was going to prom? Did I have a dress?

This channel may not have been totally free of horrors—sickness and fires and guys who spoke to their girlfriends like they were less than human. But hey, at least the streets weren't swarming with giant ants too.

A wet mouth closed around my earlobe and I flinched away.

Lear stuck up his hands like he was under arrest. "*Whoa*. Excuse me for living. Last I checked you were my girlfriend. Do I need written permission to touch you now?"

I felt the blood rush to my cheeks. "No. Of course not."

His arm slid across my shoulders and his fingers tickled my collarbone just like Officer Shelley had done.

No. Not like Shelley. Because this was Lear.

"I was only gonna ask if you wanted to drive up to Sugarman's Pass tonight," he said.

I snuggled up under his arm. My lips felt about as useful as taffy. "I'll have to see what's on my schedule."

Was this happening? Was I really about to go for a drive with Lear, only handsomer, in this new, trim body of mine, on a cloud-dappled, pink sunset evening, free of monsters, that couldn't have been lovelier if someone painted it?

"Well, don't hurt that pretty head of yours thinking about it," Lear said, "star eyes."

• • •

We passed through the parking lot, my head nearly floating off my shoulders when I slid my arm through Lear's. His letterman jacket felt scratchy soft. His eyes were pale blue. His breath smelled like chocolate milk. And he was all mine.

The dread that had built up in me over the last couple of weeks had shrunk to a shallow pool at the bottom of my stomach. It would evaporate soon. It just had to.

We got into Lear's sparkling green Plymouth Fury with yellow interiors. The smell of leather and gasoline was manly and intoxicating. Lear started the car and revved the engine, and the vibrating seat woke all sorts of desire in me.

Lear reached under the seat and pulled out a flask. He took a long pull and then offered it to me.

"What is it?" I said.

"It's hooch," he said, taking another swig. "You picky now, all of a sudden?"

"Oh, no," I said, blushing. "It's just if we're going driving in the canyon, don't you think maybe . . ."

Lear gave a little laugh of disbelief. "Someone spike your milk shake with the square drug or something?"

"Don't be silly," I said, grabbing the flask and taking a sip. The motel sign glowed a warm rose at the end of Main Street. "Oh! You mind if we stop and see Ma before we go?"

Lear killed the engine and fell back in his seat with a sigh.

"What?" I said. "I still want to go to Sugarman's Pass."

He stared out the windshield and wiped at his lips. A desperate feeling rose up in me. I just wanted him to put his arm around my shoulders again.

"I just think it's a little weird that you talk about your Ma so much," he said.

"I do?" I would've thought if I ever got a true-blue, blue-eyed boyfriend I'd stop talking about Ma altogether.

"Almost constantly," he said. "And you know, I hate to say it, but I think your Ma?" He swiveled his finger around his temple. "She's a little loony tunes."

I felt like an ant had pincered me right in the stomach. And I knew what that felt like now. Or I thought I did.

"Ma is *not* loony tunes," I said.

"What other woman do you know who can't pay her rent and keeps her daughter cooped up in a motel?"

"That's not her fault," I said. "It's my dad's. He's . . . never paid child support." The words found their way into my mouth, and whether that was true on this channel or I invented it, I didn't know.

Lear laughed, but not in a funny way. "I knew I should've listened to my old lady when she told me not to date a girl whose mom was committed."

I crossed my arms, holding my shoulders for support as I stared at the glove box.

"Oh, come on," Lear said. "Everyone in town knows your mom spent time in the hospital, Phoebe. Honestly, you're lucky I asked you to prom with a reputation like that."

My hands fell to my lap. The smell of leather and gasoline was starting to make me nauseous. I was so hungry. Had I gotten Lear to ask me to the dance by starving myself?

"My mom said this would happen," he said. "She told me that the apple doesn't fall far from the tree. And any woman who's been in the loony bin was bound to have bad seeds. But hey, maybe I'm the crazy one because I was ready to go out with you no matter how rotten the family tree is."

My jaw clenched. My shoulders were riding up to my ears. This was not how this was supposed to go. We weren't in the scary world anymore. The world filled with monsters. This was supposed to be a dream. A dream I'd never wake up from.

"Hey," Lear said, softening his voice and bringing his face close to mine. "Look, I'm sorry for saying that stuff, okay?" He ran his fingers through his greasy hair. "I just like you so much that I want you all to myself, y'know?"

I didn't budge. Before I knew what was happening, he took me in his arms and tilted my head back. He mashed his liquor-sweet lips so forcefully onto mine, I could feel the hardness of his teeth. He broke away and his eyes sparkled into mine.

"Dammit, Phoebe, if there's one thing in this world I can't stand, it's a girl who doesn't understand how *beautiful* she is."

"If there's one thing I can't stand in this world," I said, "it's guys like you. Let go of me."

Lear jerked away like I'd bitten him. He took out a pack of

cigarettes, shook one into his mouth, and lit it. "If you want to take your ma up to Sugarman's Pass and dance naked under the moon or whatever it is you do, you're more than welcome. Or you can come with me and I'll give you the night of your life. Up to you."

He stared out the driver's window and smoked. I looked at the drifting blue smoke, the mauve Letterman jacket, the golden class ring that gleamed on his finger. And I got out of the car. The engine snarled to life and Lear peeled out of the parking lot.

• • •

As I walked down Main Street, I could hear the church being rebuilt in the distance, hammers tacking and saws snarling through the spring air. Ethel was beating rugs in front of the motel and gave me a little smile and wave. She was wearing her knee braces the right way round.

Ma was asleep on one of the beds, limbs sprawled. She looked broken, like a bird that had struck a window. I thought when I saw her I'd squeeze the breath right out of her, but something felt wrong. On the other channel, *my* channel, every time I walked through the door, Ma greeted me with a smile and a bottle of pop or something.

"Ma?" I said to the figure on the bed.

I touched her shoulder and her head jerked up off the bed so fast that my hand leapt back.

"Oh," she said, laying her head back down. "I thought you were him."

I felt some relief. This woman had human eyes and a human voice. Unlike the woman in the commercial. She just looked like an exhausted version of plain old Ma.

"Him *who*?" I said.

She shut her eyes and didn't say a word.

I smelled the boozy air and saw the bottle of vodka on the table.

"Are you drunk, Ma?"

She tried to laugh, but it turned into a series of coughs. "What a question." She sat up on the bed, facing away from me, and cradled her face in her hands. "Ern left. He's gone."

"Who is . . . Ern?"

She looked darkly over her shoulder.

I searched the room with my eyes. Ern must've been a boyfriend. Ma had always said she wanted to see me safely raised before she tried dating again. And even then, with all the running town to town, it would have its complications.

"Sorry," I said. "I'm just surprised is all."

Ma scoffed. She stretched to the nightstand and grabbed a cigarette. "Surprised I haven't replaced him already?"

"What? No, I—"

We fell into silence. In the closet hung my prom dress. Purple with frills.

"And how was your date tonight?" Ma asked. She patted around the comforter until she found a lighter.

"Terrible," I said, flopping onto the bed, ready to open up about everything that had happened. To have her help me piece together this great puzzle of a channel.

Ma couldn't get the lighter to light. "Well, maybe if you dressed more respectably, Lear wouldn't treat you so bad."

I sat up. "What?"

Ma had only ever been supportive of how I dressed. When I was six and pulled her pantyhose over my head, she'd smiled and said, *I'll miss seeing your pretty face, but you'll make a killing as a bank robber.*

"Boys treat a girl the way she dresses," Ma said. She gave up on the lighter and tossed it. "It's common sense."

I looked in the motel mirror and touched my face. I was . . . *pretty.* I'd won the jackpot in this channel. I looked more like Ma than Daddy. But I didn't give a damn if this was what our relationship was like.

"I think I need to be alone a while, Beefy," Ma said, lying down.

"Oh," I said. "Yeah, sure. I'll just . . . go for a walk."

"Why don't you bring a shawl with you?" she said without budging. "Cover up those shoulders."

• • •

I walked the colorful streets of Pennybrooke, thinking.

This channel definitely felt better than any I'd visited so far . . . and yet it was horrifying in its own way. Lear was a creep. Calvin treated Rhoda like garbage. And Ma . . . It seemed people had still found ways to harden themselves even in a world without Shivers.

Daddy sat in the sky, holding his remote and awaiting instruction. *To change or not to change?*

"I don't know," I said to him. "I'm torn."

Ants weren't tearing people to shreds, Marsh was alive somewhere, and Ma was safe and sound. But what was the use in having her if she was miserable and I still missed her as much as when she was locked away beneath the desert? I couldn't believe I was thinking this, but I would trade this new body of mine and be big again if it meant I could have the old

Ma back. Even if she was buried in a cell beneath the desert.

But how could I return to a channel where I was just as helpless as a giantess and everyone was about to die? Where people already had died?

The sound of hammering led me to Saint Maria's. The church looked like a turkey that had been burnt in the oven but still eaten. Reverend Marsh was on the lawn out front. He had his sleeves rolled up and was hammering two pieces of wood together. It didn't seem to be going well.

"Hi," I said.

Marsh barely glanced at me. "You are the actress's daughter."

"Yeah," I said. "I am."

He wiped sweat from his forehead. "I fear your—"

"Yeah, yeah, you fear my mom's wantonness will bring death to us all."

His brow wrinkled as if trying to figure out whether I was sent from heaven or hell.

"I want to thank you," I said.

He froze as if trying to sense whether or not I was trying to seduce him or something.

I grew bashful and stared at my emerald green shoes. "Just for . . . being a good person. I know you don't know what I'm talking about, but . . . well, it's just important for me to tell you is all."

He pursed his lips and continued hammering.

"Hey, can I ask you a question?" I called.

He stopped hammering.

"What is your idea of a perfect world?"

"Heaven," he said, annoyed.

"No, I mean . . . what do I mean?" I studied the green of my dress. "What do you think is missing from this world?"

Marsh thought for a moment. The hammer spun once in his hand. "A perfect world is one in which people can recognize the sadness their actions bring. If that happened, we would all ascend."

"That makes sense," I said. "But what if in order for that to happen a lot of people had to die? What if . . . *you* had to die?"

The corner of his mouth ticked up in the closest thing I'd seen to a smile on the reverend's face. "For that to happen, I would gladly sacrifice my life."

I gave him a sad smile. "Okay. Thanks. I love you."

Marsh's hammering redoubled as I continued down the road.

• • •

The Penmark Roller Rink was aglow with yellow neon lights. The last time I'd seen this building, it was being carved open by a laser. It still looked broken down but for a different reason. Some of the windows had been smashed, sections of the brick chipped away, and someone had spray painted BOYCOTT across the side.

I looked at the sky where a flying saucer should have been . . . and something dawned on me. The thought flipped my stomach over with fear and excitement both. I looked at my hands.

What would I tell myself if I were watching this in a movie?

I turned in a circle, studying the streets, and made a quick list in my head: *Bleeding child in Ook's skull. Screaming girl on the test of strength. Ants climbing the Ferris wheel. Laser slicing through the roller rink.*

I looked at Daddy. "Change it back," I said. And then remembered one of the last things Beth said. "Channel five thirty-two."

He lifted the remote.

"Wait!" I said.

I felt my stomach, so close to my spine it was almost silly. I took in the colors. The green grass. The pink motel sign flickering in the distance. The blue stars. The red traffic light beaming across the shops on Main Street.

"Okay," I told Daddy. "Ready."

⚡⚡⚡ KSSHT! ⚡⚡⚡

My vision leapt forty feet into the air as cuts and burns and bruises screamed to life on my limbs. The night drained of color as it filled with screams and machine gunfire, the whine of the laser and bullets ricocheting off the flying saucer. There was the roller rink at my feet, as small as a building from a train set, in flames.

I sprinted across the parking lot, leapt over the roller rink, and snatched the saucer out of the air like a Frisbee. Keeping the heat of the laser pointed downward, I ran back toward the ant-filled carnival, the street melting to gooey asphalt beneath my feet. When I reached the Ferris wheel, I crouched and, holding the saucer like a shield, aimed the laser like a spotlight. Every ant it touched burst into flames. They screeched and writhed, a few abdomens popping in gushy explosions, as the ant army disintegrated before me in a blinding blaze.

The kids on the Ferris wheel screamed. The steel had melted under the extreme heat of the laser and the wheel was now drooping toward the ground.

But I couldn't move. The flying saucer's laser made the ground boil like lava, scalding my feet. I shook the saucer and hit it with my palms. "How do you turn this stupid thing off?"

Finally, using both hands, I crumpled the flying saucer like an empty beer can, and the laser sputtered out. I made it to the Ferris wheel just in time to catch Lear's gondola before it struck the ground. I made sure he and Duane and Manuelito were okay inside before I went to grab Ruth from the drooping test of strength. She was sweating bullets, and Pan-Cake was panting up a storm, but they were none the worse for wear.

By the time I reached Ook's skeleton, Lear had already scaled the ribs, carried Connor down, and used his shirt as a bandage for the boy's bleeding stomach.

"Is he okay?" I said.

"Okay?" Lear said. "He's a *hero*. He survived an ant attack, and lived to tell the tale."

Connor's eyes weren't glazed over anymore, but he was still pale without all that blood. Maria wouldn't stop hugging him.

"Medic!" General Spillane's voice called behind us as he and his platoon marched in from the roller rink.

A group of soldiers placed Connor on a stretcher while Lear pried Maria's fingers off of his neck and held her.

"I've gotta admit, giantess," the general said, patting my calf. "That was an excellent use of firepower. I'd say you earned a medal if they made them that big."

He saluted me, and Lear and the kids and I watched as they carried Connor back to the barricade.

"Is Connor going to be okay?" Duane asked.

He seemed shaken to the core, like he didn't expect a battle would be this bad.

Lear patted his shoulder. "One little ant bite? I think he'll be just fine."

None of us laughed.

The four remaining kids, Ruth and Maria and Duane and Manuelito, laid their heads on my foot. Pan-Cake licked the ash from my toe. Lear shivered and held himself. His shirt had left with the stretcher. He looked nothing like the Lear on the previous channel. His muscles were gone, his stomach and shoulders soft, and I could see the puckered skin on his back and sides where his father had drunk from him.

I was about to pick him up and hug him to my face when a scream pealed out across the carnival, making the kids and Pan-Cake jump. It was coming from inside the crumpled-up flying saucer.

Lear and I gave each other a look.

"Stay here," I said.

I approached the smoldering saucer slowly, ready to see the twisted face of the alien thawed from the ice in the Buried Lab. But inside was something even more unsettling. Mr. Peak was dangling from the crumpled metal, bleeding but alive. He was *laughing.*

"Ha ha ha ha ha ha! Boy, we put on a real show, kid! You picked up the flying saucer and I cranked up the juice! Liz was right about you. The big guy will stay tuned in for *months!* Ahahahaha!"

I pulled him out of the saucer and brought him close enough to prove I could fit his entire body in my mouth. His laughter stopped.

"No need for violence, now, kid," he said. "We won. The big guy may be a sicko, but he sure does enjoy a happy ending."

"Take me to the Buried Lab," I said.

I'd need a hostage so they wouldn't hurt Ma at the approach of my giant footsteps.

"They'll have evacuated by this point," he said. "You'll never find them."

I gave him the slightest squeeze. His face grew dark and he grunted.

"You're going to show me the exact spot above Ma's cell," I said.

The rising sun washed the world in grays as I walked into the desert, Lear and Peak, the four kids, and Pan-Cake in my arms. Daddy watched, exhausted and fascinated.

We went to Gray Rock first. The Navajo people were in the process of destroying some of the hogans that were still standing, though I didn't understand why. I returned the kids to their parents, who sobbed in relief. One woman started to tremble, but Lear assured her that Connor was in the Pennybrooke hospital and that he was going to be okay.

Eugene came to greet us, his confident calmness replaced with a hollow expression. I explained that the kids had run away and I'd done my best to keep them safe.

He pinched the bridge of his nose. "We lost eight kids to the ants last night, Phoebe. And thirty-three adults." He looked toward a tarp whose corner lifted with a breeze, revealing a pale arm. "It might have been worse if those kids had been here."

"But Connor might not have been hurt," I said.

He tried to smile. "Guess we'll never know for sure."

He extended his hand, and I shook it with my fingertips. I asked if they wanted any help cleaning up, but he said no. Only Maria waved goodbye.

Next, we went to the rocky outcropping.

"Where is she?" I asked Peak.

He crossed his arms.

I drove both hands into the sand and started to dig, flinging great wafts of sand into the air until my hand struck something metallic. I punctured the tunnel's steel side with my thumbnail and then peeled it back easy as aluminum, exposing the haunted hallway.

While the sun rose, making the desert sparkle, I continued to dig up hallways and rooms like I was unearthing a toy in the biggest sandbox in the world. I came to a narrow hallway with white doors that looked just like a ward at an insane asylum.

On one of the doors was a note.

Until we meet again, Sister.
—L

I flicked off the door's handle, and it slowly creaked open.

"Ma?" I said.

There was a breath of silence and then . . . "Phoebe?"

Ma, hunched and filthy, stepped into the light. She looked like she hadn't showered or eaten since I last saw her. But she was breathtaking because she was herself.

Ma blocked the sun with her hand and looked up and up and up. "*Phoebe*?"

Oh. Right.

I moved my giant head so my shadow covered her.

"It's me," I said.

Ma recovered from her shock. "Who is this cover model and what have you done with my daughter?"

I laughed and put out my hand, and she stepped into it. I lifted her up to my face so she could squeeze my cheek with both arms and kiss and kiss and kiss it. We both cried, but my tears were much bigger.

"Guess I really do look like a Framsky now, eh?" I said.

Ma touched my cheek. "I don't see it." We both laughed and cried some more. Ma wiped her eyes. "Phoebe, do me a favor and open the cell across from mine?"

"I wouldn't do that if I were you," Peak said.

I gave him a look, then reached down and flicked off the other handle. The door slowly creaked open, and a starved-looking leopard crept out. Lear took a step back as Pan-Cake started to growl.

"It's okay," Ma said. "She won't hurt anyone. She's just having a hard time changing back."

I set Ma down and then carefully scooped the leopard from the hallway. She was all bones and skin, and she slumped over on her side when I laid her on the desert sand. Ma knelt next to the leopard and petted her ears.

"Hi, Alexandrea," she said. "It's good to finally put a face with a voice." She smiled up at me. "Lex's voice kept me company through the long nights."

So, I wasn't the only one the lab had been experimenting on. There was a woman trapped in that leopard skin.

I turned to Peak. "Liz said she could make me normal again."

"Hate to break it to ya, kid," he said, "but she lied. Think about it. There's never been a disaster out there that's made creatures *shrink*. Where would be the fun in that for the big guy?"

My giant shoulders sank slowly. I should've known. There probably wasn't a charcoal pyramid room big enough to fit me anyway. I stared at my shadow, stretching across the desert.

So, this was my size now. A giantess for life. Where would I find enough food? Where would I sleep? How would I get new clothes?

"Phoebe?"

I looked down at Lear.

"Zap me," he said. "Make me big like you."

A new future flashed before my eyes. One where I was still a giantess . . . but not alone. I had Lear at my side. He wore a loincloth like Tarzan while we sat at the back of a drive-in, stuffing our faces with bathtubs full of popcorn.

I looked at my bruised fists and my bloodied legs and I remembered the locusts. Lear thought if he was big enough, he could outgrow his demons. But in my experience, they only grew with me.

"I'm sorry," I said to Lear.

I started to dig again. I dug through the hallway, past my cell, past the rooms with all the monsters, until I came to the room with the charcoal pyramids. I didn't stop smashing until it was a pile of rubble and shards.

"You think that'll help?" Peak said. "You think we don't have labs in other places? Someone's gotta keep the big guy entertained! What you gonna to do that all by yourself?"

I picked charcoal shards out of my hands. I knew this was the life I'd chosen when I decided to return to this channel. But now that I considered all the problems I still had to face, I grew so overwhelmed I thought I might collapse under the weight.

I felt hands on my leg. "We'll figure it out," Ma said. "All of it. It's going to be hard for me to do your hair in the morning, but we'll make do."

I picked Ma up and held her to my neck for a long time. She

was right. So long as we were together, we could figure it out. We'd found a way to get by since I was born.

Ma and I sat on the desert ground and caught up while Alexandrea the leopard slept in the sunshine and Pan-Cake kept a weary eye on her. When I told Ma how I finally got Daddy's attention she laughed and said she'd never thought of trying *that* before. Then she told me she whiled away the lonely nights in her cell by telling Alexandrea stories about me—about how I always found new ways to keep myself entertained in every town. That was before Alexandrea transformed, of course.

"Did you know?" I asked Ma. "Did you know that we were putting people in danger by moving around so much?"

Ma dug out the dirt in her fingernails. "I . . . had an idea. But I couldn't bear the thought of giving you up. I . . ." Ma held her tired head. "Oh God."

I picked her up and squeezed her gently to my chest. "It's okay, Ma. We do what we need to. Shh."

We held each other for several minutes, and when I'd finally hugged her to my heart's content, I saw Lear crawling out of the gutted Buried Lab, brushing sand from his pants. Mr. Peak climbed out after him.

"What just happened?" I said. "What did you guys do?"

Peak looked from Lear to me. "Nothing."

Lear wouldn't look at me. His skin was shining, like it was covered with a reflective mist.

"Lear?" I said.

"It's nothing, Phoebe," he said, and met my eyes. "Don't worry about it."

I didn't know what happened, but I didn't like it. What else could I do except wait for Lear to tell me?

My shadow fell over Peak. "You killed a lot of people."

"Yeah, I did." He crossed his arms. "Saved a lot too."

I picked him up and I set him in the room with all the dead electronics.

"You love this lab so much?" I said. "You can live in it."

And with one sweep of my arm, I buried Peak in the lab.

Lear and Ma and I sat in the desert while Pan-Cake sniffed circles around us, making little digs here and there at the sand. The sun sat bleary at the bottom of an uncomfortably open sky.

"What now?" I said. "Where will we go?"

Ma reached up and held my pinkie.

"I don't know," she said. "Then again, what else is new?"

"Another roast chicken, Miss Lane?"

I glanced at the line stretching out of the entrance to the big top tent and my stomach tightened.

"Better make it six," I said.

"Coming right up."

The carny who had flirted with me all those months and a lifetime ago, ran off to the food tent, which was packed to the gills just for yours truly.

It had been the carnival owner's idea. After he'd crawled out of the rubble of the roller rink, the laser from the flying saucer having barely singed off his eyebrows, he had seen the wreckage of his carnival and collapsed to his knees. "I'm ruined. *Ruined.*"

But then he saw me, bigger than life, wandering in from the desert—Ma and Lear, a Pomeranian and a leopard in my arms—without a place in the world to be. He said the sun was shining above my giant head, and it gave him one whopper of an idea. Ma and I didn't have much choice but to officially join the carnival. After we found out Connor and Calvin were okay, of course. And that Rhoda and her father hadn't survived the roller rink attack.

I needed to walk out my nerves before our first show started. I stayed low along the back side of the tents so no one would see me before the big reveal. It would be my first time onstage, and while throwing up in front of a live audience would be embarrassing, vomiting all over every person in that audience would end my career before it began.

I came to a tent that glowed with flickering light. The calming guitars of "Sleep Walk" played over the radio.

"Knock, knock," I said.

"Come in."

I parted the flap with my pinkie and found Lear hunched over a gas lamp, sitting on a booster seat, inking the pincers on a picture of a gigantic ant. The carnival poster read COME HEAR THE TALE OF *THE BATTLE OF PENNYBROOKE*! *75¢!* Lear had caught up with the carnival a ways down the road, having left his mom in the care of the general. He made a deal with the carnival owner to draw promotional posters for the show and was sending every dollar he earned back home. I gave him extra to replace his mom's food storage.

"How's it coming?" I said.

"Like I never want to look at another antennae again," he said, rubbing his eyes.

"I know what you mean," I said.

"How are you feeling?"

I put a hand to my stomach. "Like I swallowed a lawn mower."

He smiled, a swipe of ink across his cheek. "You'll forget all about it the moment they start whistling at you."

"Not if they start screaming instead," I said.

Lear rubbed his face. He looked tired. And while he always looked small to me, he seemed more so these days. Like he might be shrinking. His shirt hung loose around his shoulders, his belt was cinched to the last notch, and the brush was much too big in his hand. I'd stopped growing months ago, but every night when we cuddled, he took up less space in my palm.

What had Peak done to him in the desert? I remembered Lear's insistence on being zapped. I remembered his skin sparkling in the desert sun and the room in the haunted hallway, twining with sparkling mist.

I sighed and tried on a smile. I didn't want to ask about it until Lear brought it up.

"I've been thinking," Lear said, tapping the inkpot. "About your dad."

"Oh yeah?" I said, sitting cross-legged in front of the tent.

"If he's had a remote since your Ma could see him, but remotes weren't invented until 1954, and the one he has doesn't have a cord . . . what if he's from the future?"

I looked up at the sky. Daddy had been gone a long while now. Months. His La-Z-Boy stood empty, like a throne waiting for its king. At least he'd left the television on.

"What do you mean?" I said.

"I dunno," Lear said, shrugging. "Maybe he doesn't like this futuristic world, and he's looking back on a simpler time. It was just a thought."

These thoughts were too much for me. The world Daddy lived in. Whether Beth was alive there. How long our world would last. As Liz had said, sometimes it was best not to think about your insignificance in the universe. Besides, with rebuilding the carnival and rehearsing for the traveling show, I hadn't had much time to think about these things. Or the fact that Liz and the rest of the lab were still out there somewhere.

A finished poster lay drying on the floor. It showed Lear and Marsh, the five Navajo children, and me standing in the inked carnival before the lights popped on. The caption read "*The Quiet Before the Swarm.*"

"You made my boobs bigger," I said.

Lear scratched behind his ear with the brush handle. "Sorry about that."

"I didn't say I was mad."

"LADIES AND GENTLEMEN, BOYS AND GIRLS, WELCOME TO THE WONDROUS, THE GLORIOUS, THE MOST JAW-DROPPING TRAVELING SHOW YOU HAVE EVER LAID EYES UPON!"

The lawn mower in my stomach started to rev. "That's my cue," I said.

"Knock 'em dead," Lear said. "Not literally."

"You coming to watch?"

Lear started tracing pincers with his too-big brush again. "I've gotta ink this before it goes to the printers tomorrow. I'll catch the next one."

I nodded and let the flap fall shut.

On the way to the big top tent I passed Alexandrea snoozing in her cage. The leopard was no longer skin and bones, but she was still having a hard time finding her way back to her human form.

The carny ran up with a platter of six roast chickens, and I gulped them down, bones and all.

"You water Pan-Cake?" I asked, trying to hide my nervousness.

"Soaked her," he said. "Especially that little flower sprouting at the tip of her tail."

"Thank you."

I reached the big top tent.

Shit. Here we go.

I was numb from stem to stern. I couldn't feel my toes and

stared down fifty feet to make sure they were still there. There was nothing to be afraid of anymore, I reminded myself. Not even the staring eyes of an audience of thousands.

Now that I'd grown used to my crane-size limbs and tank-like feet, I had no one to compare myself to. Ook was dead and also a gorilla, and all the women I met were no bigger than my pinkie. Even Ma was just Ma.

As old Phoebe, I'd always felt like my space was not mine. But I'd outgrown that feeling now.

I slipped under the back flap of the big top tent. Ma was standing behind the closed curtain in her iconic torn dress, looking radiant.

"Ready to show 'em what we've got?" she said.

"I think I'm going to pass out," I said.

"Try not to, sweetie," Ma said. "I won't be able to catch you, and you'll bring the whole tent down." She met my eye. "Remember, if anyone heckles you, you can toss them out. You're your own bouncer."

That made me feel a little better.

"Cleavage," Ma said.

I looked down and readjusted the silken top made by the carnival's seamstress. It was comfortable enough, but it didn't have that same feeling of love and care as the piece Beth made. I still wondered if I'd ever see her again.

I stood to my full fifty feet behind the curtain with Ma standing by my side. The carnival owner had requested that we re-create Emperor Ook carrying Ma to the top of the Chrysler Building, with me hauling her up the support pole to the top of the big top tent. But we had nixed that idea and come up with a show of our own.

"AND NOW, WITHOUT FURTHER ADO," the announcer said, *"I ASK YOU TO TURN YOUR EYES UP-UP-UPWARD TO SEE THE BEAUTIFUL, THE SUBLIME . . . PHOEBE LANE!"*

"Breathe," Ma said through smiling teeth.

I put on a smile of my own and took a giant breath as the curtain started to rise.

The End.

ACKNOWLEDGMENTS

The author would like to thank the following early readers: Mark S., Breana R., Chris T., and Brooke K.

He'd like to thank his agent, John Cusick, for preventing him from submitting his bat-shit first draft; Christian Trimmer, for taking a chance on the bat-shit second draft; and his editor, Liz Kossnar, for directing the story to a more honest place (also for allowing him to include an anecdote about one of her real-life dates).

Thank you to the team at Simon & Schuster BFYR, especially designer Krista Vossen, jacket artist Francesco Francavilla, and comic artist Sam Bosma, for making the book resemble a bona fide 1950s sci-fi movie.

Thank you to the author's parents, for giving him details he couldn't find in his research; Greg of Black Cat Comics, for safely directing him through the splatter horror section; and most of all, Traci and Rebecca, for pointing out his missteps when it came to body image and race issues. The author takes full responsibility for any inaccuracies or ignorance these wonderful people didn't catch.

Finally, thank you to Hannah for being so darned wonderful through all of this.